THE ROUGH ROAD
OR THE
GOLDEN PATH?

JAMES PRINCE

Order this book online at www.trafford.com
or email orders@trafford.com

Most Trafford titles are also available at major online book retailers.

Scripture quotations marked NIV are taken from the Holy Bible, New
International Version®. NIV®. Copyright © 1973, 1978, 1984 by International
Bible Society. Used by permission of Zondervan. All rights reserved. [Biblica]

Printed in the United States of America.

ISBN: 978-1-4907-4483-4 (sc)
ISBN: 978-1-4907-4482-7 (e)

Trafford rev. 09/11/2014

www.trafford.com

North America & international
toll-free: 1 888 232 4444 (USA & Canada)
fax: 812 355 4082

CHAPTER 1

From dream to dream I think a dreamer never quit dreaming. Although, if my life is a dream come through as beautiful as being able to write Sheba's story, friend of mine, dream or reality it is wonderful.

On the first of April 2001 I had a dream where I was visiting Sheba at her place for the very first time. When I walked through her driveway a dog, I don't know if it was hers or not, but it came at me and managed to get a bite at my buttocks. I acrobatically reached and grabbed its jaws with both of my hands behind my back and I simply opened its mouth and broke it.

I walked inside her house bleeding my pans, totally ignoring the pain and I found her in a far corner of the house looking outside a window and she seemed to be very distraught. I kissed her and to my surprise she enjoyed it and she looked at me with a pleasant look of stupefaction. When she realized I was bleeding she pulled my pans down and she started taking care of my wounds.

"This must hurt a lot?" "Is it bad? I don't feel a thing. Now I'm sorry I broke the dog's mouth." "I'll put peroxide on it, but I think you should go to the hospital." "Why should I go to the hospital if I'm cured by your loving care?"

I had another dream on April fifteen. It seemed to me we were in a hospital or in a sort of a medical clinic to get the confirmation of my child authenticity. While waiting for the result of the test Sheba and I had a dance, a very nice old time waltz that was playing on the radio. When we were done I hold Sheba very tightly in my arms making all the nurses kind of envious and jealous. Some of them came to asked me if I could make them dance too, but I told them this was exclusive to Sheba. They smiled at me giving me the pretty eyes and all that; brushing their breasts meaning; 'Look at what I have to offer you.' I simply told them I love what I got.

On the sixteen of the same month I dreamed of this book I'm writing now; The Rough Road! Sheba told me once that her life has been pretty rough; this was the story of her life.

"I don't know why my life has been so much of a mess, but whatever it was, I still love the Lord." "You should keep loving Him Sheba, because your life could be much rougher yet; you know this, don't you? The Lord has the power to put thornbushe where ever He wants; you should know this. I am the guy to talk to if you want to talk to someone about it. Not that I'm an expert or anything like it, but I am interested and I can be a good listener.

We never know; I might be able to explain a bunch of things to you." "I lived through some things that would make your hair grow greyer when you're hear them." "I'm old enough for this anyway and besides, there is always some dyeing processes.

Maybe we should sit down and write your story; it might be useful for a lot of people and to yourself, who knows?" "I had a very rough road, you know?" "So did I. Let's try to smooth off the rest of it if you want to. We should meet somewhere else though; before some of your colleagues start making stories you don't want to be writing about in the book.

I have to make a trip for collecting hubcaps on Easter Monday. Do you care to join and telling me some of it?" "Would you really take me along with you?" "Sure, I'd love to take you along with me. You could enjoy the ride maybe and see what a day in the life of a hubcaps collector is like. I'll pick you up at 6; 00 a.m. Don't worry about lunch, I'll take care of it, ok? It might be boring for you at times though; especially when you'll be waiting for me to come back with my collection while I walk the road, so bring a good book to read along with you." "I'm reading your book right now in my spare time, The Precious Princess of Wonderland; so I'll take it with me. We're on John.

Should I call you John or James?" "Whatever suits you best Sheba; I don't mind either one and they both belong to me." "Where did the name John come from?" "When I was a kid still I formed a little gang to protect the young girls and boys who were mistreated by the bullies and older ones; especially the bums who were stealing from the little ones. They elected me to be the chief and I thought the name John wasn't a name serious enough or worthy of a chief because I thought it was not enough authoritarian; so I decided on the name James and they all agreed with me. Sixteen years later;

when I was walking in the street someone who I didn't recognize called me James to my surprise. I turned around wondering and I asked him why he called me this way, by this name. He said;

"You're James, my chief. You're the chief of my gang."

"I'm truly sorry not to recognize you my friend, but I'm very flattered and pleased you remember me."

I think when a person received a nickname once; it most likely follows this one for the rest of his life.

"I can't believe I'll spend a complete day with James Prince, the writer and the author of the Precious Princess of Wonderland and The True Face of The Antichrist. I have a hard time believing in this. Not only he is a writer, but he is also the hubcap king; the owner of the largest collection of hubcaps in my country. It's so exciting." "Did you pack a pen and a note book Sheba? We're surely going to need this." "Don't worry John, I got all we need to start the story and this includes a lot of my memories. It will be enough to make your hair stick up though." "You'll have a lot of writing to do for me while I'm driving and don't you worry; not much surprises me anymore, do you know?" "I can do this."

We drove north to Falkland BC and we stopped there for breakfast in a restaurant at 7.10 a.m. After breakfast we hit the road towards the lakes and the hills. After six kilometres up a swirling road we stopped at the first cattlegard, which is twelve to twenty pipes across the road and spaced every four inches to prevent cattle or wild animals to cross over. Although, when the vehicles cross them a little too fast the hubcaps fly off. The best chance people have to recover their lost hubcap is through my business or one like it. If the road workers find them before me, chances are good they end up buried at a dump site or thrown in a recycle bin.

Sheba watched me going with amazement and smiled when I stepped down to find the first hubcap of our venture. Eight minutes later I was back to the vehicle with many nice pieces.

"Now John tell me, how much those worth?" "Let's see here, ta, ta, ta, $340.00." "What? I have to work a whole week for this kind of money." "I have to wait the whole year to find this many over here. I also have to be here just on time. If I get here just a bit too late it is just too bad but I get nothing. If I get here first whoever follows me finds nothing and he might be discouraged from trying again. Timing is everything."

We arrived at the sixth cattlegard of this stretch of the road where I found a big bunch of them again. Through weeds and thorn bushes up and down embankments I found a very good value; more than five hundred dollars worth anyway.

"This was a tough road you just went through there John; now I can see why you're in such a good shape and so strong." "Yes, the road is pretty rough sometime Sheba." "It took you more time to get those little weeds off your shoes and out of your clothes than it took you to gather all those hubcaps." "I hate them but a man has to do what he has to do, right?"

From the East side of Chase we drove to Kamloops to find another stretch of road where there are six more cattlegards. There was absolutely nothing at the first one.

"How come there is nothing over here John?" "As you can see for yourself Sheba; both sides of the road here are very visible and easy to walk. I'm sure hubcaps fell off here too, but someone stopped and picked them up. I couldn't even find an empty beer can." "You pick up cans and bottles too, don't you?" "If I pick up a dozen cans in five minutes this will bring me twelve dollars an hour and it is better than nothing; especially if I don't have the luck to find any hubcap. You'll be surprised to find out how it adds up at the end of the day." "I'll bet it does." "I never know what I'm going to find. There are places where I expect to find a lot and there is nothing. There are places where I expect to find little and I find a lot. I got to know my spots pretty well though." "I'll bet you do; you seem to know what you're doing. John, there is one hubcap back there on the side of the road."

I was tempted to slam the breaks as someone said once I was doing, but I don't. I look behind first and then I stop as quickly as I can without damaging my tires or taking any risk of an accident. I parked the truck on the side of the rough road and I walked back the four hundred feet to pick up a very good hubcap in a very good shape which is worth seventy dollars.

"Tell me now John; it seems to be very unusual to find a hubcap like this out of nowhere? I mean this hubcap had no reason to fall off." "Sometime the hubcap got started off at the cattlegard and hangs on until the vibration from the rough road finishes the work. If it didn't get off here it would have probably fell off at the next cattlegard." "When you say a seventy dollar hubcap; this is the price from the dealer, isn't it?" "No Sheba, the same hubcap brand new is sold from the dealer for approximately two hundred dollars plus taxes." "Wow! This is quite a saving when people buy it from you." "It sure is, but still many people complain about my prices; mainly because they don't know what the original price is from the dealer.

Others know but they just try to squeeze blood out of me. If only they knew what it cost to sell nowadays. Maybe they know too, but they just don't care.

I usually send these people hunting for their replacement hubcap somewhere else. Very often they shamefully come back to get it after they spent a number of dollars on gas. Others will go buy cheap hubcaps from the hardware stores. In my opinion they buy a one dollar hubcap and they pay anywhere from ten to twenty-five dollars for one. This is not being very smart. Those caps either rust very quickly or break when they try to put them on. A lot of people don't seem to know the difference between good quality and cheap. It cost a lot of money to learn in some cases." "What do you do John other than pick up hubcaps? You said you have to wait a year for you to come back over here." "Oh, I have many places to go. My next trip will be around Banff and Calgary. You're more than welcome to join me if you want to. We could possibly have a couple of dances in Calgary on Saturday night and pay your mom a visit on Sunday before returning. What do you think of it?" "It is very inviting. I'll have to see." "But you better finish reading this book of Precious Princess first. I want you to get to know me a bit better. I also like to build a mention for you." "Build a mention for me? What do you mean?"

7

"Well, you'll know better when you're done reading this book, but the Lord wants me to build this place of mine for his children, the ones I know. Do you like water and fish?" "I just love water John." "I want to make a little lake over there with a fountain splashing water through coloured lights; especially made to kill mosquitoes which are going to end up feeding the fish. It will be very pretty at night. The lake will also make a nice skating ring in the winter.

I also want to make a small strawberry field with a gazebo in the centre capable to sit forty people around it. I would love to have your opinion on this." "It sure sounds wonderful John, but all of this cost a lot of money." "Not if you have the right emplacement for it and if you know how to do it. I think it would be nice to give our friends a good strawberry and ice-cream feast between Bible's studies once in a while. All of this followed by a sing along. I would also love to welcome them sometime with a good pickerel or green bass diner." "You like to share, don't you?" "It's fun. I sure don't like to be taken though. But now you should be answering some of my questions, don't you think?

You said you didn't know your father. Do you mind telling me about it?" "In her young years my mom was a babysitter and she became pregnant of the man she was working for. She never wanted to tell me more about it. As far as my father is concerned I'm in a limbo." "I know you have a Father in heaven who loves you and who looks after you. A lot of things could have happened. There is more than one possibility. It could be that she liked him, teased him and felt responsible for her

8

pregnancy. This way she wouldn't want to cause him any trouble; especially if she really loved him. He might have paid her also a big amount of money to keep quiet about the whole situation. Another possibility is he has threatened her and she was afraid not to see her child again; especially if he was a powerful man. It could be also she was raped and never want you to know who he is. Whatever it is; she certainly felt it was better for you not to know him.

I would like you to tell me about your first day in school. Did you like to go?" "I got very scared. There were people from the zoo with snakes and one of them put one around my neck and it began to squeeze me dangerously and I panicked, which made things worst. I have always been scared of them since." "One day I was walking on my property with my little Princess, her who was following me everywhere I went and we suddenly heard some little birds twittering. Princess wanted to go after them, but I quickly held her back telling her she is not to harm these little delicate beings. I told her to stay on the spot and I went to look in the high grass where the sound came from. This was under an old forty-five gallons oil stand. So I began moving the grass with my bare hand hoping to see these little birds. What a surprise I had when I discovered there was a mama rattle snake that was busy swallowing her babies. It is most likely what save both of us. I had my share of fright too that time.

What sport do you like the best and what do you like to do beside working? It is time for lunch, are you hungry?" "What do we have?" "I have beef Bologna, cheese, bananas, fresh buns, little chocolate cakes, apple strudels and seven-up. If you don't like any of this we'll stop at a restaurant." "We didn't come all the way up here to waste our time in a restaurant." "We wouldn't be wasting our time; you would have to answer some of my questions." "I can do this in the vehicle." "As you wish Sheba! I used to make ham sandwiches, but since I found out pork is an abomination to God and it's not good for us I don't eat it anymore. It is not just because it's not good for our heath, but I also hate to displease God. I'm sure He had a very good reason to forbid it too. I wouldn't be surprised to hear one day it causes cancer or some other diseases. I know pork is full of parasites and these cause cancer. This is a known fact.

We're getting close to Cache Creek now." "The ground is uneven around here, very different. It looks almost as if we were on the moon or on some other planets." "Isn't it? There is a Dairy-Queen Sheba; would you like an ice-cream or something else?" "This would be wonderful. Thanks!"

"Now, here we are at another stretch of road with many cattlegards. I didn't come here for three years now; there might be quite a bit of them."

I searched the two first ones and Sheba watched me go with total amazement. But then she got a bit worried when we arrived at the third one.

"John, you're not going down there, are you? You'll never come out of it. It is too steep." "I could climb the highest mountain on earth if I knew you were on the top of it waiting for me and ready to tell me your story." "What do you mean John?" "I mean nothing will hold me from getting back up here. Many reporters have risked their life for less and hundreds of them died in action." "I don't want you to die; I want you to write my story." "Don't you worry; I won't risk my live, but only a few scratches maybe."

A few seconds later I slipped down about twenty feet making the dirt and the rocks roll by me missing my head just by a bit.

"Are you ok John? No harm done?" I'm just fine Sheba."

The hubcap I was carrying went down about thirty feet lower than where I was. I went to get it and I climbed up sideways this time like a deer or a ram would have done. I was then out of breath for a little while and I wept off all the sweating it caused me.

"The least I can say is you can call this a rough road."

I motioned her to give me one minute with my finger to let me get my breath back.

"You're right Sheba. This was a tough one. If they were all like this one I couldn't do it all day long. Did you see Sheba the crevice in the ground over there? It looks like almost two feet wide by twelve to fifteen feet deep. It is very nicely cut too as if someone did it with a huge knife." "What caused this John?" "The water from the rain running off the road cut the ground almost like a huge knife would have done it. Pretty amazing, isn't it? God has his own tools to shape up the earth his own way. With a big tornado He can make a lake like the Okanogan one. With the wind and sand He can level up miles of land. With an earthquake he can shook up the mountains and destroy huge cities and countries in only a few seconds if He wants to. With lightning He can start thousands of fires at the same time and yet some people don't believe in Him. I just wonder what it would take for them to open their eyes. Although, I think most of the people who don't believe in God it's because of the church leaders who keep lying about a lot of things."

I cleaned up this last road and it was four o'clock already. I could have use at least another five hours to do all I wanted to do and go everywhere I wanted to.

"We should be going back soon. There are three more cattlegards to clean up by Monte Lake and there are two and a half hours to drive back home yet. Besides, when I get home I'll have thirty-eight hungry hounds to feed." "John, after all this you don't even look tired. You drove more than six hundred kilometres, you walked at least twenty-five miles up and down cliffs among thorn bushes and weeds and you look as if you're ready to start all over again." "Don't kid yourself Sheba; I'm almost worn out." "You sure don't look like you are." "I wish I have learned more about you though." "We'll meet again if you want to." "If I want to? As soon as I have finished feeding my dogs I'll sit at my computer and I'll write down all the great moments of this day." "How much worth do you figure you found today?" "More than I sold from the beginning of the year; which is around thirty-five hundreds dollars, but this doesn't beat one time where I found fourteen thousands dollars worth in one hour and this was near Brad Creek." "You got to be kidding me. You're not mocking me, are you?" "I never fool around with this kind of serious stuff Sheba and I never mock my friends either." "And most everyone who saw you today thinks you might have found five to twenty dollars worth of empty cans and bottles." "Do you care about what they think? I don't." "I guess not and I like your philosophy." "The very worse in all of this is the overhead will take more than two thirds of this value." "What do you mean?" "I mean the rent, the phone, the taxes, the helper; all those are forbidding me from getting ahead." "It's not fair." "I know it isn't, but for as long as most of the population will put up with it, this will continue. Good night Sheba." "Good night John and thank you for taking me along with you. I had a wonderful day and I am happy about it" "It was just a delightful dream Sheba."

I meet Sheba a couple of times a week for a too short of a time where she works. So one day I let her have a piece of my work and she became intrigued with my first dream.

"Could you explain to me the first dream of yours John? I can't understand that only one kiss from you could cure me of all my anxiety." "The kiss wasn't really a kiss, (too bad) but just like a kiss is sweet and pleasant to people who love each other and make them forget the hardship of the day; what I have to offer will have the same effect on you. My explanation or analysis of the situations of your life, what you call your rough road will be to you just as sweet as or even sweeter than a kiss from the one you love." "There are also the dog that hurt you and to whom you broke the jaws and also the blood and your wounds?" "The dog is someone quite mean who doesn't like our relationship for some reasons. It's got to be a jealous person maybe or just someone who will try to hurt me. This person will succeed to a certain point, but your love and your admiration for me will make me forget all the pain and the inconveniences. I'm quite happy there was only one dog. The fact I broke his mouth shows me I will win against this demon at the end; who ever he or she is." "This is very interesting. You also said you didn't know if it was mine or not." "Which means it could be someone you know or someone I know. Who ever this person is; God gave me power over this one at last." "The blood is also intriguing me." "The blood is my efforts, my work, my sympathy, my compassion for you, my desire to see you happy." "What about your wounds?" "My wounds allowed me to get naked in front of you, which means to open my heart to you completely and to let you see the bottom of my soul. Your joy, your happiness and your care are so rejoicing to me that I don't need anything else to be happy and healed." "But John, how could you explain all of this so simply?" "Because it is very simple Sheba; God speaks to me and I listen to Him." "I have to admit it; I am forced to believe you. There is something else I have to tell you John. Your book; the Precious Princess, I just can't put it down. I find it so interesting that I go over and over it again and again. I have the impression I'm reading Shakespeare or something. It is just out of this world." "Just like you Sheba, remember your song? 'A girl seems to be out of this world.'

I don't think you have the slightest idea of what you're saying here means to me and how long I've been waiting for you to say something like this. I could just cry of joy like a kid or like a woman. I gave you my book like a few months ago and every time I saw you I was hoping to hear something like this. I felt like going nuts when you said the chapter four was so sweet and I thought not as much as you."

"How come a nice guy like you is still single John?" "Up to my last relationship I always picked my women myself Sheba and my life with them has been nothing but a real mess. So now I want to let God pick my soulmate for me just like He did it for Isaac and Rebekah. Hopefully I'll be able to keep her for the rest of my life and for the eternity. I already predicted a certain woman will be my last partner. So in fact I think she is already picked. Now God has to convince her that I am the right guy for her. It is just a matter of time now, but I really don't know how long it will take. I've been alone for four and a half years now, but I trust my God; He knows what He's doing." "Who's Dana John?" "She is a beautiful young lady who not even knowing it she gave me the idea for the book; The Precious Princess and I'm very grateful to her for this. One of the purposes of this book is to make myself known to the woman I passionately love for several years now. She's actually in a process of reading my book finally." "Do you love Dana?" "I do, but not the same way I love this woman. I don't only love this woman; I'm in love with her." "I'm with a man right now, but I know he's not my soulmate." "You must feel a bit like I did at one point in my life; a kind of a prostitute in your own home?" "Oh don't get me wrong I love him dearly, but let's put it this way; he won't be the one I would want to spend the rest of my life with, even less the eternity. I just know he's not my soulmate." "You shouldn't be with him then. Don't forget heaven begins in this life and so

15

is hell and they're continuing in the next world. You've got to make yourself free and available for the right man, because the right one from God wouldn't take you away from another man. He wouldn't have God's approval and neither his blessing if he did. Besides, he wouldn't do it if he's a child of God.

I've been alone all this long because I want to be ready for this woman I love and I also want to deserve her. If you deserve a crappy partner you'll get him, because God is fair, but on the other hand if you deserve a wonderful one you'll get him too. I mean one or the other." "I learned more truth from you John in a couple of hours than I did in many years from the religions." "It didn't cost you a cent either.

'We will recognise the tree by its fruits.' Jesus said this. I'm glad you can see the difference. We also deserve the path we're on and if we live through hell it is most likely because we weren't doing God's will. Sheba, I believe God put me on your way to show you the light, because you love Him and He'll give you a chance to turn your life around to be pleasing to Him. You already have a foot in the door of heaven; now you have to make sure you don't do things to make Him slam the door on your foot." "You have a way to say things John that only a real blind couldn't see and a real deaf couldn't hear." "Thanks Sheba, you're a real sweetheart. I was hoping I could make the blind see and the deaf hear though." "Maybe you will John." "Do you see now that I'm in the kingdom of heaven and I try to make others enter too?

It is the most wonderful and rewarding job a human been could get. It is almost like being one of God's

16

angels. I know you'll do the same one day soon." "How do you know this?" "Because you're listening to me and my words are coming from God. Go read Matthew 10, 20, you'll see." "I will, but I already believe you." "God showed me how to read; especially between the lines and also how to write." "Is this why you brought up so many topics in your first book?" "He wouldn't allow me to do the things He doesn't want me to." "When do we have our next Bible's study John?" "I didn't think this was a study, but only a simple conversation. Just give me a dingo when ever you're ready Sheba and I'll make myself available for you." "I feel so much happier now. It is just like I'm having a brand new life." "This might just be what they call being born again. Your joy, your happiness, your pretty blue eyes, your gorgeous smile and your loving care are to me a great reward Sheba. I hope I'll see you soon."

I went home and I kept writing whatever the Lord is dictating me. Day after day ideas come to my mind flowing like the wind through the air or like water through a little stream carrying whatever to its destination. My Lord made me one of his tools to shape the world to his liking; the same way He uses the nature's tools to shape everything in the universe and all this to protect and warn his children about the coming wrath. He never changes, is He? He's so bountiful. There were only a few people who loved Him at the time of Noah, but He managed to save them all from the flood, didn't He? He saved Lot and his family basically the same way from the desegregation of Sodom and Gomorrah. Blessed are the ones who listen to Him and to his assistants, Jesus and his disciples.

Between writing and doing my other chores I go on the Net trying to increase the sales; which I hope one day would allow me to publish my books and my music. But the system is so corrupt it takes super and almost inhuman efforts to get anywhere. It was a time when the publishers were after the writers to get something interesting to publish; now it is the other way around and besides, now the writers have to pay to get something published and it's not cheap.

To print a book a printing company wants fifty-two percent of its value, the book store wants forty percent to sell it, the government wants its share. There is nothing but peanuts left for the writer and yet he's the motor of this industry, the brains that bring the fuel which keeps this big machine going on. If it's up to me one day things will turn around.

A good friend of mine who is also a song writer and he's in the market for forty years was just telling me lately that on an album of twenty songs he wrote the words and the music the marketing company was offering him only fifty cents a cd and twenty-five cents a cassette. Who is really making the money? So far they've sold thousands of copies and my friend didn't get a cent yet. It is always the strongest get the most. I don't know how yet, but one day with the help of my Lord I will do something about this.

CHAPTER 2

A beautiful day today. I brought a little puppy of mine to show it to Sheba.

"You should be showing the pup to my daughter John; she'll just be going crazy about this." "Alright, I'll bring it back later on if you want me to. I heard you're having trouble with your son lately." "He lies, he steals, he causes trouble at home and here at my work and now he's running away." "Just about all of us are going through this kind of troubles. I left behind my son who was fourteen at school once because I wanted to pay my daughter a visit in Quebec and when I came back there wasn't a single wall in my place that wasn't broken. He tried to blame it on somebody else too. He said they had a party and he couldn't control the others.

They put out a picture of my daughter on the wall and played darts on it. This was the exact clue which proved to me he was involve. Nobody else could ever be mad at her or even have a reason to do this. I got a lot of pictures of this mess. At the time it could have just made me throw up and I couldn't even stay in there that night. I had to rent a hotel room.

They had left raw meet on the sink that had started to rot. They had burnt utensils with drugs, name it. It was a real mess which makes you wonder why we suffer so much for our children. It is as if they want to punish us for bringing them to this world. They were so cute when they were babies. Although, there is only one thing that can win them over! Can you tell me what this is?" "All I know is I just don't want to see him anymore." "I don't blame you one bit. I felt the same way. The same kind of love and compassion our Father in heaven has for you and me is the same kind of love and the only thing that can win your son over and turn him around from what he's doing. What you and I have done to God is way worse than our sons did to us." "Tell me John, where do you get all this information?" "I told you Sheba; God speaks to me and I listen. At one point I even feared for my life and I don't think yours is safe either.

It is written that at the end time the children will kill their parents and the parents will kill their children. You can believe it. It happens every day somewhere in the world nowadays. Pretty soon people will bring anaesthesia for people and not only for animals."

"I've been thinking about your business John. I don't think it's this good after all." "What is a good business Sheba? Is it to be greedier than greed? A garage who charges three hours at sixty-five dollars an hour to change a water pump a good back yard mechanic can change in thirty minutes for fifteen dollars and the system does everything in its power to stop him? A big store like Overweight who takes ninety-nine cents a pound for potatoes or apples, two dollars a pound for tomatoes, when the farmers and the orchardists struggle and get only six or seven cents a pound and are going broke and loosing their properties? To survive now they don't only need to be farmers anymore, but they need to be good businessmen and good administrators. Is it a bank rich with billions who charges twenty-five dollars in penalty to a poor guy whose cheque was returned because a few cents were missing?

When I got in Calgary back in 1982 I was more broke than broke, poorer than poor. I had a payment of a hundred dollars a month to make at the bank for my music equipment. I had then one hundred and two dollars in my account. The bank then took four dollars for its own fees minutes before they returned my cheque for NSF and they put a charge of ten dollars on my account. Oh, they get rich alright, but they won't take their dollars to heaven and they certainly don't do this to serve God.

I just read in the newspaper about the richest people in the world. The top one has over one hundred billions dollar's worth. Let me tell you Sheba; I'm richer than he is." "Come on John, are you getting out of your mind now?" "My treasures are not in this world Sheba, but in heaven. How many of those dollars do you think he'll bring with him at the end?

I talked to one of his thousands of employees the other day and I asked her if she heard the news. She said; "Yes, I heard it on the radio, but you know on whose back he got up there, don't you? We put him up there." "Aren't you proud of it?" "My eye; he could have taking a little less and give us a little more." "If he paid you too much you would probably be without a job." "How

come?" "Too many people would have fought for it."
"You might just have a point." "He's got so much money
that even if he gives all of you a one hundred thousand
dollar bonus it wouldn't make any dent in is fortune. It
would be also a big tax write off. He's got to be a good
administrator though and it's a person like this we need
at the head of our country; as long as he is honest of
course. He's rich enough to buy this country, pay cash
for it and sell it to someone OAC, to someone who can
afford it for sure."

"My next business will be to sell books and cds
Sheba. I sure hope you will join me in this venture. I'm
pretty sure you would enjoy it. The two very best selling
things on the Net today are exactly those two items.

My first book, The Precious Princess was appraised
as best seller by a known and famous author and if I can
get you to sing some songs of mine we will do well with
this too." "I'm not this good, you know?" "We have to let
the public decide this. Although, I need to know in which
key you like to sing best or in which one you sing better. I
would like to make a few tapes so you can practice a few
songs. My first cd as you know is called; Janene, The
Smile of an Angel. If you want to I'll call my second one;
Sheba And The One Man Band." "This is cute John." "I
thought you would like it. I just love the idea. It will sell
way better if I could ever put a picture of your smile and
your beautiful face on the disk.

Here you are at the crossing of these two roads
Sheba. The choice is yours. You can stay on the
thornbush road where you seem to be on presently or
get on the golden path to the New Jerusalem with me

and the other God's children." "What do I have to do?" "Sing God's word, praises to the Lord would be a good start. Then, if you want to do more you can help me spread the word of God towards the whole world just like Jesus asked us to do. 'Go and make disciples of all nations.'

I just know from down deep inside me Sheba that you and me are bound to do something together. You are already tied up to me for ever with your smile of an angel on this cd of mine and also with this book we are working on. Besides, as you already know, the writhing stays.

There is where you are right now Sheba, aren't you? You are at the crossing. One of the two is full of the devil's traps, full of thorn bushes and the other one is a golden path with love, peace, happiness. Which one would it be? Which way will you go?

Would it be the thorn bushes and weeds up and down cliffs, a swirling and dangerous road or the happiness, the joy, love and peace on the golden path to the New Jerusalem with all the other God's children?

You must have quite a wardrobe, because you always dress as if you were a princess?" "There is no doubt; I like nice clothes." "They suit you beautifully." "Thanks John." "I like to look at a woman well dressed; especially looking at you." "Is that so?" "I also noticed lately you were looking at me as if you had some questions. As if you wanted to read my mind. Is it because I didn't put enough about me in the Princess' book? You know you can ask me anything, don't you? I will answer any of your questions directly and frankly. I have many questions about you too. You intrigue me and I think you are very special. It's probably why I wanted to write your story. This allows me to know you and also get you to know me.

Jees, I think everybody should do this. This way it would be a lot less misunderstanding within couples and in the population in general. The words die, but the writing lives forever. Can you imagine my book to last forever? Just like my love for this woman I talked to you about the other day. This is a thought which worms up my heart.

You told me one day you have talked to one of your friend about me. Would this bother you to tell me about the conversation? I think it would be good to write something else than our conversation in this book of yours. Just like it happens in real life, you know? What do you think of it? You also showed me on a piece of paper how swirling your life has been and how straight is your walk now.

You know this woman I mentioned to you, the one I love so very much has a very similar life than yours and she's just as pretty as you are. I'll introduce her to you one day. In fact you remind me of her a lot.

A few weeks ago I noticed a big change of attitude in you towards me and my book. Could you tell me what it is? You seem to be much happier and I'm glad to see you smile again. I know you're having trouble with your son, but I noticed the change and I wondered if it had anything to do with me.

Could you also tell me some of the conversations you had with your son, your daughters, your mother and friends? Did you ever talk to someone else about this rough road of yours? What was their reaction? Did you feel better after?

A few times you talked as if you have been very bad in your pass. Did you forgive yourself? My son told me a couple of times he could never be as honest as I am. This is a very scary thing to hear." "You're pretty busy, aren't you John?" "I have to keep busy otherwise; I would just go crazy waiting for this woman to make up her mind about me."

"It must be hard to love someone this much and not be with her, not been able to hold her in your arms?" "It would be way worst if I was still prisoner of my sexuality." "What do you mean John? Are you impotent or castrated?" "Not at all Sheba! You have rarely met someone as potent as I am, but this kind of question calls for what it looks like bragging answers, which I don't like to do. What I'm telling you is I'm not a victim of sexual slavery anymore. I was delivered from evil." "Do you mean to say sex is evil?" "Not at all Sheba! Sex is rather marvellous; especially with the love one, but not to be able to control it is not good. It is not my penis, this inflamed member of my body which controls me anymore when I think or I'm with the opposite sex I still love very much. Don't get me wrong, but it is my head and my heart which control the rest of my body from now on. I am quite happy about the change and this is a gift the Lord gave me; the necessary patient to allow me to wait without making stupid mistakes and this allows me also to wait for the one I really love instead of having sex left and right like I used to and most people do.

It's God who has orchestrated everything. He is so wonderful. If someone could invent a medicine which could allow men and women to control their sexual impulse without reducing the procreation; this would certainly reduce the number of assaults by at least a thousand times in the world and certainly make the inventor very famous.

Just before my dad died he was nothing but skin and bones on his hospital bed. He couldn't talk anymore because his lungs were totally shut down, but I'm sure that if we brought him a nice looking young naked girl, virgin or not, this might have killed him sooner, but he would have tried to have sex with her. His uncle who raised him was the same way. My ex father-in-law who was ninety-nine years and nine months old when he died was the same way just before his death. I guessed they didn't pray enough to be delivered from evil or maybe they didn't want to." "You're not telling me John that you love this woman without desiring her, are you?" "This is exactly what I'm telling you. I love her without being tormented and I save my desire for when I'll be able to get the pleasure. Besides, my love for her is totally unconditional; which means if she's happy without me I'm happy for her. If she can be happier with me it's better yet." "I never heard anyone talk like this before John." "Maybe it is the first time you meet a real disciple of the Lord.

My chances to have her in my arms one day were one in a billion and maybe less; now I'd say they're down to one in a thousand and maybe even better." "What do you think created the change?" "The fact she's reading my book now. She might realize soon she's actually the

Precious Princess I was talking about." "In your book you said you got married in May of 1999 and you're still single. Can you explain this one?" "Certainly Sheba; it is actually very simple." "Everything seems to be simple once you have explained it, but not before you did." "This is a part of my character. I am still single in 2001, but only physically and not morally; simply because the year 1999 wasn't really 1999." "That's a good one." "It's beyond you, isn't it? Just like the year 2000 wasn't the year 2000.

This is why the catastrophe of Y2K, the crash expected by millions of people never happened yet." "Do you mean it is still to come?" "You bet it is and I think this will happen between the year 2028 and 2033; exactly two thousands years after the crucifixion of Jesus; where and when the curtain of the temple was split in two from top to bottom; which was according to my calculations the start of the count down. Knowing for myself that God has always been precise with everything He has done; so we can expect the trend will continue.

My marriage with my princess should take place approximately twenty-six years before the end. Now, because I've learned and I know better I will never let a member of the beast or the false prophet or the devil unites me to anyone. I will only let God Himself marry us and I already know that what God has united no one can separate." "What do you mean exactly John?" "I mean we'll have a royal wedding in the face of the whole world for witnesses if this is what she wants, but no papers. As far as I am concerned I am already married to her in my head and in my heart and I have been faithful to her for a long time now.

God has put his words and his laws in our hearts and for this reason we'll stand for his word and we'll live by it. 'Men shall not live on bread alone, but on every word that proceeds out of the mouth of God. See Matthew 4, 4.

Not too many people know what year we really are living in, but don't kid yourself; the authorities know. The scientists know exactly when an eclipse happened thousands of years behind and they know exactly when Jesus was crucified, because there was one on that day. Now take that year; subtract thirty-three years of the life of Jesus and add two thousands years and you get the Y2K. Do you see that it is a very simple mathematics? The exact day the one I love so much will say she loves me I'll know then exactly what year we are without having study any science.

You and I will play a major role in the history of the end time Sheba. Now understand one thing; the end time is simply the end of the devil's reign. He wouldn't like it and this is why it's going to be the worst war ever. He's going to gather all the devils of the world to fight God and his people. I already know the result of this. It will also be then the separation will occur, because none of God's children will go against their Father and his people. But before this happens you and I have a wonderful job to do." "Why me?" "Because God has chose you to be with me in this battle.

Here's what I thought we will be doing Sheba. Tell me what you think. I think it would be the first of the kind ever. What would you say if we make cassettes and videos of our story? What if we and all the characters of this book of ours would speak each word and each line? What if our conversations, the ones about you with your son, with your mother, with your daughters, with your friends and so on would be parts live of this venture? Each and every one of us would receive his or her royalties for all the sales everywhere the story is sold according to their parts in the story.

It is so original that the book would hit the news and be seen by the whole world like lightning from the East to the West. Every one of us would become as famous as the best actor. In no time at all the book would be the most sold book in the entire world and this in all languages. They wouldn't be able to print it fast enough. It would actually be profitable to own our own printing and publishing companies. Movie makers would be after us like flies after a dirty cow's tail. I can see us in magazines, newspapers, televisions, radios and name it. I can see you organizing and orchestrating all the chorales for each show. I can see you with me every step of the way telling not only our surrounding, but the whole population of the world the Lord has returned.

We would make a tremendous fortune which we would use to feed the poor around the world physically and spiritually. God would be so pleased with us that the more we give the more we'll have to give. When people will see what we get for what we're doing; they will join us by the thousands on this golden path. Then pretty soon there will be all the good people on one side; this will be heaven. There will also be all the bad ones on the other side; which will be a hell of a hell for the people who don't love God. There will be weeping and gnashing of teeth prophesied by Jesus, my brother almost two thousands years ago."

Anyone can call me brother too if you follow Jesus' teaching and do the will of my Father who is in heaven; if not don't you dare for your own good.

"Have you ever thought about who you could have been in the pass Sheba? Did you ever think you existed before in a previous world?" "Not really John, but I often told my kids I was a queen." "You didn't know it, but you were telling them the truth" "Do you want to do me a favour and think about it? I would like you to pick three names of women in the Bible you could have been in a previous world. Would you do this?" "Sure, I will." "I'd like you to look in the Bible and see what you can come up with. I got a good idea myself of who you could have been." "Really?" "Yes, she was the wife of one of the greatest kings ever and became the mother of the wisest man who ever existed and he also became a great king. She was the wife of another man before she became the king's wife also. She was still with him when the king went to rest and wait for her to join him. She was very pretty and very intelligent and the king fell in love with her at first sight; just like I did with the women I love. Only the Lord wouldn't allow me to make the same mistakes the king made. Before King David died they brought him the prettiest virgin of the whole country to warm him up and even though he had the right to take her, he didn't.

It is very strange I was showed through dreams and vision thirty years in the future and even to the eternity for my book; The Precious Princess and now the Lord shows me over three thousands years in the pass."

Did you people notice the genealogy of Jesus in Luke is not the same than it is in Matthew? Maybe this is why there are the Christ and the antichrist in the Bible. There are the wheat and the weeds, the truth and the lies. I never ever heard anyone talk about this one. It is just to say it is God who shows me these things. According to Luke Jesus descended from Nathan, son of David and according to Matthew, you know the guy who actually spent time with Jesus, the one I believe; Jesus descended from king Solomon, son of David. It is quite a difference, you know? I am from my father, which is a total different line than my father's brother's line. Believe me my manoeuvres are quite different than my cousins' ones also.

Nathan was a good prophet, a good man, but he was never a king even though he was a son of David. Just like Jesus said it himself he was the king of the Jews. So he is a descendant of a king's line. He has to come from Solomon king of Israel, son of David. The reason why the Roman Catholic organization has chosen Nathan or I rather say; they have eliminated Solomon completely from Jesus' genealogy is because of the fact he had so many women.

This is something that goes against certain church's policies; for they don't take women at all; at least not publicly yet. But now they are ready to marry men to men, women to women and a lot of their teachers are gays and pedophiles. They will probably marry between themselves in a near future if it's not already done. All this though will have for effect to discredit the meaning of marriages and many people will pull away from this sacrament.

I heard from the news on the radio years ago; I think it was around 1965 in Quebec that the police force made a raid in a homosexual private party. One priest, thirty-eight brothers and the bell ringer were arrested, but only the last one, the civil man was to be judge by our court system. All the others were to be judged by the Catholic clergy. I'm sure they were told to be more careful next time.

"Do you remember Sheba you told me once you would like to write a book for children? I had an idea and I hope you'll like it. The idea is I could start you on this book. It could be called; From The Kindergarten To The Golden Path. If you want to I'll do the beginning; which you could change eventually and then you'll be on your way from there. I won't be too far away if you need me. You'd be better finish reading the Precious Princess first though, otherwise you'll never be able to. In my first book the Princess touches thirty-three children or so. With your book you could touch thousands and who knows maybe thirty-three millions or more; especially if it's suitable for schools. If you invite me we could even do it together. So here we are ready to go." "I'm not as good as you are though." "I'm very happy and flattered you think so, but until you try you have no way to know. When I started writing there were hundreds of words I didn't know how to spell. I didn't even know how to spell the word write properly. Not bad for a righter, isn't it? Most of the time I used the word right when I needed write and write when I needed right. But one thing I was write about is to start writing. You see, now I wrote a book you say you have a hard time to put down even to eat or to sleep.

I'm telling you Sheba; you and me will be in a book and music business and you'll love it too. You'll be so passionate that I'll have a hard time to get you off of it for supper. The very first thing to do is to get yourself a cheap computer if you can't afford a new one. Don't forget it is best the computer you use to write on is not connected to the Internet to avoid bad surprises which could paralyse everything that is on it. One thing never to forget is to save and protect everything you write. The computer is real fast to put a book together, but trust me; it is even faster to erase it.

I could have just cried one day; maybe I did when I lost six months of hard work in a fraction of a second. I pushed the wrong button after neglecting to read the question on the screen properly. Hundreds of ideas were gone too and they don't always come back, at least not all of them. Every once in a while I remember things I once wrote in the book of Precious, but they're no longer in there.

A good idea is to learn to undo, so you can get it back if you make a mistake. I think what I did is highlighting the whole manuscript that was too much on the right side and because I wanted to bring it back on the left side I pushed the backspace button, which does the same thing than deleting. Everything was gone alright and I didn't know how to bring it back. If only I would have shut down the computer then I would have had everything again. It's always better to lose a few lines than to lose everything.

So far Sheba I wrote a lot of things about you. I asked you a lot of questions and I'll need some answers to make this book a great one. Just know too that all the things I wrote are not necessarily going to stay there; they are more or less suggestions until we can discuss them over." "I know and have a great day John." "You too Sheba!"

CHAPTER 3

———— ∞∞∞ ————

SURPRISING THINGS

Today, the 24th of April 2001 an amazing thing happened to say the least. The man who in a rage broke the mirror of my truck a couple of years ago came to visit me. He needs a box for his pickup that I have and he came to discuss a deal with me. After looking at it and at different things we talked about the government and this led some how to the religion. He listened to me with interest for more than an hour and I gave him a booklet about the book of the antichrist along with a few gospel tapes of mine.

He also asked me how much the booklets were and he said he would like to send a couple of them to his religious aunts. He read, he listened and said he never heard someone before talking about the truth with so much conviction. Who could have predicted something like this to happen? See Matthew 21, 31. 'I tell you the truth, the tax collectors and the prostitutes are entering the kingdom of heaven ahead of you.'

Jesus said it. Did you see this; you the Saints Christians? I can assure you that today this is another fulfilled prophecy. I see some of the worse people receiving the word of God with joy.

Nevertheless, this man made me a ridiculous offer on the box. It is worth approximately five hundred dollars and he offered me eighty dollars worth in labour. I know he doesn't have much money, but neither do I. It is a box of a Mercury pickup 1968, which is a collected item now. I intend to ask him three hundred dollars worth in parts and labour to complete a couple of trailers I own; which I'll be able to sell for four hundred dollars each. It is quite a bit more than what he offered me, but still it's a good deal for him. The reason of his rage that time was nothing else than jealousy. I had offered him a job at four hundred and fifty dollars for a fifty hours week and he turned it down with a stupid excuse, but this was ok, it was his choice.

A young man whom I hired previously for feeding my dogs when I was away told him he was paid ten dollars an hour, but the truth is he was paid eight. Well for one thing this was a lie and it should have been private too. It was there and then this man began his anger against me.

He called me the next day and when he heard my offer; he told me I was reasonable and he will look for the parts I need. He also told me that for the first time in his life he just understood how the Bible works.

Amazing things happen. I often asked myself if I existed in a previous world too or in the pass somewhere and whom I could have been. I've seen myself I thought like a musketeer fighting with a sword. I often had the impression the pieces of music I composed could have been played by King David. One of the strangest things too is the ones I got from up there for my gospel songs are coming through the harp sound on my electronic keyboard. I also know that King David was a good harp player and he liked singing hymns to the Lord. In fact when I read how David was talking to the Lord I realized I do it the same way. David was a man after God's heart. See 1 Samuel 13, 14.

King David was a little man of about one hundred and fifty pounds who played the harp well, sang hymns to the Lord and kept the sheep of his father. When a bear or a lion came to steal a sheep from him he left the ninety-nine other sheep behind, ran to the animal, struck it and took the sheep away. If the animal turned on him he grabbed it by the throat, struck and killed it. This was quite a slap.

When the biggest enemy of Israel, Goliath the giant, the personalized devil came out of the rank of his army of uncircumcised to insult the people of God; David decided to challenge him by telling the king he could beat this monster. The king allowed David to go fight the giant beast. David did it and won with not much of a weapon in hands; at least in comparison to what the giant was carrying.

Now, what would a giant look like today? He would be maybe someone like the wrestler Jean Ferre; weighting four hundred and fifty pounds and measuring seven foot four. According to my international Bible Goliath was more then nine feet high.

A man this size and strength carrying a shield bearer, a sword, a spear and a javelin coming against a little man like David who was a young boy who seemed to be bare handed is rather disconcerting or I rather say disarming. David put the enemy down with only a sling and a polished little stone and of course with the help of God too. Then he killed the beast with the sword his enemy, this monster was carrying.

At my very last day in school in Richmond near Magog, the East side of the province in the village where I grew up the most; even though I didn't grow this much; I asked the director of the school to choose who he might think is the strongest student in the yard to come and help him separate both of my arms joined together by the wrists. He chose Gilles Delage, a six foot tall young man who put all he's got and the two of them could not do it.

The young man even got mad and tried to break my grip by putting a foot on my side and the director had to tell him to calm down a little. Nevertheless, the two of them couldn't do it. Then I asked the director to make the same grip I did and I brook him opened by myself with no trouble. He just said I was not an ordinary guy. I was fourteen years old at the time.

I am myself what most people would call a little man. One day while I was playing horseshoes on the beach in Roxton Pound near Granby in Quebec, I noticed at about one hundred feet from me a professional wrestler showing tricks of his trade to other kids of my age and younger; I'd say from fourteen to eighteen years of age. I was seventeen at the time and rather curious about these things. I was just a skinny little guy weighting one hundred and twenty pounds at the time. I was rather curious about wrestling then. I went to the wrestler then after a lot of hesitation wondering if I should or not and I told the big guy I could lift him up from the ground by his belt around his waist using only one finger. He laughed at me of course with reason too.

'You can lift me with only one finger?'

I had no problem understanding his attitude at all.

"How much do you weight?" "I weight two hundred and twenty pounds. This is enough to break any one of your fingers." "Don't laugh at me and just put a solid belt around your waist and I'll show you."

He then sent a young boy in a hurry to his car to get his belt.

"You better have a word as solid as your finger young man."

When he had the belt on I approached him, I slipped a finger under his belt in a way that him and all the others could see and up he was in the air. Not only I lifted him, but I hold him there long enough at the end of my arm. I looked him in the eyes as if I wanted him to acknowledge what I have done and then he said: 'By God, you've done it.'

It was almost funny to see the others all away around looking with stupefaction. I could tell this guy just had the surprise of his life, but the poor guy wasn't at the end of his troubles for the day. He tried to lift me up the same way; me who was one hundred pounds less and he could never do it. He almost became furious after trying for the third time without success. He hit his legs with his fists saying; 'This is impossible.'

It is true it seemed impossible. What seems impossible to us sometime is not necessarily the case, but there was no magic in this.

I never had in mind to embarrass him; I just thought this was a good opportunity to challenge myself, but I couldn't guess he wouldn't be able to do it.

Another time a very similar thing happened. It was in the same period of time. This was just a couple of days later. I was working in a blanket shop in Granby Quebec and the girl on the opposite side of the table told me her father was a bouncer in a bar for the weekends. I kept telling her I could lift him up with only one finger. She was a very little woman weighting hardly eighty-five pounds. Who could have guessed what is following?

"You better be careful with your mouth young man." "I'm telling you the truth; I can lift him up with only one finger."

She was laughing with reason every time we were talking about it. I was working from midnight to seven o'clock in the morning before going to the beach where I met the wrestler.

What she never told me is her father was starting to work at seven in the morning in the same shop. One day I was waiting for the clock to ring seven o'clock to punch my time card when I felt a big hand grabbing my shoulder from behind and I heard a big voice saying:

"I heard you say you can lift me up with only one finger young man. Now you'll have to do it if you don't want to make me mad."

I turned around and there he was with another man, a friend of his, a co-worker who was just as big as him or even bigger. There was in front of my eyes between those two men anywhere from five hundred to five hundred and fifty pounds. I asked him how much he weights.

"I weight two hundred and fifty-five pounds." "Do you have a good belt?" "I carry a belt which can carry me. Don't you worry for it; worry for yourself and mainly for your finger." "I've never lift this much before this way, but I'm welling to try."

I then approached him to try the almost impossible.

"It's going to squeeze your belly up." "Don't worry about me. Damn it."

He said looking at the other guy.

"He did it. I don't touch the floor anymore."

The other guy burst out laughing and said:

"You finally met your man my big friend."

In the same shop there was a strong man who worked at replacing the big rolls of thread. He said those rolls weight five thousands pounds. They are anywhere from eight to ten feet long by approximately two feet in diameter. One day this man called me to push a little stroller underneath the big roll once he got it up. He told me then he was the only man in the shop who could lift it.

"You have to go real fast, you know? You don't even have a second to do it."

I totally missed the first time.

"It's a failure; now I'll have to wait around ten minutes. I should be getting someone who used to do it." "Oh, come on please? Give me another chance, would you?"

When he tried some ten minutes later I succeed to push the stroller underneath on time. When we went to the other end of the big roll I asked him to let me try. He laughed at me and he told me to forget about it.

"It wouldn't cost anything to let me try, would it?"

He complied with my demand and then he showed me how to do it. I then installed myself at the end of this shaft following his instructions and he pushed the stroller underneath. He got up yelling his head off and I thought for sure he lost a finger or something. "No!" He said swinging me around.

"I waited twenty years to see someone else doing this."

He went around the shop to tell everyone he could meet about it. Most of them couldn't believe him even though the guy was so sincere.

It is only the second time I mention it too since no one wanted to believe me the first time I did. I did a lot of little tricks too like pulling two vehicles one behind the other at the same time with my teeth on the gravel back alley. The very first time I tried it and this after a lot of hesitation; which was with my old Fargo 1968 loaded with seventeen hundred pounds of shingles and this was in the back lane as well. My employee said then it must be because it's down hill. So I said, if it's the case it should be up hill the other way. I pull the truck going the other way and I basically ran with it. I have to say though this vehicle had hardly any brakes left.

I also danced an old time waltz holding with my teeth a one hundred and twenty pounds woman sitting in a chair I made for the occasion. The same evening I pulled twelve people on the rug also with my teeth. I also lifted a half ton front pickup up a pole with the help of a harness, I bent a twelve inches nail at ninety degrees using a hock attached to a piece of leather also with my teeth and many other little tricks.

But the feat of strength of my life is still to come. I now walk around with a bigger sword than the one King David had to win all of his wars with. I walk with a double edged sword and I have to cut the neck of the beast of the end time the same way David did it to the giant.

I have no other protection than God as my shield, but I know this is sufficient. The Holy Truth, the Holy Word of God, the teaching of Jesus, which the religions tried so hard to hide it to the world population is now in route for around the world.

Nothing can stop it anymore, because it is lead by the arm of the Almighty; just like no one could stop David against Goliath and all his enemies.

Christianity is the monster, the Goliath I have to fight. The religious system is on the way out and the reign of Jesus, the word of God is about to begin. Things are really going to hut up believe me and believe also all of God's prophets.

This book God gave me; The True Face of The Antichrist and the booklet to announce it are I think the sling and the polish stone of David. The truth in them is the double edged sword flourishing in the arm of God. Keep watching for the shaking of the biggest religious empire in the world; which is roman and all those who followed its steps. You'll see and hear soon the weeping and the gnashing of teeth.

There will be a day when a man says thunder and you'll hear it roll as if this was a mountain rolling and the lightning will shine from one end of the world to the other. I wouldn't be afraid, because God is my shield. There will be a day when a man says earthquake and all of the earth will shake. You'll be shaking in your shoes, but I won't be shaking, because God is my shield.

There will be one day when a man says; I want the water of your body changed into blood and then you'll see in the eyes of people who hate the true God of Israel weeping bloody tears. You'll see there mouth spitting blood, you'll see them blowing their bloody nose and they will be peeing blood. This will continue until they change their attitude and too bad for them if they never do. They'll know then their little god doesn't have much power and their ignominy will show right in their faces.

These men will be able to do these things not because they are God, but because God will be with them. Just like He was with Noah, Abraham, Isaac, Jacob, Joseph, Moses, David, Solomon, Jesus and many more and as He is with me.

When God was speaking to Moses, people were afraid to die and basically asked God not to do it anymore. Well, God did listen and spoke to people through Moses, Jesus and many more, but people still ignore the word of God; which is inflaming God's anger.

It has been a long time since people have seen wonders and miracles like Jesus was doing.

This generation will see some of them and they are not this far away. Jesus said others will do greater things than he did. See John 14, 12-13 and Matthew 17, 20. He didn't lie for there is no lie in him.

Jesus said things which when I repeat them today they hit the spot real hard. Those words were said to open the eyes of the blind and clean out the ears of the deaf.

God, David, Jesus and I are one and the same. Shocked? I can hear people say: 'This guy is a total nut.'

Jesus said the exact same thing and He was crucified for telling the truth.

David was a man after God's heart. See 1 Samuel 13, 14. 'The Lord has sought out a man after his own heart and appointed him leader of his people.'

Jesus was exactly the same and so I'm I. For the sceptical about what I'm saying I say go read John 17, 10-26. Just like David was one with God, so was Jesus, so I'm I, at least most of the time and mainly since He speaks to me.

Many people were burned alive, many others were killed or locked up in asylums for saying this truth; just like one of our last prophets, Louis Riel who was hanged which is not this far back. By whom was he killed? He was killed by the beast, the governmental and the religious system, Christianity, the beast with the number 666. Do you still wonder why I'm out of it? Louis Riel was locked up and killed because he was fighting the injustices done to his people and telling the truth about the clergy, about Rome.

King David had a good army with him. Many would have fallow Jesus into a war against the Romans. Many believers in the true God and the Masked Defenders, God's soldiers will follow me in this war against the religious system, the beast of the end time.

The truth, the double edged sword will put this monster down. It is already written. It is already prophesied. I invent nothing by saying this. My books and my songs are tremendous tools, tremendous weapons,

45

because they are words God has put in my mouth. Many good souls have suffered for the sake of our God; now is the day of the Lord, the day of revenge for his children's blood which is coming up soon.

One day soon as I predicted in my first book you'll see the system calling all the Bibles; pretending that now they have the one and only true one. They will tell you it is written directly from the dead see scrolls. Why? Because it was prophesied in Daniel that at the end time the knowledge will increase and people eyes will open.

This gigantic empire, the devilish kingdom of the beast can't afford to let the truth put him down; especially not by a little Frenchman like me. Just like they couldn't let a half breed like Louis Riel and the Métis do it in his days. So, the beast will do anything in its power to stop this truth from spreading. Let me tell you that without God I could not win this war. But also without God I wouldn't even want to try. Without God I wouldn't even be thinking or writing about it. Without God I would never have thought of it in the first place. Without God I would certainly not be doing this work.

"Hi Sheba, how are you today?" "I'm good John, what about you?" "I'm good I guess, but I've been anxious about your reaction on the part of the book I let you have. I wished you've called me to calm me down. I love working on this book of ours Sheba, but the ultimate pleasure for me would be to write one about the woman I love. See, right now I love her, but I don't really know the one I love. I have so much to know about her yet. Oh I know she's lovely, very kind and extremely pretty, but all the rest you know; all the things we don't see at first sight. I sure don't want another psycho. I had my share of someone who wants to ruin my life and kill me. I have too much to accomplish yet to put up with this kind of things. I want someone who can pull the same way and in the same direction I do. It is the only way I'll get where I should be going."

"Would you mind if I go talk to this woman John?" "Maybe we should leave it Sheba. She might just wonder what I'm doing with such a beautiful woman as you. She might not understand that all we're doing together is writing a book. She might reject you also, which would really displease me. No Sheba, let it be for now. One day soon you'll get to know her anyway." "What is her name and what is she doing?" "She's a receptionist like you, always smiling, always well dressed, but she doesn't want me to mention her name to anyone and I have to respect this. She's a lot like you as I told you before; you remind me of her a lot." "I wish you good luck. I think you deserve someone nice." "Thanks Sheba, but what about you? I told you before, you are my guideline in all of this. How's the book of Precious make you feel about the writer? In another word, how does it make you feel about me?" "I kind of wish I could be treated like the Princess and mainly be loved like she is." "How would you like to be celebrated like she was?" "This part is just incredible John. I think I read it ten times." "Could you see yourself in the shoes of this Precious Princess?" "It can only be a dream John." "Trust me Sheba dreams can be true if you believe in them strong enough.

What do you think of the fighter's side of me?" "You fight for a unique cause and I'm sure God is with you in this battle. We need more men like you." "But you Sheba, you only need one, don't you?" "Not too many men would give their lives for their women anymore." "Maybe it is just because they don't have the right partner. See, most people don't have the patient to wait for the right one anymore. They just have to have sex and they take whoever is available. This satisfy them for a while and they have the impression it's ok until they find out they are sleeping with someone they don't love at all. I went through this too.

Then they go feed the system by paying the lawyers for their divorce. Rich and poor, week and strong get hit by this. I know some fairly rich men who were just ruined by the system this way. I know others who lost a big chunk of their fortune too. Some people will recognize themselves when they read this book of ours." "Nevermind some people John, you talk about me here too." "I talk about myself too Sheba.

Do you remember a few years back I mentioned to you another book I started about heaven and hell? It is called: The Ten Virgins and The Kingdom of Heaven." "I vaguely do, yes." "You told me then it would make a good title. I wrote quite a bit in it and then suddenly nothing. As you know I never wreck my mind for ideas and for writing. I just do it when I receive the inspiration. I couldn't understand why it went totally blind after a while. Now I know and it is completely incredible. What I have done in it blends absolutely and perfectly well with this book of ours. It is so amazing that I'm totally overwhelmed by it. I remember when I told you about it; you said it would be a good one. Do you see how the Lord works? Our book was started over two years ago and both of us thought we just started it.

You don't think I had too much conversation with Dana in the book of Precious, do you?" "Most men don't know what to talk about with their wives. It's nice to see someone who does." "I just know as you can see that I could write pages and pages of conversation with you. I just want to make sure the readers will like this. There is a song I composed out of a dream on May 1st 2001. I sure would like to record it with you. I called it:

In my dreams, you're mine

When I lay down alone at night, you're on my mind.
And when I wake in the morning, you're in my mind.
There in between, there in my dreams, I know you're mine.
But all day long, I walk alone in the meantime.
Course
Him; Precious Princess
I know that you are the dearest.
Her; My charming Prince
You know now that I am convinced.
You're my soulmate;
I have no doubt, for I have faith.
It is the Lord, who worked this out, it is our fate.
2
For all of the eternity, one we will be.
There is a plan, a destiny for you and me.

For what my God has united, no one separates.
There's a mansion, He has prepared for us to take.
Course
Precious Princess
I know that you are the dearest.
My charming Prince
You know now that I am convinced.
You're my soulmate; I have no doubt, for I have faith.
It is the Lord, who worked this out, it is our fate.
3
When I lay down alone at night, you're on my mind.
And when I wake in the morning, you're in my mind.
There in between, there in my dreams, I know you're mine.
But all day long, I walk alone in the meantime.
I'll walk alone in the meantime.

My May 5th 2001 dream

I don't know if it's the fact I mentioned things of what else exactly, but I had a dream last night that is quite revealing. It could be too that God reveals to me through these dreams the things to come. One thing I know for sure is the anxiety I lived through this last week; wondering what Sheba is thinking of the beginning of our book is something I wrote down three years ago in my first book. This is something I'm not used to. It crossed my mind also that God was talking to Jesus the exact same way; I mean through dreams and visions.

I dreamed my Bible's studies were heard of through the whole world and the devil hates them just as much as he hates God. One day, as I was expecting it almost every day an army of cops came to my domain to arrest who they dared called; The leader of the sect. So of course I came out to face the enemy and I insisted to come out alone to spare the lives of the others. When I got on top of the little hill where the gate is I asked why there were so many, for there must have been thirty of them.

'You are under arrest by order of our king.'

The voice came out of a big cone similar to the ones they put on the road to direct the traffic. Then I asked them:

'Haven't you heard the thunder?'

Then almost all of them were holding their ears with both hands; some of them went to hide behind trees; others even tried to crawl under their cars. The rain was pouring so hard we had a hard time seeing each other. When the silence was back again they all gathered together and surrounded me and I asked them if they heard of the last week earthquake. Then I saw the earth shaking under their feet and most of them were terrified and screamed their head off.

'Tell me, why are you spitting blood like this? Are you guys trying to scare me or something? I see that one of you guys doesn't have blood on his lips. I'll go with him, but with none of the others. I'm still a little bit scared of AIDS, you know? Besides, God doesn't want me to mix my blood with his enemies.'

One cop came out of his line and he said hi to me:

"Good morning brother." "Hi, aren't you afraid like all of the others?" "No, God is my shield." "Good morning brother, where are we going?" "I have to take you to

51

another domain for a little while, until they can digest this last storm and this earthquake."

So this man whom I think was my guardian angel took me in his car and drove me to another domain which I never heard of. I slept during most of the trip, so I don't really know where he got me. But during this trip I had another dream or a vision of what happened to the other cops after our departure. It's not always easy to tell. They went back to their chief whom I thought could very well be the devil himself.

"Where is the man I send you for?" "One of the officers took him." "He didn't bring him here. What in the holy hell all of you did?" "There was a thunder storm like we have never seen before and as soon as this man pronounced the word earthquake the earth shook like we never heard of." "None of you could bring the fire down from heaven like this?"

At the same time the fire came down from the skies and consumed three of his officers in seconds. Another officer told his chief the rain was poring so bad that his fire wouldn't have last anyway.

"You're just a bunch of useless and stupid imbeciles. I can't get anyone to do anything wrong unless I do it myself." "I would have loved to see you and you're fire against the rain of this storm." "Go the hell right now; you're not supposed to love anything or anyone."

CHAPTER 4

⸺ ◦⊱⊰◦ ⸺

MY MAY 6ᵀᴴ DREAM

Dreams are wonderful and also quite strange sometimes, to say the least. It is three in the morning, I just woke up, the temperature is too high, I'm thirsty, I opened a can of pop and here I am writing what I just dreamed of.

I rushed all I could to be at church in time with my sister Emily, her son Patrick and her husband Adam who invited me over.

As far as I know none of them go to church. Not only that; they are in Montreal; which is like three thousand miles away. I don't think they go to bars either. I got there just in time to hear the last phrase of the sermon. The priest was saying it is not what you hear that is the most important, but what you're doing with it.

After church Adam took me to the bar; which is in the same building than the church. Both places are probably owned by the same people. He wanted to buy me a drink and play me a game of pull. He ordered two drinks for us, one glass of milk for my son and one pepsi for his son. The two kids took off with their drinks and Adam asked the waitress how much was the bill.

'Nineteen dollars.' The waitress answered.

"What? That's all I got. I'm sorry, but I can't give you any tip. How much is the milk?" "Four dollars a glass!" "Shit, this must be thirty dollars a quart. How much is the pepsi?" "Actually, it's not pepsi, it's coke and it's the same price than the milk." "Damn, my son won't even drink it."

"Dad, I don't like this stuff; it's not pepsi."

"This is probably the reason why coke sells more than pepsi; we don't always have the choice."

"Can you give him a glass of water?" "It's two dollars." "This is the place to come if someone wants to swear after church."

"John, can you lend me two dollars please?" "Sure; that's probably all I've got anyway, but you can have it." "Here's your drink John; cheers to the freaking trap we're caught in. I had twenty-five dollars for my expenses for the week. It cost me six dollars for our seats at church. Now this is nineteen and I owe you two. I don't even have two dollars to play you a game of pull. I worked all of my life and I'm almost ready to retire. I have a good job and I hardly missed any day. Let me tell you; I'm not much more ahead than I was thirty five years ago." "Let me encourage you Adam; you would have been lucky to get a shut anyway; I just feel like a winner." "Ah, ah, you can brag; words are cheap." "they are cheaper than drinks over here, this is for sure. Let's go play horse shoes; I brought them with me." "Let just hope it doesn't rain now." "If it does; I'll beat you on cribbage." "This is still to be seen." "Thanks for the drink and don't forget to ask for the price first next time." "It goes to show you how often I go to the bar." "It's not cheap. This is a place for those who like to pay down the debt of the country. I think they even tax milk and water for children over here."

DREAMS

Some dreams are very strange. They can take you years ahead, years behind, thousands of miles away with people you never met yet or others who are long gone. Jesus said we will be like angels. Can you imagine? You think Japan and in a fraction of a second you're right there seeing a tourist ordering a dog of his choice from the butcher; a cook who kills the animal in front of you and cook it to your liking. You think of Israel and you can see thousands of pilgrims talking to a holy wall slipping notes through the cracks between the rocks and waiting for an answer, expecting to be heard by God. Some of them feed the system thousands of dollars for their trip. It just shows how little they know God and how much they were brainwashed.

I heard this week on the news that in the world at least two millions children were kidnapped and sold for prostitution every year. There is a lot of money which is spent on stupid things or trips that could be used to stop this abomination. There are a lot of people who think there are good people and they feed the beast billions of dollars which could have been used to stop evil. A lot of people are afraid of God's coming so much some of them kill themselves. Personally, I wish He had stopped and destroyed this abomination longtime ago.

Today, May 7th, another amazing thing happened. A man who is a bit strange, I have to admit came to get some information on the supposedly st Paul, the supposedly apostle. This is a guy who I talked to a few years back about it. This guy kind of like to preach to everyone he can. He was really mad when he left me last year when I told him about the lies that were in the gospel of John. I told him the one who lies in there couldn't be the John, the apostle of Jesus. I believe there are two Johns in this gospel; for there is some truth and a lot of lies and contradictions.

You could call this the wheat of Jesus (The truth) and the weeds of the devil. (The lies) See Matthew 13, 24-43. One of those Johns actually made Jesus a liar. Well, I know Jesus wasn't a liar and the John of Jesus wasn't one either; so I came to the conclusion there was a writer who was a big time liar. I figured he is the John of Paul and he is an impostor. See John 8, 39-44. This Jesus told them they were not the sons of God and neither the sons of Abraham, but they were the sons of the devil. Now go look a bit farther in the same conversation with the same people, in John 8, 56. Jesus would have said: 'Your father Abraham rejoiced at the thought of seeing my day.'

No, don't blame it on Jesus; he's not the one who made the mistake or this lie.

Anyway, this man was very furious against me that day for telling him the truth; that one John was a liar. This same man deceived me a few years back. He came to see me all distraught; telling me with proofs in his hands he was going to lose everything he owns to a storage company to which he owes some money. On his request I lent him two hundreds dollars and he was to pay me back fifty dollars a month out of his welfare cheque. He gave me one payment and then he was hiding from me and doing everything in his power to avoid me. So one day I simply went to sit with him and I told him he didn't have to hide anymore; that I didn't want him to go the hell for this little bit of money. So I gave it to him. I'm not rich either, but the fact is I hate to be taken.

But today he was hungry for my words, for what I know about the antichrist; just like a dog who didn't eat for three days goes after everything he can get. He wanted to get my booklets, but I told him they sell for three dollars. They cost me four. He said it was cheap and he will bring me the money. I told him there was some truth in there which might drives him crazy.

"I am already crazy, it will make no difference." "I know you are, but I don't want to make you worst. I am also a bit scared you use my writing to your credit, do you know? I wouldn't want you to bring the wrath of God on yourself."

Then I showed him another twenty or so contradictions and lies which disturbed him quite a bit.

'Those Bibles are no good; we should destroy them, burn them all.' He said showing rage in his statement.

"What proof would you have and how would you be able to argue differently when they tell you one day those lies and contradictions never existed?"

A week later he brought me three dollars saying he had sold enough cans to buy the booklet.

Some people already say today; 'Don't read the King James, it is outdated.' Others say; 'Don't read the international, it misses a lot.' Again others say: 'Don't read the Louis Second, they have changed too many things in it.' Others would tell you not to read the Bible at all; it could drive people crazy. It's true it could be very confusing to read a Bible with so many lies and contradictions in it; which is supposed to be the absolute truth; especially if we believe the teachers who lied so much to us.

The Gideons have already taken out the entire Old Testament and distribute only the New One; which means kissing goodbye the whole law of God for millions of innocent people in the world. What they actually do is turning innocent people away from the true God and bring them to the god they have made up, Jesus or Paul. At the time of Moses they made a golden calf. With Jesus they say he is God and also the lamb of God. They sure like to make an animal out of God. They made a god out of a man they say was God made man. God is God and man is only a man who likes to manipulate God, but God the Almighty doesn't let men and neither beasts manipulate Him. His enemies are just about to become his footstool. Do you know what this means?

Two days later the man who wants the pickup box called me. He said he would like to come the next day to clean it out. He told me also he sent the booklet I gave him to someone and this someone wants to copy it and send it to many people including a priest in Penticton.

Wow! Among all my acquaintances, relatives, love ones and friends, none have done this much yet. He is the first one I hear of who actually sent it. He is the first one who is anxious to spread the truth, the good news to my knowledge anyway. This too is a truth that hurts and I am the victim. To see my ex enemies coming to me to get the work I have done for my Lord before any of my love ones, it hurts. My mom whom I love dearly told me she likes my work, but she is not much for the propaganda when I asked her how many booklets she will order from me. I told her she knew a lot of people I don't, but she said she doesn't like fighting. A sister who doesn't work had no time to read it even though she likes it. It is only a half an hour reading, but a good friend of mine didn't have the time to read it in forty-five days.

Many are saying they don't like fighting, it is though a very small cross to carry.

Many religious people reject God and his word and refuse to spread his word. I just wonder what they'll have to say when the Great Judge ask them; 'Where are your deeds that come with your faith?'

On May 21st I composed what I think is one of my nicest songs and it's called; Tonight

I also think it will be a very good song for marriages and weddings.

Tonight

Tonight if my God is willing.
Tonight you'll know of my feelings.

Tonight I'll put my head to rest.
And I will lay it on your breast. (Chest)
I have been waiting for so long.
To hear from you, to tell me too.
I wrote it in my books and songs,
How much I love and I want you.
Chorus: How much he loves and he wants you.
Tonight we'll start a brand new life
To lead us through eternity.
Tonight we'll be husband and wife
The golden path is so pretty.
It's for us two that I've believed
In our love, in our destiny.
For this reason we will receive
All the blessings God promised me.
Chorus: All the blessings, He promised him.
Tonight you'll be for my own eyes
The tree of life, the tree of joy.
Tonight will be for you and I
The root of pleasure to enjoy.
My Lord has shown me how to reach
The very deepness of your soul.
The kind of love for me to teach
This one is to fulfill his goal.
Chorus: This one is to fulfill his goal.
Tonight if my God is willing.
Tonight you'll know of my feelings.
Tonight I'll put my head to rest.
And I will lay it on your breast.
Chorus; and he will lay it on your breast. Tonight.

THE ROUGH ROAD OR THE GOLDEN PATH?

THE GAMES OF LIFE, THE GAMES OF THE WORLD

Games are fun for someone and can be miserable for others. At seventeen I was playing horse shoes on the beach. I had a little sign saying; '$10.00 a game, anyone is welcome.' It came to a point where no one wanted to play me anymore at least for money.

One day my oldest sister where I was living woke me up in the early afternoon telling me my scooter was gone. This was my only way of transportation too and I didn't report it to the cops right away, because I neither had driver's licence nor registration nor even a plate on the bike.

It was a brand new motorbike (Scooter) I paid five hundred dollars for. It wasn't new anymore when I got it back from the police though. The three brothers who stole it kind of learned to drive with it. They got one month in jail for this. Well, I didn't think this was fair, that it was enough punishment for what they did. When they got out of jail I was looking for them and when they heard about it and even before I could find them; they stole a car and drove it right to the police station and right into a police's car. I didn't know I was this much scary, that I had such of a reputation. When they went to trial; I went to see what was going on. They were kind of having fun and laughing.

The judge asked them how much time they want, for they seem to enjoy jail. 'Ho.' They answered. 'Give us what you want. A year or two, we don't care.'

So the judge looked on his desk for a few seconds and asked them if three years time would be pleasing to them. This was the very maximum he could give them. Their laughing kind of stop right away and I waved them good bye. In those days three years meant three years too. Today it costs too much to keep them in jail this long even if they deserve more time and still jails are full, mostly with Christians who have faith.

While I was without my bike I had to hitch hike to the beach where my horseshoes were and this was eight miles away from my home. One day a nice man picked me up and he asked me if I wanted to drive. He told me he has been driving for a long time and he was very tired and sleepy. 'Well sure.' I told him. So to the wheel side I sat and I drove the car to about half a quarter of a mile away from my destination. Then he asked me to pull over on the side of the road that he needed to take a piss. So I pulled over on the shoulder. He opened the door and he went in the bushes. He's going pretty far I thought, but some guys are really shy. I waited for about ten minutes and then it clicked in. I looked around in the car and I found a pistol and bullets. I grabbed this because I was always interested in those things, probably for having too many enemies. No one likes to lose. Then I wiped out the steering wheel and the handles. I quickly walked to the beach where six people were already waiting for me; for I was two hours late. An hour later I saw the cops questioning people on the beach. They didn't come to me and I didn't bother telling them anything either. I was there every day so I had good references. That day I beat my own record in scoring ringers. I put twenty-one of them in a row in the pin. The old guys I played against said this was something they never heard of. I earned more money this way than I did working my night job. When I found out I had to wait at least twenty years to get a day job in this shop I simply quitted it.

I must have travelled at least twenty thousand miles while hitch hiking. I've been attacked three times by homosexuals. On one occasion I had to fight a man who was just a little too insisting and I know I broke his nose, because I heard and I felt it brake when I hit him. As far as I am concerned they all deserve the same treatment. He took an exit from the highway saying he needed a shit. He had already two occasions to stop at a garage, but he didn't. He kept saying that maybe he'll take me all the way to my mom's place where I was going.

Being young means you don't know everything and you can be a bit slow sometimes. Once the car was stopped he asked me twice if it was alright and I said no pushing his hand away. The second time he did I opened the door at the same time. When he did it the third time, I hold his hand on the seat and bang to his nose full blast with my right hand. He wanted a shit and he got himself a shitty bloody nose. If they could stick to their own kind it wouldn't be so bad, but to try to force themselves on young innocent people as I was, well, put it this way; it is a punch I never regretted and it's got to be true there is more satisfaction to give than to receive. Women could probably argue this though.

Another time three guys in a car decided to give me a rough time. Well, I knocked down the two guys on the back seat and when I told the driver to stop and let me get off the car, he didn't argue with me.

The very first time I played pull I had to climb on a wooded pop bottle wood case, because I wasn't tall enough otherwise. From the time I was eleven I couldn't get a cent from my dad even though I worked six days a week from six to six for him. I managed to get a quarter from my mom pretending it was for the church. She knew it was to play pull I wanted it.

I always tried to play the first game against someone I had at least a chance to win with a bet of ten cents. The price of renting the table was also ten cents a game. It was a flip to know who was to put the first dime. In 1959 I won a big tournament. Then twenty years later I suddenly quit gambling completely, because it has come to a point I couldn't call a shot anymore without earring behind me; 'Ten bucks he doesn't get it and I'm on.' After the shot I heard either; 'He did it on purpose or you guys are cahoots; so one way or the other there was always someone to blame me.

I won another tournament for my fourteen years old son astonished eyes back in 1982. Up to a few days ago I couldn't comprehend what happened in the very first game. A very strange thing happened in the very first game against my first opponent. After the brake I apparently had no possible shot at all. Everybody said it including the referee. I took an extra minute and then I called the shot. One bank, combination, double cross side.

It was the kind of shot that requires enough power and a bit more and the cue ball would be on the floor; which makes you lose the game and the tournament. I hit it just right for the ball I called slowly fell in the name pocket. Then the cue ball came to locate itself on the same spot again, living me with no shot one more time. Again everyone agreed I had no possible shot.

Then out of I don't know what or where I called another almost impossible shot; the corner of the right side central pocket to make a combination in the corner of the same left side. The ball went in to the grumblings of everyone around, but what I didn't understand for a very long time is the cue ball came to locate itself on the same spot again for the third time. Again there was no shot I could really do and the referee and my opponent told me so; basically telling me to pass on. I told him this was an important tournament and I should at least have a minute to look around the table. The referee then said; 'One minute!'

There was one of my balls against the bank a foot from the corner pocket on my left. There was only one way to hit it and this was from the same corner of the side pocket again and on the opposite side of the table. I called it for I had no other choice anyway and guess what, I did it again. I tried the same shot hundreds of times later on and I came close, but I could never do it again.

Then I didn't have to look around for anymore shot, because my opponent quit and threw his cue in a corner and he went away. With those three first shots that were out of the ordinary I had demolished all faith in this man who was the very favourite to win the tournament. I strongly believe to this day that if he had hanged in there he would have won this game and possibly the tournament too. I was very lucky to make these three shots, but no one can say I was lucky to get these three positions.

After the tournament I played two games to satisfy a defeated participant and he won both of them. I had nothing else to prove, he was happy, but I had the trophy. I was gambling with bowling also. I was playing in a team in Montreal where I had an average of two hundred and ten and in a team in Granby Quebec where I had an average of two hundred and five. The two captains didn't seem to like my scores, but I didn't want their positions. In Montreal where I was also working at that time I was playing on Wednesday night and in Granby I played on Friday night. I had a girlfriend who worked in a store every Friday night and Saturday all day. I had to get something to do. So all day on Saturday I played and bet against anyone who wanted it too. At times I had up to ten people betting against me. If I scored two hundred or more they had to pay me two dollars each and if I score less than two hundred I had to pay them two dollars each. I made more money gambling this way than I made on a day with my construction job.

It was during one of those Saturdays I scored seventeen strikes in a row without getting a perfect game. I had two hundred and seventy-nine in one game and two hundred and ninety-one in the other.

A perfect game of twelve strikes for a score of three hundred would have given me a bonus of three hundred dollars and since the pinner would have earned also fifty dollars he just ran to see if I had it. Unfortunately it was not the case for either one of us and he wasn't the only one to be disappointed.

I also started gambling with poker, but then I couldn't win much with this one. The best skill you can get in this one is to know your opponents are honest.

One day after losing many of my pay money I didn't join the others where I had a rented bedroom in the house where we usually play. The lady came to my door to call me, but I pretended being asleep. It was there and then I learned I had no chance to win anything or very little. I heard them in their conversation picking the key words. If one says the word <u>blue</u> it meant he had a full house. If they talk about a car it meant he had three of a kind. If it's a big car he's got three high cards. If he says small car he had three little cards. If he talks about the house he has four of a kind. Again big house meant big four and small house meant small four. So I had no chance to win much, because only the best hand would bet against me and at the end they would share the three hundred dollars I have lost. So everything I worked hard for all week got in their pocket. All of the five or six of them shared my money once I was washed out to play among them. One of them was a house builder and another one was a car deader.

I think I was lucky to learn this in early age. There are so many people stock in this habit and not able to pull away from it.

One of my uncles told me once the only time he ever won anything with poker he was followed, beaten and stolen of everything he had by four of the guys who were at the table he played.

One time my dad and his cousin where working in the wood and when they were ready to come home my dad's cousin got caught in a poker table where he lost everything he had earned for his wedding the day before his return. The income of six months of hard labour was gone in four hours and his dream life with his love one was chattered to pieces too. He actually was on what they called then; the wedding round. The guy just cried his honeymoon, but it was too late.

He was also my dad's best friend and dad felt sorry for him. So dad with the luck of the devil sat at the table and got up again when he got all of his cousin's money back. Dad was not a gambler, but he was the kind of guy who seems to know where every card is. I'm pretty sure today he could have supported us better with gambling than he did with working; for he was not working most of the time.

CHAPTER 5

THE WORK FORCE

My father took me to the woods since I was eleven. That year during the summer we were skinning trees and he had hired a good half a dozen young men from fifteen to eighteen years old. Dad was falling the trees; some poplar. Mom and dad's uncle were branching off and taking off a strip of the back to give us a chance to start peeling off with our blades. The first one to finish his tree could yell and had the right to the next one. I did up to ninety-eight trees a day and no one could beat me to it. If another one would yell at the same time I did; the other guy would get the tree.

Everybody knows they all tried to beat me with the will of the devil. This was like peeling five cords of wood in a day. We got five cents a tree. Well, put it this way, I never got paid. He paid all the others in front of me on Saturday afternoon; anywhere from fifteen to twenty-five dollars and when I asked him for a quarter; he told me he had no change left. This was a lot of pull games I was robbed of.

The next year dad hired a bunch of men, lumberjacks. We were six teem. Among those teem there were my uncle, my dad's brother and his son who was twenty-one at the time. Anyway they were two full grown men. We were working from Monday morning to Saturday noon, time of the pay. My dad being the foreman wasn't working on our production from Friday noon until Saturday noon, because he had to measure everybody else's production and figure out how much every other teem had earned. Even so, no other teem could beat us and everyone knew my dad wasn't the best or the hardest worker anyway.

One of these Saturdays when collecting his pay my uncle look at me and said from his height: 'You little son-o-a-b.'

He was a person who was dribbling while talking and he was dribbling more than ever then. He was beaten in production; he didn't like it and he blamed it on me who was the height of three apples. Those men were collecting two to three hundred dollars a week each, but I never got a cent for my work that year either.

There is one thing I learned out of this though and it has always been helpful to me in my business as a construction contractor. This experience taught me that two men who work together are worth twelve hours out of an eight hours day and two men separately are worth almost sixteen hours out of an eight hours day. This was the trick for us to beat all of the others. All the others were professional fallers or lumberjacks.

Dad was falling the trees ahead of me and he never had to watch if I was in the way or not. For this reason he never had to wait either like I've seen my uncle do. Dad was way too selfish to tell them too. I was following behind branching off, marking the tree every four feet and clearing off the branches. When dad had finished falling the trees at the end of the road he came back at the beginning cutting down the trees the way he wanted to. When at my turn I was done I came back at the beginning too and I put the logs away. I never ever wait for him to move a log no matter if it was seven or eight hundred pounds. I would find a way to move it with a lever I made up and I rolled the big logs where they had to go on the side of the road where it could be picked up easily with the horse.

There was apparently only one danger really I faced every day; the forest was infested with bears. Every day I saw some of their marks on the trees I was working with and also on the ground. But God, my real Father was watching over me and I'm sure if a bear came after me I would have given him a bad time with my axe.

One time after lunch I asked my dad to roll me a cigarette and he told me that when we smoke the work doesn't get ahead. I got up and I started throwing logs at him for he was sitting down right on the pile of wood where the logs needed to go. I don't think I ever saw him get up as quickly as that time. 'Go smoke somewhere else than in my face.' I told him. 'At least if you don't want to bother giving me one cigarette.' I am happy my Father in heaven is fair and just; with Him justice will be done to me.

I quit school fairly young at the beginning of my grade seven. It was a new school for me in a new town and totally different from where I used to go. The teacher also was different than the ones I had before. He was a tall man in his thirties. One day I watched him pulling back the hair of another student and I thought to myself; 'If you ever do this to me, you'll be sorry.'

The next day from the blackboard where he was standing he threw a brush aiming at the student behind me for what ever reason. One thing I know is I didn't like it one bit for he missed me just by a hair. I got up, I walked to the back of the room, I picked the brush up, I walked back towards him and I threw this brush to his face telling him to get my quitting notice ready. I walked out of this jungle class of his and to this day I never regretted it.

I went to look for a job which I found within a half an hour in the biggest restaurant in town. It was a job of six days a week, twelve hours a day and the place was opened three hundred and sixty-three days a year. I was fed every day as much as I wanted to eat and twice a week I could bring a guest of my choice. I didn't realize it then, but working this many hours kept me away from troubles. I got home that day after I quit school to face my strict mom.

"You're home early today." "Yes, I quit school." "You'll have to get yourself a job." "You bet I will. I already have one." "And where is this?" "At Belval's Restaurant!" "They didn't think you were too young?" "No, I lied on my age. I don't care what they think, I got a job." "You'll have to bring twenty dollars a week for your room and board." "This won't let me much for my expenses though, but that's fine with me. I think you should settle for fifteen, because I'm fed on the job." "How much does he pay you?" "I will be paid fifty cents an hour."

This was in 1959. She didn't need to know how many hours a week I had to work. I also let her break the news to my dad. I already had so many fights with him that I was afraid one day we would kill each other. But he wasn't mad at all this time. He was rather happy I bring some money in rather than costing him anything. All I can say is from my early age I paid my due and financially I don't owe my parents much if I owe them anything.

Since I was eleven years old he took me to the wood where he worked just as often as I was at school or more. All of my summer holidays from that age I spent working in the wood also. From the age of six I was the one to empty the shit pail, bring in the fire wood and light up the wood stove the mornings of the winter. I was in the hospital at ten years old for an operation in my growing for over doing. I was in there again at eleven for having cut my thumb off with an axe while splitting wood. I made the kindling a little too small, because I was the one who light up the stove in the morning at thirty below and even colder than this. I wanted to put the match in and run back to my bed again before freezing my ass. Then dad got up when the house was way warmer and so did all the others. There was basically no insulation at all in the outside walls of that house.

Coming back to my restaurant job some how dad found out I was working seventy-two hours a week and the price of my room went up from fifteen to twenty $.

He didn't even have to feed me a bite and on top of it, I was already smoking for three years; which took a whole five dollars a week. He was responsible for this habit of mine too; for he wouldn't even roll his own cigarettes. I had to do this for him. Well, as you know we don't play with the fire without getting burnt sometime. But he was the boss so I swallowed until one day I had enough of the whole situation.

I went to rent a bedroom and to my surprise it was only six dollars a week. Shit I thought; I was really ripped off at home. I had a girlfriend by then and the land lady was afraid we sleep together. She was watching us like a hawk. I didn't know why for she was the president of a doggies club. You know women who go with dogs. She had to go to the hospital one time with a dog that was stuck with her. So it had to be for a legal reason she had the rule. It could also be because we were both straight which wasn't right in her book. Nevertheless, this girl I was going out with was just as much of a virgin the day I left her than the day I began going out with her. I was proud of it too and mainly free of guilt. She's the one who liked my mom too much.

We got to my mom's place one time as we did every so often and there was nobody home. At eleven o'clock that night she went in her room telling me she couldn't stand anymore that she wanted to go to bed and sleep. This was understandable and acceptable. An hour later my mom got home and the two of them chatted until five o'clock in the morning. Well, this was her choice, but I wasn't this stupid after all. They talked the whole night and kept me awake too. This is the kind of things we can forgive, but we have a hard time forgetting and when they reach the high number it blows up.

I kind of liked the job at the restaurant, but there was a guy who was working there for over thirteen years who didn't like me for some reasons. He kept pushing me around and looked at me as if I was a dirty old dog until one day he did it a bit too much. I pointed it out to the manager a couple of times who simply asked me to try to put up with him. This is what I did until I punched him in the forehead. He lay down on the floor until the paramedics came to pick him up.

This was the end of that job for me too. Ho, the manager tried to fix things up telling me he would like to keep me and all that. I told him then that one or the other had to go; if it wasn't him it would have to be me. So out I went as soon as the guy was ready to come back to work. When ever I met him after that day he was very polite and respectful with me. It was like many people say; kind of a bad thing for a good one.

I soon found a job at a bubble gum shop. It was there I learned to lift some sixty pound boxes with one finger. Next thing I found out is I could lift a one hundred and sixty pound man by the belt with one finger also and this quite easily. It was him who had a good bike to sell me for twenty dollars and this at $5.00 a month.

One time after giving my parents my pay cheque for several months I asked my dad for an additional five dollars a week and this for four weeks to buy a bicycle I needed to travel to work with. There were a couple of miles to walk to work back and forth. He turned my demand down and that night he, my mom and my two older sisters were going out for a dance like thirty miles away. It was an injustice I just couldn't put up with without a fight. I got really mad at him and I turned his bedroom upside down. When they were back at four in the morning and dad saw in which condition I left his room I heard him telling my mom he should wake me up and give me a correction. I was still awake and of course I was expecting this. I got up on the couch for I had to sleep in the livingroom and I told him to come I was ready for him. I guess he was afraid the neighbours would call the cops. Anyway, my mom came to tell me to go to sleep and she sent him to fix the bed. She knew that wrong was done to me. She knew too I was ready for anything even to die for my rights, for a bit of justice.

Dad very often told mom I will never eat enough bread crusts to measure up to him. One day I got to their place and my young brother who is bigger than me and dad were fighting and didn't want to listen to anything. I grabbed my brother by the belt with one arm and I threw him in a closet telling him to stay there. Then I grabbed my father and I turned him the other way and I told him this was enough. This was the end of it at least when I was there.

When dad and I had our worst physical fight I was seventeen. My mom and my two oldest sisters were working. The two oldest sisters were helping also financially. I was unemployed living on UI and so was he. I was collecting twenty-two dollars a week and I had to pay fifteen for my room and board. This was fine, but one day he left when I was lying down on the couch watching a movie on TV.

He told me when he left the house he wanted the dishes done before he came back. Most of the time when he left it was for a couple of hours, but this time he was back within a half an hour and the movie wasn't over yet.

Of course the dishes weren't done either. So he went to the kitchenette and then came to get me. He grabbed and dragged me; then he pushed me at the end of the kitchenette. I told him I won't do it and I tried to pass by him. He punched me then in the face and I flew to the end again. I went to the sink as if I was complying, but I grabbed the whole pile of dishes with the bucket and I threw it at his feet repeating that I won't do it. When he came to punch me again I just ran at him, wrestled him down. I was on top of him holding him by his shirt my fist ready to nail him, but I didn't hit him. Honour your parents if you want to live longer, but then I was far away from remembering those words.

I know though it was God who stopped me then; for sure it wasn't the devil who would have loved me to do it, because I was in a total rage. I told him if he ever touches me again I will kill him. He never tried this again either.

Today I realize it was God who stopped me from committing this crime. The devil would have been really happy for me to break this God's forth commandment. There were many of these traps set up for me by the devil.

Next I went to my room, grabbed a few things of mine and I went to stay at a friend where I was treated a lot better. There were seven girls and one woman in the house and the cops couldn't understand why a father would want to beat a young man of my age to do the dishes. My young sisters hated the dishes and what wouldn't he have done to please them.

No, nobody's perfect except the hypocrites of course. The ones who are not honest enough to look at themselves to see who they really are. Take my word too; the ones who point the finger, accuse and condemn the others are the very worse. Just like Jesus accusers were worse than the ones who actually killed him. See John 19, 11. 'Therefore the one who handed me over to you is guilty of a greater sin.'

Nobody's perfect, just look at our government politics. Even if God was at the head of our country; people would find a way to accuse Him of something. I could think of dictatorship! None of our politicians can open his mouth anymore without risking a lawsuit. This means that all we'll have for leaders in a near future will be none but lawyers. They are the worse, but they know what to say and what not to say, what to do and what not to do to be safe. Stockwell Day knows something about this after receiving an almost eight hundred thousand dollars bill from the province of Alberta.

What is following will be nothing but hell on earth and you know what; it will be well deserved. When people can't forgive a simple act like the king of USA who had an affair with a beautiful young adult woman willing to go with him for what ever reason! When we already know the vast majority of the population is adulteress. What do you want, God up there? You'll have Him and let me tell you what; most of you wont like it. But I will and I will still be working for Him with joy. To me it will simply be wonderful working for Him without risking to get killed for the truth.

Some of you will say God doesn't need me to do this. Then I'll tell you He didn't need Moses to take his people out of Egypt either. He didn't need Moses to bring down the ten commandments from Mount Sinai. God didn't need Jesus to convince the world He was the Father, the only true God with all the powers! If only you knew God; you wouldn't be talking or thinking like you do.

I saw Sheba today again and every time this happens my heart pounds harder than the usual and I noticed too that my hands sweat like I never saw this happened to me before. What is it exactly that makes me feel this way? I don't even sweat when I face a crowd of two hundred people. I hardly sweated at all when I faced a big bear one time with a little one shot twenty-two riffle. I guess she's more important to me than any size crowd after all.

She was a little more distant than the usual though. So different than she was four days ago when she promised me with emotion in her voice she will call me at the beginning of the week. Every minute was like hours and every hour was like days. I didn't dare go away from the house just in case the phone rings. When it rang I picked it up as if it was a matter of life and death.

A day prior to the usual I travelled the one hundred kilometres and I went where she works just to see if everything was ok. Then I found out her young daughter was sick and required all of her attention. The poor young teen had to stay home by herself because mom is forced to work. This is the cost of living, the cost of the lifestyle of nowadays. I know Sheba felt bad about it. I could tell she was at work but not by choice. God I wished I could have done a miracle right there and then and be able to send her home with her kid or something. Wouldn't it be nice if I could cure her daughter from a distance just to ease the mother's mind?

'It is just one thing after another.' She said almost in tears. Then I gave her three sheets of the book including the song; Tonight and I told her I won't let her read anything more until the book is completed. She smiled when she picked up the envelop as if I just understood her wishes.

Six days ago she asked me if I was real busy and I told her I will be free one day for a pretty woman. She smiled and she didn't say anymore. But yesterday all of a sudden I thought; 'What if she needed me and this was the reason for asking me?' I could just have kicked myself for not catching on earlier, but today she told me smiling it wasn't the case. What a relief it was. I just know I would travel the whole world to help her if she needs me. But talking about being busy I wish she wasn't quite as much and she could give me a bit more of her time.

I just realized I made a huge mistake before by telling her she should make herself free and available for the right guy when he'll come along. By doing so she would give the man she's with a chance to find a woman who would love him and be with him heart, mind and soul which she's not. It was the right thing to tell her, but it should have come from someone else than me.

After seeing Sheba six days ago I heard a strange story on the radio. A little episode called: Focus on the family. It was the story of a guy who loved a woman desperately; something like my story with Sheba. A doctor was telling the story of this man who started to write to the one he loves a couple of notes a week and she didn't respond to his advances. So he continued to write to her letters after letters, hundreds of them until she married the postman. The poor guy wasn't the postman either. But the story could have been a good warning for me. Maybe without knowing it I could have been pestering her. God is good and I know He loves me. I got to pay attention to all of the little clues. This is why I have decided not to let her read anything more until the book is completely done. This will give her time to get hungry for more reading; especially if she likes my writing. At the end I'll know if I should call this book fiction or non-fiction.

One thing which works in my favour though is the fact I delivered all my letters to her myself. Then if she marries the delivery man I'll be in heaven. My song; Tonight then would actually be a fulfilled prophecy.

God do I want a chance to spend a couple of hours with her. I have so much to learn and so much to know about her yet. Somehow I know that everything will be fine, but the wait is just unbearable. There is nothing else I can do though. I got the feeling I already pressured too much to get in touch with her. Her changes of moods could just be the result of this pressure.

It could be too that at some point she thought and believed she was the Princess of my book. Then at other times she thinks the Princess is someone else. I asked her if she knew who the Princess was and she told me she didn't. I think she might be confused about it sometimes.

The thing is I didn't want her to love me because I love her, but because of whom I am. But my God and I know it is not easy for me to love her without desiring her. She must be the most beautiful woman I have ever met. She will be the very perfect queen. I can just see her captivating the whole world with me.

Sometimes as if she wanted to show me a cold and tough side of herself, she tells me things like out of sight out of mind; talking about her son being away and her younger brother she didn't see for years or her father who she doesn't know and she has never met.

There is a lot of emotion suppressed in her and I think the Lord is using me to help her out. I thought she'd cried the other day, but she assured me when I asked this was something that doesn't happen to her.

She told me she went to a rodeo with friends last weekend by Falkland; the first town on the route of my hubcap collecting and she found herself looking over the cattlegards; thinking it must be what I'm doing. I might have been out of her sight, but not out of her mind then. I thought this was very encouraging for me. I just know I can't act by men standard if I want to be with and keep her forever. I have to let my Lord lead me all the way to the golden path.

I have seen Sheba happy and excited only three times in just a bit over four years. The first time was at Easter when I gave her a card. She was dancing of joy on her seat and the card made her hands agitated until she couldn't hold it anymore and then she dropped it on the desk until I was gone. The second time was when I gave her one part of this book with an article of me in a Toronto magazine even though she told me she could wait. The third time was when I gave her some more of my writing.

Well, I really enjoyed seeing her this way and this encourages me to do one more thing. Her birthday is coming pretty soon; on the 5th of July this is. This is only five days after we're celebrating my mom's birthday; which we're doing every five years. Mom's birthday is on July 31st, but some circumstances made that we have to do it on the 30th of June this year to get everybody together. I mean celebrate big time. This is a gathering of almost one hundred members of the family including her children, grand children, great grand children and great, great grand children. In my first book the Precious Princess is a Leo and when I asked Sheba when her birthday was she sadly told me she was a Cancer.

'Don't worry.' I said, 'I think God gave me a cure for this disease.'

This is as simple as to stop eating the food He has forbidden and stop feeding the system. Sheba also asked me when and where we were celebrating mom when I mentioned it. I told her then it was in Quebec. Then she told me it was too far away. But it is only five hours away by plane.

So I got her a birthday card, a pile of pictures of the last celebration and a letter with a declaration of my feelings for her. Just like I wrote it in my first book; either

I will win her forever or lose her indefinitely. Is it too late? Is it too soon? I think if I do it; it is because it is just the right time. One thing I know for sure is the fact she's going to go through a lot of emotion. People can lie for all kind of reasons, but on the spur of the moment the reactions are genuine and more revealing than anyone can think of. Here is the letter I wrote to her with her card on May 25th.

May 25th 2001.

"Hi beautiful. You told me lately you didn't want your name involved in my writing and I respect this. I have decided to call you Sheba. I don't know if you know her or not, but she's the one I love desperately. She's the Precious Princess of my first book. She's the one I spent thousands of hours writing for. She's you.

There are forty days to go before your birthday and I thought it was time for you to know. I don't know if you're going to be mad or happy about it though. If you dislike it I'm asking you to forgive me for intruding in your life and wanting to make you happy. I sincerely believe I have followed God's guidance in all of this. One thing I can say for sure is the whole thing, my love for you and you have inspired me a lot. As you know the stories, the music and the songs are just incredible.

The way I described my love for the Precious Princess in my book is the way I feel about you. It was you I was talking about. It was you I was talking to in this book. If you're mad about it I'll back off and you will never hear from me again other than from the books and the movies made out of them. I thought it was time I was honest to you about the whole situation. This is the reason for this early birthday card to you. I wanted you to recover before the fifth of July in case it was a big shock to you.

Our story is unique and will be heard of by the entire world. I believe it would surpass the Titanic and the Forest Gum in popularity. I think Emily Dion will like it a lot and so will Michael Douglas, the movie maker. I'll leave it up to you to change what ever you don't like in it after discussion.

Please don't mock me if I'm shaking and sweating when I give you this envelop, because I did a lot of things in my life, but none of them as crucial or important as this one. Either I'll have my dream life fulfilled or shattered to pieces. Either way, I put my whole life, my whole destiny in the hands of God. He knows what is best for me. One thing I know for sure is I could never love another one as much as I love you and I will never settle for less. I might not even be your type I don't know. All I know is my heart is an opened book and this book is in your hands.

I personally think you could put me out of your sight if you wanted to, but never out of your mind anymore. Happy birthday to you with eternal love and may God bless you as He did me.

John Prince a fervent admirer."

THE ROUGH ROAD OF CHILDHOOD

I talked to one of my sisters about what I'm writing on my childhood and some stuff about dad and she told me he was dead and buried. Maybe so, I said, but I'm not. All the dead will have to come out for the judgement anyway, I said. "Our dad is buried and what he has done is buried with him." "Yes, but I am alive and what he has done to me is still alive too even though I have no resentment against him." "Don't you think we should keep the dirty laundry within the family?" "Well, this is just it; there is some dirty laundry that was never cleaned.

There are some members of my family who told my ex-girlfriends I was a little pervert when I was a kid. I too thought it was buried. See the one I love now is about to enter our family and she wouldn't find out from others; I will tell her myself how I was. There is a big load of dirt in our family that was never cleaned. There is quite of an accumulation and it stinks. Maybe it is just the right time to take it to the Laundromat."

Yes, it is time we get pure and clean to get before God. It is time we stop being hypocrites and saying; 'What a nice family we are.' Some of us can't even speak to each other ten minutes a year. What kind of a brotherhood this is? The Lord said; see Matthew 5, 24; 'First go and be reconciled with your brother.'

Now you know why He doesn't always listen to you. Yes, we have a lot of dirty laundry and you can try to bury it all you want; it will always stink until it gets cleaned out.

One of you was irritating me until I couldn't see straight anymore and then she was hiding behind dad for protection. He was kind of her chum. She was just a little pest and could do as she wished, because she knew he will always protect her.

One morning on the way to work to the wood dad was driving at one hundred miles an hour; he who could hardly go sixty. I told him if he doesn't slow down I would jump out of the car. He told me to open the door and do it if I wanted to. This was the same day when not realizing it he happened to stand just behind me with his running chainsaw. When I picked up a log to throw it, which was my job, I hit the chain with my hand. I was very fortunate the chain located itself between two fingers. When I saw him and I realized what he was doing; I just ran as fast and as far as I could away from him. I ran at least a good mile before he could reach me. I knew too he was running behind me. I had my little finger ripped off to the bone and that time at least it wasn't because of my awkwardness. He knew I was injured, but he didn't know to what extend.

Not everyone have the chance to have a dad in this world, but many would have been happier without any. It was certainly not because I didn't help him that he was mean to me. Yes, the road is sometimes very rough. God said He will bless up to forty generations those who love Him. I do love Him with all of my heart and for this reason I know my posterity will be happy.

Yes, my dad was a demons possessed man and he couldn't rid of them. I know he regretted some of the stuff he did, because I saw him cried at different times.

Nevertheless, evil is from the devil and we can't rid of it as we wish. We have to love God with all of our heart and pray that He delivers us from evil as Jesus told us to do. If you love Him He will deliver you and if you don't, why should He?

The Almighty is full of compassion for the ones who love and obey Him. He can pull you out of the hell you're in. This includes anything like, drug, alcoholism, smoking, sex slavery, gambling, theft, murder and all immoralities.

There was an accident last week, well sort of. There was a fifty-eight years old cyclist riding his bike in an early morning in the streets of Tofino and he was blinded by the lights of an incoming car. I guessed he didn't like it and pulled the middle finger, the finger of honour at the driver. The driver didn't appreciate it so he stopped his car; put it in reverse and backed it up to the cyclist breaking his wrist and both of his legs. This one I will call it; hit on purpose and run. This shows you it is dangerous to meet more evil than we are and we should be polite even with the enemy.

Now, if this driver would have hurt the cyclist with a firearm the authorities would say we have to take the guns away from people, because they are too dangerous. What will they do with all the cars? Anything can be a weapon in the hands of a devil. There are thousands of times more accidents and deaths caused by cars than there are caused by firearm.

Did I ever thought of killing someone else than my dad? I never thought of killing anyone; otherwise I probably would have. There are people who kill and others who call for it, who are killable, I think.

88

I was fifteen when my dad and I were just finishing building our big house. Dad took a bad decision or I rather say; he took the right decision with the wrong people. We worked for months in the wood and at the sawmill and at home to get all the lumber we needed to build it. There was just a bit of the finishing left to do when he ran out of money. A lender came home and talked my dad into getting all the material he needed to finish it; that he would back him up. Dad had not much education and the guy had good references. So dad blindly went and ordered everything he needed. When it was time to pay the bill the guy went back on his word with the reason we didn't have running water and neither sewer. The bill was three thousands, five hundred dollars and was already in collection. My dad was framed.

One of my uncles who was working for the church told my dad to go see the priest who just received a big inheritance. The priest, abbot Tremblay from Richmond took all the information he needed; telling my parents he will help them and he went to buy the credence and gave our family of twelve forty-eight hours to clear the site. Before the time ran out he started to paint the windows watching one of my sisters undressing in the bathroom and when she saw him; he just smiled at her.

I thought of it then and I still think that this priest, the lender and all the people who could have helped us saving our house and didn't do it deserved to be buried in the well I was digging by hand. I was down to the water by then at fourteen feet deep, but the well wasn't big enough to bury everyone who deserved it.

It was harsh to lose our house we worked so hard to get and build, but it was also our first step away from Catholicism and the first one toward Jesus' discipline. It was not too easy to forget it either. Now I know we were blessed by this misfortune. Again only God could hold me back from killing this man who was no doubt in my mind a demon possessed.

It is not something I like to talk or write about, but they are things that happened. My brother tempted me a couple of times too. One day I went to the garage where I usually got my repairs done and my mechanic who was also a friend of mine told me my brother and my brother-in-law were looking for me and as they said; they wanted to kill me. My wife left me and they thought they had to make me pay for it. To this day I sincerely think they were lucky I never found them that day.

I also think the brother-in-law really had killer's instinct, because he was jailed for murder a few years later. Guess who gave him a job when he was back in Canada coming out of jail. Sure, no one else wanted to hire him. We forgive, but to forget completely I think it is humanly impossible. Oh there are some who pretend, sure, mainly the hypocrites.

I have a sister who is just a year older than me. She was looking for a fight with me all the time mainly when my parents were away. But that time she found me. I just had enough of her tomboy's habit. I thought to myself; 'You want to fight like a boy, just be ready to take it like a boy.'

That day my parents were gone to get their groceries and her fun was to slap me in the face. That time it was enough for me; when she did it I didn't slap her back as usual, but I punched her in the belly. Not as hard as I could, but enough to make her bend down and lose her breath. Well, this was the very last time she ever hit me. I felt sorry I didn't do it sooner.

When my parents arrived they all got together as usual and they told dad what I did and of course I was the instigator, the bad guy and the only one to blame. He came to my bedroom door and when he opened it I was waiting with my hockey stick in the air ready to hit him in the face. He shut the door behind him saying; 'Let him go for now.' He knew damn well they lied. He had also a number six sense which told him when there was danger to cross the line. I was fifteen then.

He mainly liked to teach her how to drive while she was sitting between his legs. I still wonder who was driving when the car hit the hydrogen bomb in the middle of the boulevard. She too knew he would defend her no matter what she did. She took advantage of the situation. There is a lot of dirty laundry and it stinks.

It's got to be washed though before the final judgement. I could tell you hundreds of this kind of true stories, but I think you have a drift now of what my childhood was like. I was no angel either and I will never pretend I was, but I sure had to fight a lot of injustices until now and this is something I will do until I die. Yes, I had a dad, but neither me nor my mom has to count very far to mention all the good things he has done to us.

One of my brothers-in-law told me one day after he heard me play the fiddle that I had inherited from my dad and all the others had nothing. Poor innocent I thought to myself; my dad never spent five minutes in his whole life to show me something that wasn't for his own benefit and he never showed me a note of music either. Discouraging me from it he often did this. He didn't want any competition with his fiddle either.

He put a lot of efforts to teach his girls some dancing and how to play the guitar, but try to remember when and where he tried to teach me anything. I got an answer for you and this is never.

I forgave him and I also forgave all the others, but there is some laundry to do. No matter how rough was my road in the pass, it didn't stop me from finding the golden path which led me to God. The devil tried in many possible ways to get me to fall in the irreparable as you know now, but the Almighty loves me and He keeps me under his shield. He kept me from thousands of dangers and I'm sure I didn't notice half of them.

There are a lot of people who say the ones who have condemned Jesus were bad, but those people who did it didn't throw the first stone at the adulteress woman. Today though, there are a lot of people who have thrown the stone at Clinton and at Prince Charles and they are not the least better. Jesus said it was necessary the scandals happen, but woe to the ones by whom they happen. Those two paid a lot for their fantasies, because they are public figures. The ones who are not known will have to pay too.

Just before I had a big fight with my dad at sixteen I went to a studio to learn how to lift weights and I was told by the trainer I had it all to become a champion of my category even to the Olympics. I could put three times my weight above my head then which I believe could have been a record at the time. But then this trainer liked to take my measurements a little too often and he was getting closer to my testicles each time. So one day I just told him off and I stop going.

I couldn't afford to buy some equipment with my five dollars a week for expenses; so I made my own with a steel pipe and two big logs from a maple tree I got from the sawmill near by.

One day through the window I saw my dad tried it, but he didn't know I was watching. He could hardly lift it from the ground. This was three hundred and three pounds. His dad, my grand-father Prince was seen lifting a two hundred and ten pounds anvil above his head with one arm only. My mom could arm wrestle down many men. She tried me for the last time when she was seventy-one. I told her then; 'Somebody else maybe mom, but not me yet.' She's eighty-nine now and she is still surprisingly strong. She will be ninety this year and she remembers everything since she was two and a half years old. She could tell you a lot of stories too. I intend to write some of her life stories soon. A book I will call; The Tour of My Mom's Garden.

After I hit the big pig with an axe when I was seven the manager of the farm where we had a rented house ran after me all the way to our house. I yelled and I instinctively went directly to the axe for my defence. My mom came out of the house right away and challenged him and she swung a bucksaw in front of his face until he took off. She spoke English to him and I didn't understand what she was saying at the time, but I clearly understood what she was doing. At her seventy-fifth birthday's celebration we, all the children were asked to tell a story of our childhood concerning her. I told them this story adding that when we have a mom like her; we don't go hide behind our father, but behind our mom when the need is evident.

One day I surprised and intrigued my girlfriend's father. He was a very strong, proud and heavy set man. He was mad at one of his daughters once and he punched the wood table. The two sides of it flew to the walls under the pressure. He also killed an ox that didn't want to move with a punch in the belly. He was often bragging about it too. He told me once his mom could walk with two one hundred pounds bags and this quite easily. He was a school bus driver when I met him.

One morning it was freezing rain outside and he was stock in the snowbank when my girlfriend asked me to do something and to go and help him out. I asked her what on earth she thought I could do in my dancing shoes. I got out anyway, just to please her. I could hardly stay up on my feet. Then I got an idea. The bus had its nose in the snow and the driveway was sloping toward the front of the bus. There was no way that even a towing could pull it up without chains.

I was a general contractor in construction at the time and I always carry some asphalt shingles in the trunk of my car in the winter for weight and also to put under my tires when I was stock on ice. I was very careful so he didn't see what I was doing. I went to get a few pieces of them and I put them behind the back wheels of the bus. Then I went to tell him to keep the bus in reverse and slowly touch the gas when I'll give him the ok. Then I went behind the bus again and I put the shingles under the tires with the sandy side on the ice. After this I grabbed the bumper on the driver side in a way he could see very well as if I was going to pull the bus back and I gave him the sign to let go. The bus came back the six or seven feet he needed to free him and go; for he was late and he had no time to check out what I did. So he left in a hurry.

When I think of it today; it was the bus that was pulling me. He kept telling his brother and the other co-workers all of that day I pulled the bus on the ice upward. They kept telling him I must have done something he didn't see even though he was watching.

I saw him thinking at the table during supper, but he didn't say anything until diner was over. Then I saw it coming. He sat smiling in his rocking chair and then he asked:

"Now you're going to tell me what you've done this morning to get the bus out of there and don't tell me you pulled it with you arms?" "I thought you saw what I did." "There are things I saw, but I think there are also things I didn't see."

I burst out laughing and I told him my trick adding strength doesn't come only with physical; there was a lot of it up there. He didn't think this was funny though.

CHAPTER 6

THE SABBATH

When I woke up this morning I wished my Lord a good day. Then I wondered what I could do to make his day. In no time at all He filled my mind with ideas for this book. So I turned the light on, I grabbed a sheet of paper and my pen I keep by my bedside just in case this happens. I'm kind of lucky I found a pen I can write downside up with. This way I can write while I'm lying down in bed. After a while my light went dimmed, because the battery was weak. So I got up and I went to sit where there was a better day light. Then my pen no matter how wonderful it was got empty anyway; so I decided to call one of my sisters in Montreal who had not much time to talk, because she basically have to raise her three grand-daughters that her son doesn't support and neither raise.

He's only twenty-one and he already has three kids with two different women. I don't know what they think, but what beauties this guy gets and make babies to. I told my sister that if I wasn't a born again man I would get a membership in his club. I let my computer and my generator be quiet today too for they can be tiresome after a while. Today is a resting day, a day to please the Lord.

It was very quiet in my house for the last nine months, but for a couple of days now a new family of mice found their way in my ceiling. Those little creatures can be noisier than five or six puppies running and playing on the floor. Those mice woke me up the last few days at five in the morning. But yesterday I predicted today they will let me sleep.

Yesterday I went shopping at the hardware store. I tried to catch them in a couple of traps I got, but it seems their knowledge too has increased. It is almost impossible for them to get in and out of those traps alive, but one of them did it three times though.

I hurt my fist punching the wooded ceiling above my head to get them to move somewhere else. They irritated me to the point I thought of making some holes in the ceiling to put some traps in there, but there is not enough space anyway. So I got up in the middle of the night and I got my hammer to release my hand. I could hear the dogfood dancing up there when I hit it again. When I hit it often enough they moved above the bathroom and I could hear them just as much. So I went to hit the ceiling there too and then the light fell off its socket. There is the hole I needed I thought right away.

I know it was said we should not kill, but I was faced with two choices here. Either I can rest or I can't on the Sabbath day. It is in the law of men also that we're not allowed to feed wildlife, but hey, they don't have to live with those miserable creatures. Back from my shopping last night I put some rat poisoning up there by the hole left by the falling light. It is something I can't use everywhere, because of the number of dogs I got. It could make them sick and even kill them too. When I got a bit sleepy from writing, I went to lie down and get a nap.

I woke up after a little while from a phone ring in my dream and right away I went to look at my call display just in case it really rang. But it didn't and I went back to bed. After a few minutes I heard four mice, one after another running up there above my head and then they slowed down and then silence. Great, I thought, it works. Another one came running and then went back. It was going too fast to notice dinner was served. It kind of slowly came to lay down with the other four. I too very often feel sleepy after a good meal, especially after a good spaghetti. I heard a few scratches and then nothing. I counted twelve of them and I thought; this family was just as big as my mom's one. They made more noise than we all did too, up until I found the truth anyway.

Then came another one from a different direction this time! Maybe it was the foreman. It was running and then slowed right down; probably when seeing all the others laying down wondering why they lay down when there was so much work to do yet. This one too went above the bathroom for dinner and came to lay down with all the others.

Now it's quiet again and I can have my resting day to be pleasing to my God. It was said that even your animals should be resting in your land or on your property on the Sabbath, the seventh day. See Deuteronomy 5, 12-15 and Exodus 20, 8-11.

On May 29th I went to visit with a friend who his also a neighbour of mine. He is a singer and a guitar player. I took my last song and the music recorded on a tape along with me. He's a Frenchman but he speaks English much better.

He said he loves the song. He's got to sing at a wedding fairly soon and he asked me if he could modify the song to suit him. Here's what I thought to do. He's got a 1955 Cadillac convertible which is just like bran new.

"I would like to make you a suggestion Don." "What's this?" "What if you would take the two bumpers off your Cadillac and replace them with two Volks Wagon bumpers I have at my place? I also have a nice hood and a trunk lid. I'll bet you anything it would make people laugh and cry at the wedding like you never seen before." "The same song was changed to suit Elvis, Hank Snow and Hank William." "I'll bet you the original is still original though and every time a singer would change it; the writer would be notify and make money with it or at least he should have." "I think you're pretty touchy today." "What about you Don? What do you think about my idea for your Cadillac?" "Oh, I won't want you to change anything on it. It is pretty as it is." "So is my song Don! Anyone can change anything on any car in the world, but I don't think the designer would appreciate it." "You wrote this song, didn't you?" "Yes I did and I think it is prettier than your Cadillac as it is. To me it is worth more than your Cady too; probably because I created it. Go to the wedding and sing it the way I wrote it and you'll see how much people like it. If you're applauded, I'll leave it the way it is and if you're booed, I'll change it your way. What do you say about this?"

Amazing things happen all the time. Today June the sixth, my ex girlfriend called me in the middle of the afternoon. At first it was to ask me if I knew someone who needs a P.A. system and an electric guitar. I need one, but I don't have the money for it even though it is a good deal. Then she told me she left her husband a couple of weeks ago. This was of no surprise to me at all. Her brother and I were giving her less than a year for this to happen.

It is not because someone buys a licence for fornication that it makes it better. Not to the eyes of God anyway. Later on in the evening I called her back; for I sensed she was quite depressed about it. After talking for a while I sang her my last song. She could hardly believe I wrote it and she was totally amazed about my improvement with my singing. Later on I read her what I wrote on my vision of the judgement and hell. Well she was totally blown away as she said.

'It is not you who speaks but the Lord Himself. 'John.' She said; 'You really are a prophet of God.'

Now she can't wait to get her house back to start Bible's studies in it; for she rented out for a year. I'm just overwhelmed by all of this. My ex-enemies buy and spread my writing almost before I do and my ex-wife wants me to use her house to give Bible's studies. What is this if not a miracle? She also paid to get two hundred and fifty booklets of mine printed out. More yet, she made me a cheque of ten thousands dollars for me to get the truck I was interested in and she gave me the electric guitar, the amplifier and a bran new banjo she said she couldn't play.

She must have had some remorse during this year of honeymoon for making me lose forty-five thousands dollars with my property and another three hundred thousands dollars from an inheritance. I was also a beneficiary before she left me. The lady told me before she died I was going to inherit the same amount than her. But my greatest inheritance came to me from above.

I just finished supper and I thought of a little story I have just made up. I laughed it before I wrote it down. Here how it goes.

I got home after work and the dishes weren't done as they usually are. I was wondering, because this never happened before and I asked the wife if everything was ok. She lied a bit to me and said she had work to do for the Lord. So I asked her if she would mind telling me what she has done. 'Not at all!' She said thinking. "I prayed for a friend for a couple of hours." "He must really need help this friend of yours. Do you think I can do something for him?" "No, he'll be fine now that I prayed for him." "It's good to have faith. Now you know I love you and it would hurt me a bit if I found out you lied to me. You know this, don't you? The Lord speaks to me, you know this too, right?" "Yes I do."

I saw her getting a little red and I let go of the torture. Later on I asked my son why he didn't cut the grass as he promised he would. He didn't know where to look and of course he was ashamed for not keeping his word as he always did. He gave me this excuse.

"A good friend of mine insisted he needed my help and I thought it was a priority; so I went. Is it alright if I do it first thing in the morning?" "Yes son, it's alright if you keep your word this time. You know the Lord speaks to me so, if you lied, I'll know."

I heard him taking a deep breath as soon as I left.

"Hey son, where is your sister? We were supposed to practice my last song tonight. She has never missed it before." "I don't know dad, I didn't see her yet." "What is wrong with everybody today?" "I don't know. What do you mean Dad?" "Something is strange, that's all."

Then the Sabbath came and nobody lies on that day at least not in our home. At lunch all of them wished me a nice father's day and admitted this was why they had to cheat a little to get things organized and some shopping to do. All of them had the same question for me though.

"What did the Lord tell you?" "The Lord told me you would come up with the truth soon or later."

THE KNOWLEDGE HAS INCREASED

Even a young kid of nowadays can understand if God is Almighty He has all the powers and He knows everything. Then He didn't have to come down as a man to know how it is like to be tempted, how it is like to love and to have enemies and pain, how it is like to live and die. If He has all these powers He knew all this even before He made people. Even a three or a four year old kid could show you on the calendar where is the first day and the last day of the week and that the Saturday is in fact the last day. I am glad to know there are people on the earth who know God, love Him, pray Him and truly obey Him. This is a consolation to me.

Today God showed me in a vision why I have to wait for the woman I love so much. If I was to take her before she's ready to commit herself totally and completely to me and she would go with someone else; even though he was an ex husband or an ex lover; I could never again go with her or take her as a wife.

Someone would ask me if I couldn't forgive her. I could forgive her anything alright and so would God if she repents, but I could not commit an abomination to the eyes of my God. This would be hell on earth for me since I could not stop loving her. I prefer to be in hell on earth for a short time than to be in hell for the eternity though.

King David has sequestrated until they died his ten concubines who slept with his son Absalom for the same reason. David cried over his son who rebelled against him just like God cries over any of his children who turns away from the truth. For any of you who doubt what I'm saying go read in Deuteronomy 24, 1-4. Millions of people have committed this abomination and still do. We are wondering why there are so many divorces. God can simply not bless those false marriages. Marriages from an adulteress to another! They are not married by God, but by the beast. Those marriages are not valid to the eyes of the Lord and neither to mine.

There are people who ask why God speaks to me and not to them. To this I would say; if He was to do it; you might be scared to death and go hide behind trees or under cars. If you don't listen to Moses, to Jesus and the other prophets God sent you, his voice will be like thunder; which will make you dizzy like it did to the people at mount Sinai who were afraid to die when earring the voice of God.

THE JUDGEMENT, THE CONSEQUENCES AND HELL

Here's what I saw in a vision on the judgement and hell. The inhabitants who were complaining still do it to the devil now though, but they do it in vain for he has really mocked you and he's still doing it. Now he does it while laughing, crying, and gnashing his teeth. He is faithful to himself and listens to no one, but his power is now reduced to nothing at all.

Before he had the power to tempt the good souls, but he doesn't have this pleasure anymore. He became very small. He doesn't even have pleasure with his own little demons anymore, because all he sees is ugly, monstrosity and abyss. They also see what we have and this is real hell to them.

Some people had the surprise of their existence when they arrived at the judgement. When they appeared in front of the Great Judge with their little luggage! God knows and sees everything. I heard a woman tell Him she was faithful all of her life and she never stopped praying God. Here is what He told her.

'Yes, I see you prayed all of your life since you were a little girl and this gave me a lot of itching in my ears. I see your smile is fading down now. I heard you pray thousands of times, but not even once for my pleasure. All of your prayers were concentrated on yourself; selfish and proud person you are. You wanted good notes to look good in class. You wanted nice clothes so the boys could look at you when you passed by in the street or at school. Then you wanted your parents to stay together so they can baby you. You prayed for a strong and handsome husband who doesn't cheat on you and doesn't give you too much trouble. You prayed for good children who don't give you too much sadness. You prayed for good friends, peace and happiness. You prayed for a nice house, a nice car and a big swimming pool." "And You God gave me all those things." "Yes, I gave you all those things you attached yourself to and when I sent you my servant to ask you to take your little cross and to follow Me (my word), what did you do? You told him; 'Let God talk to me Himself.' And you sent him for a hike. Well, he went and he went to tell other people I wanted to warn.

Today I'm talking to you as you requested, but you're not going to like what I have to say to you. You have ignored the words my servant Immanuel suffered to bring you. You also ignored the law my servant Moses gave you. You ignored my feasts and my Sabbaths that you celebrated for the pleasure of my enemy, the devil. When you were singing on the day of the sun, I was hiding my face away, because I couldn't stand seeing or earring you. You, to whom I gave all those little vagaries of fashion.

I sent you other of my servants to open your eyes. What did you do then? Them too you sent for a hike. Now it is my turn to send you for a hike. Go see in hell, there is a place prepared just for you. It is not the worse, but it is not the best one either. It is the one you deserved though. Although, it is far from being like the ones reserved for the people who took their cross and followed, listened and obeyed Me.

There was also a big fellow who I saw in front of the Judge with a big pile of luggage for he was a rich man. He told the Judge all the good things he has done on earth. It was then the Lord told him what his deeds were worth.

'You gave for your own satisfaction to people from whom you expected a return or recognition for your own self-esteem. 'Look at me and see how generous I am.' Do you recognize yourself? Very seldom you gave something you needed for yourself.

You have spread out the lies rather than the truth; this is what your money was used for. You gave thousands and thousands to the beast, but very little to my children. You helped others for your own satisfaction. When finally one of my disciples knocked at your door, what did you do? You threw him out the door and you despised him. You made yourself called a child of God, but I'm not your God. Your god is the one whom you served. Where is he now? He was happy with you, but I cried over you. Think only of all the money you spent on foolish things. If only this money would have been spent to stop abortion or else feed the poor of the world; the earth would have been populated a bit more to my liking. You have ignored people in misery even some of your own family.

No, my children didn't do these things. Oh, you were very good at making faces in the assemblies. You were brilliant to disfigure yourself even though my servant Jesus told you to go in your room to pray." "Yes but, Paul told us to pray everywhere." "What did Immanuel tell you? He told you that if you don't gather with him you were scattering. Why didn't you listen to the one I sent you? You have listened to the one who disguised himself as an angel of heaven to deceive you. You too have listened to the liar, my enemy, the one who worked for your lost.

There is a place prepared for you according to your deeds, but it is not with my children." "Yes but, didn't Jesus died for my sins? Jesus sacrificed his life to bring you the truth you ignored. I'm sorry for you, but you had the opportunity to do the right thing; to spread the truth and you have chosen the liar and his lies. Now go see the one you served; he's happy with you and he is expecting you."

CHAPTER 7

ANGIE, THE MIRACLE DOG

Angie, a little black female dog not very attractive, I most say and is totally submissive every time I talk to her just because she was a bit too long under the control of her bigger sisters. The whole litter was actually unwanted. A dog I don't like very much, a boarder collie that gave me a lot of troubles and bred her mother. This male dog belongs to a man I moved in this area from BC.

I managed to give away Angie's brother to a lady who just loves him to no end. I knew right from the moment she picked it up this dog would be spoil to the fullest. Angie's sister was picked up by my employee along with another male and both of them are quite intelligent. I strongly believe that both of them outsmart their new owner.

I put ads in the papers quite a few times trying to give Angie away, but as soon as people looked at her putting her tale between her legs and crawling like a snake when she's talk to, they just turn around leaving her behind with no regret at all. So I decided to give her a bit of training like how to sit properly, walk on a leash, come to me when I call her and be quiet when she seems to bark at nothing in particular.

One day though while she had to stay put for a certain amount of time on the same spot, all of the sudden she started to howl like a wolf. I asked her what was wrong and all at once, I heard the horns of a big semi coming behind me that made me jump out and call her off the road at the same time. I have to say this is not a busy street at all.

She was already at the point she wouldn't move unless I ordered her. This was quite strange I thought; wondering why she howled instead of barking. Did she really try to warn me about the coming truck and the danger I was in? Anyway after a whole month of training I thought it was time for me to put some ads in the newspaper again just to see if I could give her away.

Since I hate to put a dog down unless it is absolutely necessary and that very often giving it to the BAAC means certain death; so I did everything I could think of to find her a decent home. I got a few calls, but no one would actually come to look at her. A woman asked me over the phone if I would drive her out to their town sixty miles away. I couldn't help asking this woman if she wanted a one hundred-dollar bill on top of it. A man said he will come to look at her, but he never did.

I looked at Angie with despair and I asked myself what I was going to do with her. She seemed to understand what I asked and she put her head between her front legs making a strange sound, a kind of a little cry.

'You can hide your face, but it's not funny.' I said. 'You've got to go. You're just not the kind of dog I want to breed.'

So I kept training her knowing very well it was probably the only chance I have to get rid of her without causing her to die. I thought if she was well trained enough and behave normally one day or another someone would pick her up. It was just useless; no one would come and if someone came they just turned around saying she's not what they were looking for.

One day when I was walking her with the leash she started howling again. 'What's wrong now?' I asked kneeling beside her? I lifted my head and I looked in the direction she was looking and suddenly I had shivers all over my body. At about 500 feet away there was a huge wolf running towards us. Lucky for us we were fairly close to an old garage where we ran without losing a single second. We just had the time to make it and shut the door behind us. This ferocious beast was hungry enough for both me and this little malamute and Border collie crossed dog that without a doubt just save both of us a lot of troubles. This is the second time she warned me of something dangerous I thought.

Is it just coincidence or did she know what she was doing, I asked myself? But this beast was still scratching at the door and no doubt it was still interested in us. The poor little dog was scared to death and I wasn't too sure about my safety yet either. I found there in the garage a three foot long by a one and a half inch round steel pipe and from then on I thought; 'it's alright if you come in now, I'll handle you bastard.'

A passer by saw the beast and honked making the beast go away.

After this experience I wasn't too sure anymore if I wanted to give this dog away or not. I didn't think it was this stupid after all. 'Ah, this is just a fluke.' I told myself; she's too stupid and useless to be anything but a good pet for somebody. But then again doubts went through my mind as well.

What if she knew exactly what she was doing and her timing couldn't have been any better? Well, it could have been a bit sooner, but she sure wasn't too late and maybe sooner I wouldn't have realized what was going on. Besides, if we were any farther from the building it would surely have been trouble.

I had a hard time to go to sleep that night. She sure gave me a lot to think about. The guy who scared the wolf away said it was very unusual to see one of those beasts around here, especially by itself. I don't know why, but since I'm very young there have been all kind of unusual things that happened to me. At the age of seven I punched a big black bear on the nose twice and he left without hurting me. Then I mentioned to him what Angie just did to protect us.

"Mh," He said, "She did huh." "Yeah, and this is the second time she warned me of danger." "Is she good with cows?" "I have no idea because she was never tried." "Do you think we can try her out soon?" "Maybe, but I'm not too sure if I want to give her away anymore. You know it's not every day a dog save your life or protect you this way." "I could buy her if she is good for me." "It doesn't cost much to give it a try." "Well, why don't you take her to my place one day, so we can see how she will behave around the cows?" "Sure, I'll do this. Just tell me when it's convenient for you." "Anytime, tomorrow is ok." "I'll see you tomorrow then at around 9 o'clock. Bye." "Bye." "Ho, what's your name?" "I'm Larry." "I'm John. See you tomorrow. Thanks again for your help." "That's nothing; I blew the horn for a lot less, believe me. Here is how you can get to my place."

I dreamed that night of Angie being a spy for the police and for the government. What a foolish dream I thought. I can't even give her away to anyone. But then, I couldn't forget the way she kind of saved my life either. Of course it's not an easy thing to forget. What do we do with a dog that just did such a thing? What if Larry wants to buy her now before I really have decided what to do with her? Ah, we'll see how she behaves with cows anyway.

Little after the 9th hour the next day I was at Larry's place with Angie. We took her to a pasture where there were a couple of hundred cows. As we got close to those big creatures my little Angie crept down with fear. She was shaking so bad I had to take her in my arms.

"I don't think she likes cows." Larry said looking at Angie. "She's just terrified." "I don't think you'll get a cow dog out of her either." "No, you're right, but she might be good with sheep. Let's go try her if you don't mind."

As we walked where the sheep were Larry asked me to let her go.

"Are you sure it's a good idea?" "We wouldn't know unless you do. Let her go." "Ok, we'll see."

I took the leash off her neck and I asked her to go pointing out the furry animals. She went alright, but she didn't go with a dead mouth and she jumped the first little one and held it down by the throat and if we didn't rushed she would have killed it in no time. I concluded that what she thought I wanted from her is to get an animal for me. Well done I thought, but I didn't tell Larry this.

"She's not what I need John. I need a dog that would be aggressive enough with cows and gentle with sheep, but she's neither." "I understand. I think she can only be a good pet for someone." "I'm still impressed with what she did with you yesterday though." "I got an idea of what I'll try with her next." "What's this?" "It's just an idea, that's all. I'll put her to test." "Well, thanks for coming anyway John. I had to know and I think it was worth the try. If you ever have a dog that is good for me, let me know. You know what I need now." "I sure do and I will Larry."

So we shook hands on this and we parted from each other. I went home with Angie thinking how smart she was. She actually did everything not to be adopted by someone else and I also think she knew exactly what she was doing. So I said to Angie.

"You don't want to go anywhere else but with me, do you? We'll see where this leads you."

As I was driving home on this stretch of highway she started howling again on the back seat of the car.

'Oh shut up.' I said. 'What's wrong with you now howling in the car like this?'

As I look back in front of me I slammed the brakes as hard as I could and I pulled completely out of the road for there was a vehicle coming toward me on my side of the road. This stupid driver was passing another vehicle in a curve and in his blind side on top of all. He would have not done any better if he was suicidal. If I didn't pull off the road when I did it, it would have been a head on one with no chance to survive for we were both at high speed. I was driving the speed limit at sixty miles an hour and the other guy was even faster.

It's got to be a drunk driver or a European who is not used to the road regulations of North America, I told myself, but Angie, this little angel felt the danger again. She couldn't even see this other vehicle coming. I had no more doubt in my mind then; this little female dog could sense the danger ahead of time, a few minutes before it was crucial.

I better start paying attention to this dog, because she's something else. I think she's a miracle dog. This makes three times now. Could this be just coincidences? I don't think so. I hugged her with so much love when we got home and I knew from then on I couldn't let her go anymore.

Angie is a little dog and the daughter of Bonnie. Bonnie is a young female survivor of a disaster in British Colombia Canada on July of 2002.

Six of my precious dogs were spared from this disaster, six out of seventy! They are Buster my oldest who has been prisoner of the Tofino BAAC for four months and came out of there sick with a cough that never left him. This disease was also contagious, because he gave it to some other dogs as well. Fluffy, a dog that was left in Taylor at my hubcap collection with Leo; my employee and Precious also got it till the end of their life.

Poor Precious, she could never run without coughing anymore. I wanted to be specific about the Tofino BAAC here, because they're not all the same. In fact the Saskatchewan officers, the ones I know so far have a lot more common sense. I should cross my fingers though and touch wood, we never know. I should mention also that Buster has never been sick in almost thirteen years before this incident.

The assistant manager of the Tofino BAAC; Elizabeth Turnell said on the news that my mutesheps dogs weren't adoptable because they have never seen a kitchen floor, a TV set or heard a door slammed. S. B. They are outside dogs with fur which could resist -60 degrees. They are dogs that like to make their own dents, their own bed in the ground; so they don't have hip problems when they grow holder like so many dogs do. You and your associates are too stupid to know how cruel you were to my animals when you put them in small cages on cement floor. This is why I say it now so you know.

One of their employees told me one of my dogs wore out his paws completely trying to make his bed in the ground like he used to and they put it down to avoid criticisms. This might just be one of the reasons why they got a shrink coming from Vancouver to evaluate my dogs. The few dogs I have now have their own houses with real doors, real floors, but they can go out when they want to and no; I cannot afford TV sets, especially in colour for them just yet and they don't care about it either.

Bonnie senior, a female dog who was close to a dirt pile always made a beautiful dent and she brought her puppies in it just like wolves do with their pups. I would take all the seven or eight of them and put them back in her comfortable doghouse, but she would always take them back to her dent in the ground. I would repeat the process and give her heck, but she brought them back again. Then I decided she knew better than me what was good for her pups and herself. Of course in her dent she didn't have as much of house cleaning to do with her tongue. Then I decided to build doghouses without a floor. This way the dogs of either sex could make their own bed to their own liking.

The last year of Buster's life I tried to keep him inside the house to spare him from the bad weather because of his age. He was not happy at all even with a huge pillow. He ripped this pillow to pieces twice and then I put him outside again.

There and then I saw him smile again and be happy. I will never forget the day he couldn't walk anymore and I had to put an end to his life to cut down his suffering days. This was the D day; the day of the disembarkation, the 6 of June 2004. He was then fourteen and half years old. He was the very best friend I ever had on earth beside God and I thank my lawyer for getting him back to me.

The other five dogs save from the disaster are Fluffy, my beautiful Precious and her three daughters; Bonnie junior, Fanny junior and Princess junior who were only four days old at the time of this disaster. My precious Precious was hit by a car in the village of Goodadam Saskatchewan where we live now. She was my eighteen generation. She was the daughter of my precious Princess, one I'll never forget.

This is how quiet my mutesheps are. Precious with three young females puppies of four days old never made a sound the whole day the Tofino BAAC officers were there at my place along with two vets, a dozen employees, two big trailers and their drivers and a policeman. This is not too easy to believe from four females.

Princess senior, Precious' mother was killed by a car too while trying to save her son, a beautiful young male. The one they called; Chewy, the one Kat Riley wanted to adopt and they won't let her have him. You can see his picture on animaladvocates.com website. When you're at it take a good look at Elizabeth Turnell with my dogs on the picture as well and tell me those dogs are vicious. This picture was taking a few days after they were seizes if not the same day.

They couldn't find anything wrong physically with my dogs and this is why they got coming from Vancouver a psychiatrist to evaluate my dogs. They had to get something to explain their criminal actions to the public. They had already lied to a judge twice to get the two warrants against me; now they had to find something to tell the public, like my dogs had Giardia like you and me and most of the living beings on earth have.

Two drivers who were driving as fast as a hundred kph or more in a fifty kph zone killed both Precious and her mother Princess. Princess died in Elkford BC trying to save her son. While I was visiting her this friend of mine turned her young dog loose and he went to the road where my precious Princess who was always following me everywhere tried to bring him back into the yard. This was her son. I gave this pup to my friend, but she later returned it to me. When I picked Princess up on the road I shed a tear, because I had just lost a very dear friend; an every day companion and I noticed a very strange thing in these circumstances. She had no mark on her body other than her heart lying beside her on the pavement. There was not a drop of blood either. This is the kind of dog she was. She would poor her heart out for others. She died like she lived. The Tofino BAAC employees wouldn't do as much; especially not the managers.

Both Princess and Precious, her daughter were killed at the beginning of a village by speeding drivers. Those drivers couldn't stop for a dog and they couldn't stop if they were kids either.

Princess was by a long shot my very best friend along with Buster. You should have seen her and me hunting. She could smell a deer a half of a mile away and a mouse from a quarter of a mile. I have a lot of stories to tell about Princess, but I'll come back to it later.

Precious was killed in Goodadam when I was in Tofino BC at my trial charged by the Tofino BAAC for a crime I absolutely didn't commit. While I was gone the same male dog that bred Bonnie; the father of Angie came to my place dragging his chain and tangled up with Precious who got loosed and I figured she went looking for me since I was long coming back home.

Not only this dog tangled up with Precious that time, but he also tangled up with Princess Junior, the sister of Bonnie and Fanny. My little Princess was loosed too when I came back home. She could have been killed too.

My friend Mike who took care of my precious animals while I was gone had to call the owner of this run-around dog to come and help him untangle them, because he couldn't do it by himself. He was tangled up with Bonnie this time. They were tangled up so tight he said he couldn't even slip a finger under her collar.

What a mess and all this started with the Tofino BAAC and by the ones who forced them to perform this monstrosity. I now keep my dogs inside. I gave a house to Fanny and Princess and a garage to Bonnie and Angie. This S.O.B dog broke into the garage by breaking the glass and bred Bonnie again. I asked the mayor and also the cops to do something about it and nothing to this day is done.

I'll have a doghouse trap built just for him soon. I caught the S.O.B a week later and his master who probably let his dog go on purpose was mad as hell when he found out I kept his dog prisoner. When he came to get it I told him that if I catch him again he'll never get his dog back alive.

Back to the disaster I can tell you it was a nice set-up. The regional districts of Okanogan some how managed to get the Taylor Indian band to force me to move most of my dogs out of the reserve. My lawyer said I had enemies and it was political. We understand they can be dirty. This Indian reserve is where I kept what is believed to be the largest hubcap collection in this country with one hundred and twenty-seven thousand pieces. This though was before I got many thousands pieces stolen by my employee.

On March 12, 2002, the day before my birthday the Taylor Indian Band forced me to get rid of my dogs or to move them out within 30 days. They told me for many years I needed a kennel license to sell and to keep dogs at my hubcap collection.

When I asked for one they refused it for stupid reasons like I didn't reduce the number of dogs like they asked me to do when they were the ones who forbid me to sell dogs without a kennel license. On April 9th Tom and Elizabeth who are investigators for the Tofino BAAC came to Taylor at my hubcap collection asking for my dogs. I told them they have been removed to Elkford on my property. I was not over worried because all of my dogs were healthy and had everything they need.

On April 10th along with 5 more employees they came to Elkford to inspect my dogs. I didn't mind this because everything was alright with my dogs as far as I am concerned. They asked me to surrender 4 dogs. They were mothers that have fed puppies for the last 8, 9 and 10 weeks. For this reason they were a bit thin, which was perfectly normal. They were Minie, Bear girl, Blanche and Buddyna. But then they wanted another female pregnant called Golden.

She was so big anyone could see she was ready to explode. Minie, Blanche and Beargirl were on my list of dogs to give away so I didn't mind this too much to see them go. But Buddyna is one of my favourites and I got upset then. All they had with them were only four kennels so they decided to trade Golden for Buddyna, but Golden is my pet too and besides; she was my bread and meat of the present time.

Besides, she was just about to give me puppies and the sale of puppies is very important because it allows me to buy dogfood for all the dogs. Before the number of dogs was this big the cost of dogfood and the income from the sales of dogs were almost the same, but with this many dogs the cost of feeding them was about eight thousands dollars a year and the income from them was about six thousands. This is nothing to get rich on.

Anyway, I didn't want to let Golden go and Elizabeth said then they will work it out with me on this one. I told them if she needs to see a vet I could take her down to my vet right away. They said they wouldn't cover the bill then. I said; what if I refuse to let her go? Tom told me then I will be charged. If this is not blackmailing I wonder what else it could be.

I went three times the following days at their location asking for information on Golden and her pups and they refused to give me any. It was through the news in the papers I found out she had thirteen puppies. This must have brought them a couple of thousands dollars besides giving satisfaction to a dozen of their customers. I'm not without knowing that many people who didn't want to pay my price for my dogs complained to the BAAC in the hope to get my pups from them at a lower price and with their shots on top of it paid by the general public. I was selling my females pups for $250.00 and my males for $350.00.

They came back twenty days later on April 30th with a warrant saying I had over thirty dogs chained to trees as if it was illegal to tie out a dog, which was not true anyway.

They were seven BAAC employees, 2 vets, two cops in two cop's cars and it was one of them who advised me to call a lawyer. They seized up then 3 females with their pups and 2 young adults. The mothers were Belle with 6 pups of 24 hours, Clementine with 3 pups of 48 hours, Fluffle and an 8 weeks old pup. This was nothing else than stealing from me and with the help of the police and the court on top of all.

None of my dogs had sign of illness. Then Buddyna, the supposedly dog in distress on the 10th of April according to Tom and Elizabeth was inspected by 2 vets on the 30th of April and they couldn't find anything wrong with her. Her condition was one hundred per cent without any exterior help.

As I was walking by the female vet I over heard her telling her assistant the dog she just look at was skinny. I took this dog in my arms and I asked her if she really believe this dog was skinny. She then told her assistant who was writing the results he was normal. I was sure ready to get a second opinion on this one. I understood at this point and time they were ready to do anything to indict me and lying was nothing at all to them and this was part of their plan.

A few days later I retained the services of a lawyer. On June 11 Tom called telling me that 2 of my dogs had contracted Parvo Virus, which is a very contagious disease. There was no sign of this disease on my property. On June the 13th they came back again for what they called a quick inspection, but they didn't pick any dog.

The BAAC officer from Grand forks told me then I could do any kind of business I want on this property of mine that it was in zone E. He also told me he and his staff had to put down twenty-one dogs in his establishment, because they contracted Parvo virus. This kind of told me my dogs were much safer on my property beside of being loved and well treated.

One of my young adults had a sore leg without showing any sign of injury. I think he squeezed his leg maybe between the tree and his chain. They told me the dog needed to see a vet right away. I said I was going to town the next day. Tom said this was ok. Having many years of experience with animals, especially dogs, I knew the dog would most likely be alright in a day or so. It is the same thing with me, if I get hurt and if it doesn't get better in a day or so then I go see a doctor, but if I get better I know then I will be alright.

The next morning the dog was 100% better as I expected him to be. At 5 o'clock Friday the 14th Tom called asking me if I saw the vet with the dog. I told him the condition of the dog and he said he will have to see him. Saturday morning, the 15th I asked a neighbour who owns five dogs and has a lot of experiences with dogs also to come and inspect this dog of mine. Just like me he said the dog was a little sore but could walk and put all his weight on his leg.

Monday the 17th Tom came to my place, but I wasn't home, so he left a paper at the gate with the date, the sixteen of June 2002. Tom came back on Tuesday the next day with a woman to inspect the dog he thought was still limping. He said it doesn't seem to be the same dog. I said it was him and he is fine. He asked what I have done to him. I told him I know how to take care of my animals. He asked me then if he could give a quick inspection to the other dogs. I told him on their way out they could. They then stretch their way all over my property again and at one point I told them it was enough; I had other things to do and I escorted them to the gate.

CHAPTER 8

⸺⊷⊶⸺

They were back on July the 3rd 2002 at nine o'clock in the morning with a warrant saying they believe I had an animal in distress on my property.

When the cop showed me the papers and asked me to open the gate I asked him to give me a few minutes to get the key, but within four minutes they had already cut the wire and moved in. I asked him what would happen if I turn all the dogs loosed. He said I would be charged with obstruction of justice.

They came with the police, 2 vets, 2 large trucks and trailers, a dozen employees, water and dishes. All of this for supposedly an animal in distress, but there was none of them in distress until they were in anyway.

At 9.30 they started to put my dogs in cages and load them in the trailer. They left at 12.30 with the first load, but the water was still untouched on the grown in front of my house when they left. This was a hot day too. I have reasons to believe my dogs in their care were 4.5 hours without water and this with all the stress they were going through.

They spent more than 20 minutes trying to catch a young adult from inside a dog pen. I offered my help when I saw in which condition they were putting my dog and what they were doing to this dog. Tom said then they didn't want me in there. Five minutes later Elizabeth asked me to pick him up that she didn't want to put more stress on him than it is necessary. The poor dog was ready to collapse. The foam was leaking from his mouth. I told them they were a bunch of idiots, that they should raise dogs; this way they would know how to handle them. Before this I asked the present cop who was watching the whole thing who was cruel to my dogs. He just plainly told me they had to do their job. Their job is to protect the animals, not to hurt them like this. I showed him also what it was written on the warrant; especially the animal in distress. He told me there was nothing he could do about it.

Then I went in the pen and I called my dog that came to me immediately. I took the dog and I put him in the damned cage he has never seen before. I didn't do it for them, but for my dog they put in an incomparable distress. A bullet in the head would have been a lot less painful to him and if I knew what they were going to do to my dogs; this is what I should have done to most of them, but they would have charged me anyway and this for doing a lot less cruelty than they did.

Most of my dogs were put in terrible distress that day. This is kind of taking the children away from their parents and be taken where they think they going to die or else never see them again. There is no need to be a psychiatrist to know and understand this.

There was another dog they couldn't load also mainly because they were afraid of him. He is a dog I invested three years training him for a wrecker. He is the one who was tied up close to a truck with auto parts in the box. They took them all including my oldest one of 12.5 years. Many dogs could suffer depression now in their hands for being away from me whom all of them had a lot of love for. When I go away and I have someone to care for my dogs I asked them to give my dogs steaks and gravy if they stop eating their every day dogfood.

I couldn't reach my lawyer that day, because he was out of town and I got kind of desperate; so I called a neighbour to come and witness the condition of my dogs. His name is Tremblay and he came with a camera. All of my dogs had an insulated doghouse, trees to give them shadow, water and a lot of dogfood, since they weren't allowed to finish their last meal at my place.

Tremblay repeated afterwards the condition of my dogs was not as the members of the Tofino BAAC were saying. In fact everyone who came to my place other than the members of the Tofino BAAC of course could tell that all of my dogs were well treated and they could testify of it too. I'm sure the cop who was at my place that day could testify of it too; if he wasn't paid too much to keep his mouth shut of course.

The same cop told me it's got to be someone I could call. There and then I think I got the best idea of all. I called all the media in Tofino and I asked them to go and ask for the sick or the injured dog at the BAAC in Tofino. I asked them to go look for the animal in distress, to go and ask for the injured, the sick or the skinny one.

All of the reporters said and this was on the news that the dogs seem to be healthy to them, but they were refused any access inside their building.

I have a sign above both of my entrances in Taylor and in Elkford saying free dogs on appointment with the phone number. But some puppies got stolen. Those thieves probably thought they were doing me a favour.

Long before all this on October 13th 2000, I offered the BAAC of Tofino up to 20 dogs for adoption. Robin Rogers (the manager) told me then they couldn't take any, because they weren't fit for adoption. At that time also the female officer, his assistant with him congratulated me for my dog holding system and my doghouses. I told her she was too nice for this kind of work.

I didn't know what they were after. I had no idea human beings in a civilized country like Canada could be so cruel, way more vicious than any of my dogs anyway. I made a song on them called; My Dogs and it is posted on my WebPages at www.hubcap.bc.ca. I didn't know they could forge so many false proofs.

I never heard as many lies at once as the day the crown attorney read my file to the judge. What I wrote in my song; My Dogs is true; they are more vicious than my dogs. I pleaded guilty for one reason and one reason only. If I had pleaded non guilty the trial would have cost me at least ten thousand dollars and my chances to win were basically nil. Since I have no money so no money to waste; this is why I pleaded this way.

My lawyer assured me I would have no criminal record. So this way I had to pay seventeen hundred dollars to my lawyer and two thousand in fine plus some luxury taxes of three hundred dollars I couldn't afford to pay to this day.

To go to a trial my lawyer said I have to pay two thousand dollars to have an independent vet report; money I didn't have and besides, by that time half of my dogs were already assassinated by the employees of the Tofino BAAC with needles to the heart, I heard afterwards; which is apparently very painful and illegal or else they were sold. Who's cruel to the animals and to a pet owner, really?

I was also told by my lawyer that without this report we were doomed. This way I was saving at least six thousands. I wouldn't have hesitated a single minute to spend this money if I had it in my possession and if I had at least one little chance to save even one dog. I thought I've lost enough in this ordeal anyway. Just like one of the journalists wrote in the newspapers that I was accused, I was seized, I was condemned and I was punished before my trial and found guilty.

Talking about money I couldn't forget the exorbitant cost of room and board for the time my dogs were in the BAAC custody. They sent me a bill of sixty thousand dollars after thirteen weeks ($60,000.00. Yes, sixty thousands, you read correctly. This is not all. The bill was up to one hundred and ten thousands dollars three weeks later. Yes $110,000.00. I don't know if I can call this blackmailing or not, but it sure looks like it. They also lied about this one to the public.

My lawyer who makes tons of money told me that even he couldn't afford this kind of bills. He also said they acted with heavy handed.

They forgot to mention in the agreement that I have to supply a TV set, house doors and a kitchen floor to my dogs. Why not a Jacuzzi when you're at it? $400.00, the cost for one dog returned to me. My Buster who was born with me thirteen years earlier on Christmas eave and let me tell you that he was quite a gift. Why would someone want to neuter a thirteen years old dog anyway? Buster fathered I'd say two hundred pups. What can I say? Most females didn't want anyone but him. When you're hot, you're hot.

Sixty-seven or seventy dogs at $400.00 a piece for care doesn't add up to $110,000.00. I don't know who made the calculation, but someone could agree with me; this is just as stupid as my dogs were not fit for adoption, because they have never seen a TV set, a bedroom door or a kitchen floor.

According to what I learned in school it adds up to about $28,000.00. Besides, I'm sure they didn't spade and neither neutered all of my dogs, because it was said by some of their own employees who witnessed a young female in heat was put in the same room with three males that fought to get her and took turns to mount her and all this without knowing if they were her brothers. Then if they have spaded or neutered the dogs they have put down, they have wasted the money of the poor innocent people who paid for the misfortune of my dogs.

They (BAAC management) beg and get money from the public every time they cry on the media. This is a real good business they got there. Good way to eliminate the competition also. Seriously, someone has to investigate what is going on in this institution. As far as I know, they have three ways income and maybe more.

First they receive grants from the government. Then they have a very particular way to beg for money through news papers, television, radio and even maybe Internet commercials using the soft hearts of people who love animals no matter to whom they belong to. Then as you know now, they can charge people, animals owners like me either they're right or wrong to do so and charge them an arm and a leg.

They blame breeders for running puppy mills, but they do no better. They can and they do also sell dogs just like any breeders. They blame dog owners and accuse them of running puppy mills, but they too like to have some on display and piled up in cages and on cement floors contrary to decent breeders like me.

I knew all the way from day one that one of the things they wanted was my puppies when they took Golden. At the beginning of this ordeal or plot they seized the pregnant females in perfect shape and in perfect health probably because they had many customers to satisfy. One thing is sure; it was not because my dogs were sick or anything like that, because they were all well treated. There was a good reason for them to return Buddyna and take Golden though; she had dollar signs written all over her belly.

Buddyna, the one they returned was a bit on the thin side, because she had just finished feeding four puppies. This is not this easy on a mother; especially at the end of the second month and I challenge anyone to prove me otherwise. The big one (Golden) is the one who had thirteen pups at the shelter a couple of days after she was kidnapped. She must have been worth at least $2000.00 to them. The very best thing for this dog was to be left alone where she could have her pups in her own environment. She was doing just fine and she was secured where she spent all of her life.

The mother who killed and ate her pups at the shelter did it because she was too scared for her puppies. This never happened at my place. It wasn't me who caused her this much distress. She was just fine at my place. Did you ever think how you would feel if you were kidnapped and taken were you think you're going to die? This is exactly what my animals went through, but I'm the one who was accused of cruelty. Besides, dogs even though they are very intelligent, they don't have the faculty to understand what exactly happened to them.

They probably thought these stupid people that my dogs were crazy and this would explain why they got a shrink for animals coming from Vancouver.

I feel like saying what Jesus said when they crucified him. 'Father, forgive them for they don't know what they're doing.'

I can ask God to forgive them and I can forgive them myself, but no, here they knew exactly what they were doing. They were trying to destroy a man's livelihood and his career. I wouldn't say they were destroying a breed of dogs, because I strongly believe they are still breeding my race of dogs to this day. They simply used the law backed by the cops to steal my Kennel. I desperately asked for an inquiry into what they were doing, but to no avail. Who cares nowadays for a Frenchman in the West who disturbs so many people?

With all the reports you can read on the animaladvocates.com website; we can tell that a lot of people care about animals, but don't give a shit about people. They cry and they lose sleep and appetite over my dogs that were killed, but never had a word of compassion for the man who lost them all. I'll tell you something, my dogs missed me too, this I know. All of them did. I miss them all too to this day. It never occurred to you I might love my dogs and my dogs loved me? Haven't you heard of a one master dog?

If Buster didn't come back to me he would have died from affliction. I'm sure too that many of my dogs didn't responded to their treatments because the only thing they wanted is to be returned to me, to my place where they were happy. I'm glad today that my precious Princess didn't have to go through this mess. She wouldn't have survived it anyway.

Contrary to what it was said by the people of the BAAC my dogs were well sheltered, well fed and this was said also by the manager of the Tofino BAAC Robin Rogers. They were never at any time out of water except the day they were taken to the shelter and there is nothing I could have done then except shoot them all maybe.

My dogs were petted every day and they were played with. It was euphoria every time I came out the door. Each and every one of them wanted to be the first one to be petted. When I got the harness out, every one of them wanted to be the first one to get in front of the sleigh or the buggy, depending on the season of course. Princess was so possessive; she wouldn't let Buster have his turn. I had to put her in the house to give Buster a chance to have his turn.

Some of them loved to let me take their hair off and some were more possessive and thought I was stealing from them. Their hair is worth about $400.00 a pound. I got some from every single one of them. One of these days, when I have enough money for it I will get a coat done with their hairs from at least eighty different dogs. Each one's name will also be written on it also with their hairs. All these names will testify about the cruelty of those who killed them.

I also created a half of a five gallon pail to set at the base of the trees where I could collect the male's urine. What a crazy thing to do most of you already thought? Don't judge too soon, you might just regret it. I created a repellent to keep the deer off the roads. The deer smells it from at least 400 feet away and turn around as soon as the smell hit their nose. The deer is the animal that by far is the biggest killer of people in North America.

There are more than one hundred and fifty people a year killed by this beautiful wild animal. I offered my repellent to the BC. Government. Their response; 'Not interested for now.'

Only when I'm dead I thought! I could go on this way, but you got the message. In fact, I suspected I could be charged for disturbing wildlife.

I actually tested this product of mine near a water spring where the water doesn't freeze even at thirty below. The deer and the moose were going there just about every day until I spread this product over and then only the cougar made it there after.

Buster, the one they called grandpa was heart broken when I picked him up in the lawyer's office. I couldn't recognise him. He was mostly black when I lost him and mostly white when I got him back. He didn't want to give me the high five as he was accustomed to. I said this is not my Buster. Then the secretary said; 'Oh yes he is.'

He died at fourteen and a half, but this dog was built to live at least twenty years. I also think the shots giving to our animals are shortening their lives.

Do you remember too dogs used to live nineteen, twenty years without shots? Nowadays a twelve or a thirteen years old dog is very old. One of my aunts had a dog, a collie that lived to be twenty-one years old without hip problem and without any shot of any kind. Her dog was born in 1936 and died in 1957. I strongly believe these shots are there to enrich the veterinaries and the shots makers. I over heard today from doctors on television there were only twenty-four cases of rabies in Canada since 1954; yet millions of dollars were spent on shots.

One woman veterinary in Penticton BC, told me back in 1991 there were only three cases of rabies in this province in more than twenty-five years. This province must be the wildest province in Canada as well. Maybe this was another reason they wanted to take my dogs away from me. They were afraid I can prove that shots are shortening our animal's lives.

Belle, Buster's mother was the granddaughter of my oldest sister's dog. Her dog won the first price for obedience, behaviour and beauty. The kind of dogs that would die on the spot rather than disobey! I brought Belle from Quebec in 1987. It took me two days to get her to accept the ride in the vehicle, but then she wouldn't eat, pee or poop for the next two days. All she wanted to do from Victoriaville, Quebec to Calgary is riding in the vehicle.

I discovered later on why dogs like riding so much. The only thing that could take Buster away from a female in heat was a ride in a vehicle, especially a truck. If there was something else; then it was to lock him inside a building, but this would have meant trouble inside this shack. It had to be something quite powerful in the ride at least to keep Buster away this way from a female in heat.

The dogs have their senses developed way more than people. I heard today from an expert lady on television it is a million times more developed than our senses. Their senses like earring, their smelling, their sense of danger and a lot of other things, but also their sexual feelings are extremely sensitive. The vibration of the vehicle is what they like so much. No one can blame them either. A lot of people would die riding.

Even though Belle was very intelligent and I loved her very much, I couldn't get her to shut up. She was a pure German shepherd. Maybe they don't hear themselves when they bark. Someone would walk the road towards the hubcap collection in Taylor and she would start barking when the person was a thousand feet away and she would still be barking when the person was long gone, as far as fifteen hundred feet. Luckily the closest neighbour was not too close, because she would have caused me more troubles yet.

I couldn't count all the times I walked out of the house with a roll of newspapers trying to shut her up. On the other hand, she was one of the best guard dog I ever had. I'm sure the BAAC, the Indian band and the dog control had a lot of complains about her, mainly from thieves who were afraid of her and God knows they were a lot of them. This is why I bred her with a pure Malamute to get a quiet dog, some mutesheps.

I wanted some intelligent dogs that don't bark too much, but still do when it is necessary. This is what I got from them, some adorable mutesheps. Maybe this is what the authorities didn't like; me having a bran new breed of wonderful dogs. I don't care of what they think; I know what kind of dogs I own and they are the very best; enough anyway to make the BAAC envy me and my dogs.

CHAPTER 9

Buster was six months old when I heard him bark for the very first time. For some time I thought it was something he would never do. He was three months old when I tried the first trick with him. Although, this is something I advice everybody not to do! At least not with the same article! I had a golf ball in my hand inside my sixty feet long shop in Calgary and I sent it at the other extremity. Buster then was standing beside me, simply looking at me as if wondering what I wanted him to do.

He looked at the ball rolling, but he never moved. He looked at me again as if demanding what I want him to do. I asked him to go get it pointing the ball, so he slowly walked all the way straight to the ball and looked at me again without touching the ball. I said; pick it up. He did. I said; bring it back. He did and I petted him as a sign of appreciation. He never failed to bring what ever I wanted since.

I could certainly appreciate it a lot when I had to retrieve a hubcap that was hard for me to get. Some places it was forbidden for a person to go but not for a dog. Don't get me wrong I have what it's believed to be the largest collection of hubcaps in my country, but

I never ever stole one in my entire life. The pieces I'm talking about were on industrial properties or on ranches and the owners weren't interested in them at all.

Sometime the owners would find them before me and they would hang them on the top of the fence posts. Other times when the cap wasn't too far; I could retrieve it with a sixteen feet pole I brought along with a hook at the end. The farmers also hanged a lot of hubcaps for me this way.

Belle, Buster's mother could jump a six-foot fence with a chain in her neck. Her mother jumped my dad's eight-foot roof trying to catch a bird.

Buster jumped a six feet high coral as if it was just a pothole. I trained him to jump me as if I was the enemy, which he liked particularly to do and he never wanted to miss the training. I had to stop it though, because he became to take it a bit too seriously and he became a bit too aggressive with me and the very last time we did it, he made two large scratches on my chest with his teeth. His job was to run and jump me and mine was to catch him and throw him on the ground. This last time we work this one out I got scared when I saw him coming, so I moved aside and he caught me when he passed by. He must have been coming at thirty miles an hour this last time. This is the reason I thought it was enough of that. I spent a lot of beautiful hours playing and training him.

Buster and Chimo spent hours competing ferociously, because neither one of them wanted to let the other one get the ball. There were times when I laugh a lot when Buster couldn't make it in time and he would put his nose between Chimo's back legs and flip her around. This was

139

just hilarious; especially when this would allow him to get the ball before she did.

Although, Buster was way stronger than her and to give Chimo a chance to get to the ball before him; sometimes I hold him back a few seconds before throwing the ball, but this is not something he liked very much. He was a winner, a great winner and a proud competitor. On the other hand if I didn't send the ball too far Chimo could get it before him. When Buster had enough of playing this game he would keep the ball in his mouth and there was no way to pull it out of there. I tried a couple of times, but there was no use, his mouth was just like a vice.

Buster was also impressively manageable. One day while I was walking in a park with my girlfriend and holding him on the leash; he was walking ahead of us without stretching the leash. I was quite amazed to say the least. I then swung the leash to the left and he slowly turned on the left; then I swung it on the right and again he turned on the right. I asked my girlfriend if she saw what happened and she asked me what it was. So I repeated the process for her eyes and she had a hard time to believe it too. He was only six months old at the time and this was the very first time I was trying this.

He seemed to know everything even before he was trained for it. I was completely impressed by him one time when I called him over while he was playing with two other little dogs. We were at my girlfriend's son's farm and we were just leaving. I called him and he came immediately. I asked him to get in the car and he did it right away. I asked him to go on the back seat of the car and he did just this with no hesitation at all. Then I asked him to lie down on the back seat, which he did too right away. He executed to my astonishment four different commands within one minute and he was only four months old.

Not surprising he also won the first price of his class of twenty-six, all kind of different breed for obedience at a Taylor training kennel. There were a lot of pure dogs among them too, but he was the only bilingual one. He was a blessing to me and I knew it too. All of my dogs that were killed by the Tofino BAAC could have been just as good with a little bit of love and time.

I could give Buster orders in French and in English and he would obey them in both languages. At first he wasn't too sure between sit and shit, but he learned the difference pretty quick about this too. The pureness of an animal doesn't mean much to me either. Many people told me Buster wasn't a pure dog, but to me he was a pure shepherd and a pure malamute at the same time, a pure muteshep, a quiet shepherd.

Someone would ask me why so many dogs. Well, I didn't plan this and I didn't really want to have this many either, but it was just like a family, when a kid is there either you wanted it or not, you keep it, at least I do.

Did you ever try to control a bitch in heat? Try thirty. The year before the seizure, I asked Robin Rogers, the manager of the Tofino BAAC to help me find home for twenty females of mine. He refused. I asked him in person and I asked him again a third time over the phone. He refused. I told him though, if he was going to kill them it was something I could do myself. His response: 'It didn't come from me, but you might just have to do this.'

It crossed my mind a couple of times the reason for me to have so many dogs left to feed could have been caused by the animal lovers, pet shops owners and the Tofino BAAC who spent a lot of time working to ruin my reputation, the reputation of a man who breed some of the best dogs in the world and was taking care of them just like a good mother would take care of her children.

I kind of got the proof of this a few years back when after I sold a puppy to a family who begged me for it and this for the moderate amount of ten dollars. The man brought it back a couple of months later telling me his wife found out I had troubles with the BC BAAC and for this reason they couldn't keep a dog which came from a man with this kind of reputation. The least I can say is, it is disturbing.

This is a man, a stranger to me, who came to my place a couple of months earlier begging me to lend him money one day, because he couldn't pay his rent and his family was going to be kicked out of the house in the middle of the winter. I just couldn't let down this unknown man in distress who was crying for help if I could help, so I lent him the two hundred dollars, which he paid me back. Here in Saskatchewan it's not like it is in Quebec, if you don't pay, you're out, even in the cold winter.

The whole trauma of the disaster of Elkford BC, might just have been a bit of my fault in a way though. After killing a dog I considered unfit to anyone and was fighting with others every single occasion, I prayed God to do something about it, because it did affect me to put down a dog even if he deserved it. This dog accidentally bit me when I tried to separate them during his last fight and he refused to obey me, which is something I don't allow from an adult dog, but this still broke my heart.

I just didn't expect God would let the devil do so much damage to me. We have to be very careful for what we pray for; especially if we know God the Father listen to you, which has to be my case.

God must have had a very good reason to get me out of BC though. Today I got the feeling I went from hell to heaven, but I also know that in paradise, in the garden of Eden there were also some dangerous snakes.

Just before I left this province I said something bad will happen to Tofino and to BC even though I never cursed it. There were a lot of fires since and now there is a lot of flooding as well. My suspicion is that it's not over yet. Those are the exact same words Robin Rogers, the BAAC manager told me the last time he came to my place before the Elkford disaster. One could believe this was a premeditated plot. My lawyer told me that out of six houses in his street only his didn't burn. I told him it was most likely because he helped me out.

As you know now the man who was my landlord in Taylor is an aboriginal and he mentioned once the power the Indians will finally get when they got the money. He kind of said this will be then the day of victory over the white men. I couldn't help telling him they already got their revenge, their day of glory.

The Indians showed us how to smoke (The pipe of peace) and the smoking now is killing millions of white people among others. So I guess they won at the end.

More white people died and still do from smoking than there were ever Indians who were killed by white men's hands. Did my landlord ever laugh when I told him this!

One law officer of the Taylor Indian band told me once they didn't just want my dogs out of the land, but me and my hubcaps too. I looked at her straight in the eyes and I said; 'Before you kick me out of here, I'll give my whole collection to my landlord and then I'll work for him. You then try to kick him or me out of here.'

She turned around on the spot and she knew I had the better end of the stick this one time.

Harassment, harassment, always harassment! I was harassed for more than ten years and by the Indian band and by the Tofino BAAC. They both used each other to do it.

I concluded a charge by the BAAC against me on the Indian land wouldn't hold in court. This is why they managed to get me to take my dogs somewhere else. Not only they wanted to rid me of my dogs, but they also wanted to make sure I couldn't breed no more. This is why they neutered Buster. Buster might be the only dog they neutered though. This was done illegally too, because Buster was never surrendered to them and I would have never given my consent for it either and I was forced to pay for it on top of all. There was not a better dog in the whole world.

They are extremely intelligent and don't bark unless they have a very good reason. This is probably why they didn't understand my dogs; they were all too smart for them. If one of my dogs barks, even if it's three in the morning I get up, because I know it is important.

In Tofino a dog is not allowed to bark more than five minutes at the time and more than fifteen minutes in one day. A dog is not allowed in the front yard. You only allow lighting up your fireplace the days they say you can. The clothes lines are not allowed either. It's a good thing we are in a free country.

The only time Buster went to the hospital is when he fought with a porcupine at four o'clock in a morning. Thinking there were thieves hiding in the ditch close by, I turned him loosed and I send him after what ever was making him bark. This was a big mistake from my part. I should have gone with him and be holding him. He had quills all over his face and inside his mouth. I tried to help him, but it was no use, I was just making things worst. I called the emergency animal hospital and got him in at five. He was put to sleep right away, but I don't think he was operated on until much later. I picked up sixteen quills out of his face up to a year later. They were coming out of his head through his ears and a lot of them by the sockets of his eyes. I think he survived by a kind of miracle. I had to call him back twice because all he wanted is to finish what he had started. He would have probably killed it, but he would have died too. This was in the summer of 2001 and one day when I was working on a roof in the summer of 2003, suddenly I felt a terrible pain in my left forearm. I also felt like I was paralyzing.

There was one of this quills disappearing in my arm. There was only one quarter of an inch left to go when I noticed it. I had to use vicegrip to get it out of there and if I didn't get it out, this thing would most likely have killed me. No doubt in my mind, this quill came out of my

Buster's body, which I most likely got when I hugged him or when I was ridding him of wood ticks.

My kind of dogs is also very clean and self cleaning too. I never gave Buster a bath in fourteen years and as far as I know, he never ever smelled bad.

I can imagine why the people of the BAAC got tired of the complaints. I guess they were tired to hear; 'We found one at the Hubcap Collection.'

Of course they like to sell puppies too and they sure proved it without a slice of a doubt. I can see now too they were pressured by a great number of animal groups, animal lovers and pet shop owners. I'm with them one hundred per cent when it comes to protect the animals, but not when it comes to compete with breeders. They're supposed to protect animals, not to harm people and kill dogs.

The first warrant stipulated they had one phone call to complain about me having fifty dogs chained to trees on my property in Elkford. The officer from the Grandfocks BAAC told me afterwards it was him who phoned the Tofino office to make the complaint. 'I like dogs to be loosed and to be allow to run all over the property.' He said. This is how dogs get kill on the road dummy.

But my dogs weren't chained to trees at all. In fact, I was praised by an officer of the BAAC of Tofino office a year earlier for my doghouses and for my dog holding system.

The material I use to build my doghouses is the same material your houses' doors are made with. In fact, this material is a part of the door they cut off to put the window in. My doghouses supply coolness for my dogs in the summer and insulation against the cold in the winter. Dogs love to lay on top of the flat roofs for the height and to make a change from the ground.

She couldn't believe the shape my Buster was in for a twelve and a half years old dog. She too said that my dogs were not fit for adoption. She had received the message before she came to my place. She would have taken two of the most beautiful four and one half months old male puppies though. I told her the money for feeding all my dogs comes from the sale of puppies. I personally think she was too nice for this dirty kind of work and I told her so.

They have actually took my dogs from a dogs dream land with more than three thousand trees and put them on cement floors where they tried to make their beds as they were accustomed to. The results were pretty bad too as one witness said, one of the BAAC employee. Some dogs wore out their paws until they had no more. The dogs were put down as idiots, because this would have been evidence against the BAAC.

They took my dogs from a guy who hates to see them dead and they took them to a place where they would kill them. I actually predicted this. I disparately pleaded to spare my dogs from this disaster, but this was in vain. Other people did just that too.

The holding system is a rope going from tree to tree at approximately forty feet apart, six feet high. Rolling on the rope is a pulley with a swivel snap holding a nine, ten feet leach or chain that is attached to the collar of the dog. The reason for putting the swivel up high is to avoid the tangling up with dog's hairs. If a BAAC officer ever sees your dog choking because of his hair stock in the swivel, watch out. With the kind of dogs like the ones I have with hair sometime six inches long this is something that could easily happen. This way the dog has more freedom than when someone is walking it on a leach, because the dog goes where he wants to go when he wants to, not where his walker wants to.

A dog I sold a few years back saved his master's life. The thieves tried to get the BAAC and the dog control to destroy it saying he was vicious. The thing is the dog never hurt the jerk, he just held him there showing his teeth and growling until the cop came to pick him up, but he never bit him. Another one of my dogs was chosen as being the best in search for avalanches victims.

Thieves tried to break in hundreds of times every year in Taylor. They succeeded too a couple of times. I surprised many of them myself. At time I wondered if I had more hubcaps sold than stolen. Today I am sure of it, because my employee stole thousands of them and the cops didn't want to do anything about it. I have a few witnesses too who are certain he stole money from me as well. So yes, it was important I had dogs there and on my property in Elkford also.

I know for sure too the BAAC had a lot of complaints from the pet shop owners who would have loved to see my kennel destroyed long time ago. I strongly believe my best witnesses in a trial could have been the Tofino BAAC officers and their employees. They were at my collection at least twelve times a year to inspect my dogs and for unfounded complaints and this for more than ten years.

The only thing I was told by Robin Rogers, the only one thing he complained about in these many years that was not quite up to standard is he would like me to put a little more wood ships in the puppies' kennel. I put some in immediately. He said a couple of times that what I had for my dogs was much better than what they could ever given them. They sure proved this to be right later on.

On October 3rd 2001 after inspecting my place in Elkford with one male vet, a policeman with a camera and another BAAC officer; on their way out Robin said it wasn't over yet. I guessed it was a warning I didn't pay enough attention to. But, what could have I done differently anyway? It's not this easy to move away with fifty-three dogs and not too much money. Ho sure, I could have killed forty wonderful dogs like they did, but if I did this I wouldn't have been able to sleep to this day, but they could.

Not once he and other officers had something to nail me with in more than ten years and it's not because they didn't try enough. This must have been very frustrating for him and for the animal lovers who didn't like me to continue the breeding.

The previous three weeks I was in Quebec visiting my family on a trip where I left my cds at forty-six radio stations across the country. Family too is important to me. They came to visit my animals while I was gone. I supposed it was a great opportunity for them to catch me with my pants down, sort of speak.

After their visit it was said by Robin Rogers in the newspapers the condition of my animals was acceptable. Apparently there was a little problem though, because the only guy I could get to feed the dogs and take care of them while I was gone didn't like to rake the poop very much. We all know this could be a reason for persecution by the BAAC. He was supervised though by my Taylor employee and another Elkford friend of mine and also by another friend who introduced this guy to me.

Here I'm going to tell you things which even the shrinks from Vancouver don't seem to know nor understand and the BAAC officers and their employees even less.

We have to understand the dogs' philosophy to know that when we take the dog's poop away from him he feels stolen; dispossessed of something that belongs to him. Their shit just like their urine are use to mark their territories. When a dog is alone at home he doesn't feel the threat as bad so the problem then is not as serious.

Although, when there are many other dogs around their shit becomes very important to them; so if you remove it too far away from them every day; they will try to find a different spot all the time to make their deposit, one of the only thing they produce. You most likely have seen a male or a female dog spinning on itself a dozen times on a spot before dropping its fortune. A lot of times they will try to find something to hold their deposit in place like a little tree or even the fence, which I hate passionately, because then it is not easy at all to pick it up or to rake it.

Although, you have to admit it yourself, this is very smart from their part. If you deposit your money at the bank you just don't want the BAAC agents to come and take it away. So to calm down the dogs with their pangs and stop them from shitting all over the places it is better to rake their droppings with a little bit of dirt and pile everything as close as possible to them, but out of their reach and then you'll see they will always shit on the same spot close to the cake, which will save you a lot of work.

The morning of October 3rd when they came to my property I was raking when they arrived. I think I was not supposed to be around. It was supposed to be a surprise party for me. I surprised them. It was only nine o'clock in the morning. They must have been a bit upset for missing their shot. They were four of them, two police officers, Robin Rogers, the Tofino BAAC manager and one vet. All of them were armed with cameras to try I supposed to catch me with my pants down, sort of speech. I mean trying to accumulate enough proofs against me while I was gone, so they thought anyway.

Robin told me that day he didn't like at all the man who fed my dogs and took care of them while I was away. I got to say I didn't like him too much myself either, because he burnt my beautiful wood kitchen table.

What do we do when we don't have enough proofs against someone we want to demolish? When we are the BAAC of Tofino behind Robin Rogers and Elizabeth Turnell, we lie and we make some up. This goes for Tom Kuisk as well.

One day before all this an old lady came one time to the hubcap collection, parked her car illegally on the highway where there is a lot of traffic, walked all the way around with a cane, came to my yard and asked me how many dogs I have. She could hardly walk with a cane and see three feet ahead of herself. I told her the BAAC already knew how many dogs I have. I told her to go home and rest in peace and let others live in peace too.

There was a woman I was told who used to feed her dog in an expensive crystal bowl and she complained to the BAAC because I feed mine dogs in hubcaps commonly called dog dishes. When I told Tom Kuish about this his response was: 'They were thirty.'

My caps were just as clean as his plates on his table before his meal. At least I hope his dishes were just as clean as my dog's dishes. I have learned longtime ago that a clean cap sells much better than a dirty one.

A nice and young couple who were opening a restaurant in Tofino once came to my place to buy fifty regular hubcaps and half a dozen of motor home wheel covers to serve salads in them. I would think if it's good enough for people it's got to be good enough for dogs.

This big bunch of responsible and respectable people from the Tofino BAAC came to my place on July 3rd 2002 like thieves and they acted like thieves too. The first batch of my dogs went through the trauma of being caged by strangers from 9 till 12.30. They have never seen a cage before. The cages were loaded in trailers and piled like war prisoners and taking away without a drop of water. None of them rode in a vehicle before with strangers. They have also forbidden me to feed them either food or water. They were probably afraid of the mess the dogs could make; especially the mess they tried to make. I was earlier than they thought or wished I would be. My dogs already had their food which they never had a chance to finish eating. Not even a last meal for these poor creatures. It was time for me to bring them water. So in the heat of July there was no water for the prisoners.

The cop gave me the warrant stipulating an officer of the BAAC had a suspicion an animal could have been in distress on my promises. I told the cop and I showed him the an Animal. I asked; "Do they need twelve employees, two vets, two trucks and big trailers and a cop for a suspicion there is an animal in distress?" "There's nothing I can do." He said. "What if I turn them all loosed?" "I'll have to arrest you for obstruction of justice." "You dare call this justice? It's nothing but lies." "There must be someone you can call." "My lawyer is away."

So I went in my house and I called a neighbour who I thought was a friend of mine. Lucky for me he doesn't own any dog so he didn't have to be afraid of them about retaliation. Tremblay came with a camera and took a lot of pictures that might be of good use some day.

Somehow it helped a little bit. I didn't feel so much alone against an army that invaded me.

After he was gone I still felt helpless. This is when I thought I had the best idea. I called all the media I could think of. Yes, it's me who called the radio stations, the newspapers, and the TV stations. I told them my dogs were on their way to the shelter and I'd like them to go take pictures and videos of my injured, my sick or my thin dogs at their arrival. Of course there were none and the managers of the BAAC were still at my place, so they couldn't interfere with the journalists. Surprise, surprise. All of them were refused access.

A couple of days before they came for the seizure they brought me a big pile of bags of dogfood. Not that my dogs were out of food, but a little help is always appreciated; especially when you don't have too much money. I noticed that most of the food was puppy food. I was not suspicious enough and I didn't pay enough attention of the trap I was set in.

Well, you know what puppy food could do to adult dogs, don't you? I'll write it down anyway for the ones who don't know. It gives them the run badly. The very least thing I can say is they came to my place to stir up a lot of shit. I knew this for a long time already and I wouldn't give it to my adult dogs. Well of course, in the morning of the disaster Robin Rogers and a few others were going all around my dogs with their nose up in the air trying to find my dogs wet shit. The running shit they wanted to cause on purpose. Pictures and videos with dogs having their paws full of poop is a good trick to get the population sympathy and a lot of cash.

They already had all the mothers, the puppies and pregnant females earlier, so why bring me some puppy food other then trying to set me up?

The Bag of Puppy Chow and the bag of Dog Chow are basically identical. Only the writings are different. I went to look at the bag again, lifting them all up, then I realized what they were trying to do and this was to cause a lot of shit and they did. It won't hurt the dogs, but it sure doesn't look good on the ground near the dogs. If they can catch you with dog's shit stock in the dog's paws, you're cooked.

They had mentioned giardia before and Nicko who had wet stuff for the longest time was pointed out to me. Out of all my dogs he was the only one with the run. I was giving him medicine for it for over a month. He was according to Tom Kuish a vicious dog. Tom was afraid of him anyway, probably because the dog was a very good guard dog.

I took this dog to my vet and I got him a complete check-up. Nicko was afraid of the floor that of course he never saw before. It was very shiny and slippery and this was scary. I'm scare too to fall when I walk on ice. I hope I'm not quoted as not fit for adoption for this and besides, I know what the ice is. It was not found any giardia in him and the vet who was a total stranger to him had no problem at all doing his job.

He's the one who told me that most of living creatures on earth had a sort of giardia. The dog had a bit of a problem with the floor coming in and no problem at all with it going out. If my wildest and most vicious animal could adapt himself with a slippery floor, going through two doors for the first time, meet a pure stranger and let him work on him with a needle and other instruments within ten minutes, why then all of them couldn't adapt? This is on file in Taylor BC. His name was Nicko.

Shortly after my dogs were seized I asked the management of the Tofino BAAC for the permission to visit my dogs accompany by my vet. I was refused. I thought everyone had the right to a second opinion. Within a few days after they took my four first dogs I went to the shelter and I asked to see my dogs. I was refused. I went there three times. I was refused to see my dogs. Some seventeen days later I was told I lost my dogs because I didn't claim them within the fourteen days grace I had. I noticed a lot of shit on the floor as if I was shown that with all the employees who work over there, they weren't doing any better than I did with my fifty-three dogs by myself.

I was mixing their poop with dirt and pile it close to them, but out of their reach causing an incentive for them to always poop on the same spot instead of all over. It was much better than what I saw at the center and it smells a lot better too.

I asked them for my collars back and I was told they'll give them to me, but they never did, which constitute a theft, an aggravated offence and this with the collaboration of the court and the police.

CHAPTER 10

The least I can say about the whole ordeal is it was a very rough ride. I wish I had Angie, my little miracle female dog with me before this misadventure. Maybe I would just have had a chance to move my dogs away before the holocaust, at least my Buster. One thing is sure; there must have been a better way to handle the whole situation.

Many thoughts went through my mind during this ordeal and they were not all very nice either. First I thought of loading my semi-automatic 3006, disarm the present cop, make all these employees unload my dogs at the point of my gun and make this bunch of dirty people get in this trailer, even the drivers of those two trucks instead of my dogs, then lock them all up with a padlock. Then take them all on the top of a very steep hill on their way to Tofino, stop the vehicle, put it in neutral and let the hazard do the rest.

Another thought I had was to back my truck in the front wall of their building at the BAAC center and put a one hundred litres tank of propane in the middle of the floor and shot it with my gun and blow the whole thing up, but just the though I could hurt my dogs was enough to change my mind.

My lawyer to whom I gave my first book; The Precious Princess of Wonderland to read told me afterwards he wondered what kind of man I am and he went to read it to see if I could be a risk for this bunch of liars. It is not he thought I was a bad man, but rather I think, because he thought they deserved such a fate.

There are people who kill and there are others who deserve to die. This is not the first time I say this, but luckily for me and many others my God said; 'You shall not kill.' Exodus 20, 13!

There are always two voices speaking to us. I have always tried to refute the voice of the devil and I'm happy God gave me the strength to do it in moments like the ones I went through with this ordeal in Elkford BC. They might not be so lucky when they do the same thing to people who don't have God in their lives like the man who killed four cops in Alberta.

Another thing I realized afterwards is the dream I had many years ago could very well have come through after all with the BAAC invading my property. Here it is again.

I dreamed my Bible's studies were heard of everywhere in the world and the devil hates them just as much as he hates God. One day as I was expecting almost every day an army of cops came to the domain to arrest who they dared called; The leader of the sect. So of course I came out to face the enemy and I insisted to come out alone to spare the lives of the others. When I got on top of the little hill where the gate is I asked why they were so many for there must have been thirty of them.

'You are under arrest by order of our king.'

The voice was coming out of a big cone similar to the ones they put on the road to direct the traffic.

'Haven't you heard the thunder?'

Then almost all of them were holding their ears with both hands. Some of them went to hide behind trees, others even tried to crawl under their cars.

When the silence was back again they all gathered together and surrounded me and I asked them if they heard of the last week earthquake. I saw the earth shook under their feet and most of them were terrified and screamed their head off.

'Tell me, why are you spitting blood like this? Are you guys trying to scare me or something? I see that one of you doesn't have blood on his lips. I'll go with him, but with none of the others. I'm still a little scare of AIDS, you know? Besides, God doesn't want me to mix my blood with his enemies.'

One cop came out of the line and he said hi to me. "Good morning brother." "Hi, aren't you afraid like all of the others?" "No, God is my shield." "Good morning brother. Where are we going?" "I have to take you to another domain for a little while, until they can digest this last storm and this last earthquake."

So this man whom I think was my guardian angel took me in his car and he drove me to another domain I never heard of. I slept during most of the trip; so I don't really know where he got me. But during this trip I had another dream or a vision. Sometimes it's hard to tell which it is. So in this short dream I saw what happened to the other cops after our departure. They went back to their chief whom I thought could very well be the devil himself.

"Where is the man I send you for?" "One of the officers took him." "He didn't bring him here. What in the holy hell all of you did?" "There was a thunder storm like we have never seen before and as soon as this man pronounced the word earthquake, the earth shook like we never heard of." "None of you could bring the fire down from heaven like this?"

At the same time the fire came down from the skies and consumed three of his officers within a few seconds. Another officer told his chief the rain was poring so bad that his fire wouldn't have last anyway.

"You're just a bunch of useless and stupid imbeciles. I can't get anyone to do anything wrong unless I do it myself."

"I would have loved to see you and you're fire against the rain of this storm." "You go to hell right now. You're not supposed to love anything nor anybody."

I think the thunder storm and the earthquake suffered by the cops of my dream are the blames and reproaches suffered by the manager, the assistant manager of the Tofino BAAC, the BC BAAC and their officers, from the animals lovers of the Okanogan Valley.

One thing I know for sure is if the members of the Tofino BAAC did love dogs as much as I do they wouldn't have killed them, but they would have found homes for them, especially the ones their own employees wanted to adopt. If they loved my dogs as much as I do, at least they would have found a faster way, a more human way to put them down and mainly less painful. I just want to say they have many deaths on their conscience. But what I'm I saying here? There is no use, because to do what they have done they have to be without any conscience. It was certainly not because my dogs were vicious, because they let pure strangers to my dogs walked them around in the streets and parks of Tofino and among other people, unless they really are this much of dummies to put people at risk.

Today I have fourteen wonderful, happy and loved mutesheps that will be trained for pulling the sleigh and this only because I had the wisdom to listen to my God and to move away from BC. They tried very hard to destroy my breed and myself. They hurt a lot, they caused a lot of damages, but they failed, because I'm still standing and so are my dogs. If I rely on this dream of mine though concerning the invasion on my property, my stay over here is only temporary. As I said it before, today I have the impression I moved from hell to heaven, but I just happen to know that in paradise, in the Garden of Eden there were dangerous snakes too. Even though that here in Saskatchewan it is like heaven in comparison to what I went through in BC, I had a certain number of misadventures here too caused by the least good ones of the society, the rotten ones, some demons possessed people.

Goodadam, Saskatchewan in October 2001. Everything started very simply when I moved a couple and their belongings here from Taylor BC in the falls of 2001. I knew this couple from buying my truck from them. They found a house with a garage on a nice piece of land of four acres in the village of Goodadam for the reasonable amount of twenty-two hundred and fifty dollars.

This couple left BC on a kind of no where trip, go as the wind pushes us to search for a good deal on a house somewhere or anywhere. I'm sure it's the money for this truck that allowed them to buy this property. I might just have bought myself innocently the troubles to come along with this truck.

What ever it is, this couple met on this trip a man from Goodadam at the bus terminal in Saskatoon and it was during this conversation the couple found out there were properties for sale at very good prices in this village.

In fact at first he didn't want to sell me this truck, because was he saying, he will need it to move shortly. There is when I told him I will move them when the time comes. He was extremely surprised I stuck to my word when they came to ask me to move them here basically for the price of the gas. This was not an easy trip either, because the truck was loaded to the fullest and on top of everything I had to pull his minivan behind. It took every bit of this truck power on propane to claim the Rockies with such of a heavy load. It was even worst on my way back, because I had to face a very bad winter storm where I couldn't see much ahead of me.

Although during this trip, this moving task I had the chance to look around for cheap properties just in case maybe one day I wanted to move somewhere too. Of course if you read until now in this book you already know the problems I had with the BAAC of Tofino. My precious Precious and her three little puppies of three days old were missed by this bunch of fools from the BAAC who have never seen nor heard them.

They didn't take them, but I knew very well they weren't in security on my land anymore. This was not because of me or the coyotes, but rather because of the two legs wolves from the Tofino BAAC. For this reason I had to find a safe and friendly place for them and there was no time to waste. Of course I had good reasons to fear.

It was then I had the idea to call this couple I moved the previous year. They understood very quickly my situation and for having visited my property and my dogs a couple of times they knew very well there was nothing true about my dogs being in distress. They have accepted to take care of my dogs until I could do it again and this with a little compensation.

For the first time in a long time I could leave my property without worrying about my dogs left behind, because the ones I own from then on were riding with me on this trip of one thousand miles. This was at the beginning of January 2003. It was a bit of a long trip for them who never travel before, but they did a good job. I installed them in their own dog's houses, so they didn't feel too much out of their elements and for myself, I didn't have to worry too much about what was going on in BC.

I quickly found a house for sale on a beautiful piece of land of an acre and a half and this for one thousand dollars, which I couldn't afford to buy right away. I had to rent it for one hundred dollars a month for six months before I could actually buy it. This house is straight and solid, but without adequate insulation which caused me my first real problem in this village.

Once everything was settled I had to go back to BC to get my furniture and my personal belongings. Before going I made some deals with the mayor of the village to keep an eye on my house and especially on my cat who had to stay behind mainly because he gave me a bit of troubles on the last trip. I left him everything he needed for the time I was gone, which was a full pail of water and a full pail of catfood.

I just knew that if I left him somewhere else he would have left to come after me and I wouldn't see him again. I just asked the mayor to look through the window from time to time to see if he's still got enough food and water. This big black cat of mine that I love so very much; Miowe took off on me twice while I stopped at the gas stations on the previous trip.

I called many times when I was gone to require about my animals. They all told me everything was fine, so I could sleep well and not worry about them. When I was back after five weeks I received what I could easily call the largest demonstration of love of my entire life.

I myself missed my dogs and my cat a lot, but it was nothing compared to how much my cat missed me. He had his mouth dripping like I have never seen before and he could not control his bowels either. Lucky for me he settled down after forty-eight hours. I sure was impressed by his reaction and I never thought a cat could love and miss me this much.

I keep dogs for many years now and I know they can miss me even just after one hour, but either it's one hour or twenty-four hours or yet many days their reaction is the same at my return. I missed them too, but ten minutes later they are already settled down and back to normal as if I have never left.

I had the gas furnace going again and I adjusted the thermostat at fifty-five degrees for the time I was gone, but since I had many wood stoves I got the gas disconnected when I was back around the fifth of February. Although this winter, especially that month the weather was stable around minus forty degrees. What ever, when I received the gas bill I could not believe the numbers I was looking at.

This was five hundred and twenty-eight dollars for a little less than five weeks of use of this furnace which was inspected and lighten up by a specialist from the gas company. Also the fact this furnace was located just under my bed in the basement was playing with my nerves each time it was starting. I could just not get out of my mind a couple was blown up in Peachland BC in the Okanogan valley just a few months earlier and it was caused by the gas hit by lightning.

This mayor who was watching my place while I was gone has never said a word about the T top from the Camero 1986, which worth many hundreds dollars and is parked behind my house until I mentioned it to him. When I talked to him about it he said; 'Ah! You noticed?' Then he told me he thinks a young blond man took it.

There are two young blond men in the village, one of the two is the today mayor's son and the other one is an employee at the coop across the street from my place, but I had no reason at all to suspect this last one.

Although, when it comes to the today mayor's son it is a much different story. He came to my place many

165

times and he also told me many times on the street he wanted to buy this car for his younger brother who was about twelve at the time. This was in 2003. What he actually wanted is to put the car back with the wheels and the rooftop he already owns. He talked to me about this car many times a year and every year for the last seven years. The very special wheels of this Camero were stolen also, but this was done before I own it and I have no problem figuring out who has them now. There was something else, but I'll come back to it a bit later.

This mayor who is also a roofer was interested to form an association with me at fifty, fifty on all of his construction work contracts. He already knew I was a journeyman carpenter. He also assured me I wouldn't have any problem with my animals, that there were already two ladies in the village who were breeding and selling dogs freely.

The three first contracts went without too many serious problems even though I noticed my new partner was taking off a bit too often, but even then I was making a good living anyway.

Then came on a much bigger contract which was the residence of a priest near a church in Itunara, a little town of six hundreds people fifteen miles West of Goodadam. I basically did the whole work by myself. I worked sixty hours in a very high temperature of one hundred and five degrees and this on the roof where it is warmer yet. My partner worked less than twenty hours on this job.

The priest saluted me a couple of times, but he never offered me a fresh glass of water even if he saw me sweat as if I was coming out of a shower. When came dinner time I went to the hotel to get a couple of cold bottles of beer and I went to sit beside the church to drink them in the shade. I was just waiting for the priest to come to say something about it. I can assure you that I was expecting him with a brick and a lantern and also with a few empty bottles. I have to mention too that I went all over the church property trying to find a faucet with water.

This was kind of different for me, because everywhere I worked to that day; people were giving me something to drink and something to eat. One woman even offered me a bed saying it was way too hot to work in this temperature. She also gave me a few cold beers and this was the first time in more than twenty years when I drank more than two bottles the same day.

The priest never showed up though, but I had quite a message for him which comes from Jesus and it is written in Matthew 10, 42: 'And whoever in the name of a disciple gives to one of these little one even a cup of cold water to drink, truly I say to you, he shall not lose his reward.'

It is little to say this priest needed to hear it but, how can a blind man see the sweat on a forehead of a hard worker?

The next evening the mayor, my new partner came to settle our accounts on the church job. The only thing is he wanted to get fifty per cent of the money for it.

Before we settled this last one we started to replace the shingle on a house near the village. Everything went fine to take off the old shingles and we were four guys to do it. There was the owner of the house who was helping and he had his tractor with a big bucket to take away all the waste. There was also a friend of the mayor, the mayor and myself. Within a little more than one hour half of the roof was ready to receive the new shingles. But then the mayor said he forgot to take his compressor, his nailers and his nails with him, so he went home.

He went to get his tools which were indispensable to us to complete the work. All three of us were waiting for this man (if I can say) for two and one half hours for this guy who was gone three miles away. We asked his friend what could have happened. His response was: 'What do you think?'

No doubt there were most likely a few drops left in the bottom of his bottles.

When he came back a little before noon we started covering this roof right away, but guess what, he was doing it backward. Instead of covering form left to right he was doing it the other way. So I told him he was working backward and he seemed to be all surprised. I told him it was hard enough to work on a roof without having to do it backwardly. His friend said then that I was capable to do it too. I said no way; if he can't work properly I rather go home. Then the owner who was looking from the ground level told the mayor he was going all crooked. It was true. So I had to take over and start covering this roof normally from left to right. Luckily we only had six rows done by then. At around four in the afternoon we had this half of the roof done and everything was fine except these six first rows. I told the landlord this was not hurting the quality of the roof and he would most likely never look at this part of the roof for another twenty years. This was accepted, but he really had the intention to make the mayor fix his bad work. Everything was bad but ended well.

When the evening came my associate came to my place to settle the job done at the church. He had made his calculations at fifty, fifty. "I don't think so", I said. "This is not the way I learned to count. We are at fifty, fifty at work too. I can understand that you have to leave from time to time, but other than this you have to work too. If you want to be fair you'll pay me $15.00 an hour for my hours and do the same for the hours you worked. I allow you $150.00 more to you for getting the contract. You owe me $1225.00 and you earned $575.00. If you can't be fair I have no more business to do with you." "I'm the one who got the contract." "And you are largely paid for this too."

He grumbled a bit, he gave me my money and he went home. I was waiting for him to pick me up the next morning but he never showed up. I started to look for him three days later and I found him in Itunara, the next town, a town of around six hundred inhabitants fifteen miles West of Goodadam. I found him, but he seemed to want to hide. I went to talk to him anyway and he told me that our arrangement wasn't working for him anymore. This is perfect, I said and I went on the spot to put a little ad in the newspaper. One more time I was on my own again and this with only a few dollars.

I don't know if he realized it or not, but by setting me free he did me a great favour. I am not a quitter and it would have taken me a lot to let him down, but this way everything was fine with me.

Three weeks later the owner of the house where I worked on half of the roof came to see me and he asked me if I would go finish the other side of the roof. I was working then on my own property demolishing the rest of the shop I bought. Of course I will I said, "But I thought it was done long time ago." "No, I didn't see him since." Talking about the mayor, my ex partner.

"You will get paid by the insurances." "I hope they're not going to take months to do so, because I can't afford to wait too long." "If it's too long I'll pay you myself and they can always pay me back." "If it's the case I'll do it."

Two days later I was on his roof and with his help I started to clean the second side of his roof. A couple of hours later the mayor with his drinking body came to get his tools thinking probably I was going to use them. The owner of the house I guess saw this coming and for this reason he stayed on the sight, because beside for getting his tools these guys wanted to make a number on me.

I started at eight o'clock in the morning and I finished with the sundown. All I had left to do the next day was the cap, about one and a half hour. I did the whole thing with a hammer. In fifteen hours I earned $1100.00.

I talked to the mayor about the other side of the roof I worked on and he told me to claim the whole thing from the insurance for myself. This is what I did without any remorse. I didn't waste any time to go buy myself a good compressor and a roofing air nailer. This was the last roof I have done with a hammer.

The reason why the mayor didn't go back to finish this roof was because he could not get the money from it for a long time and he needed the money every day for his drink. This is why he was in this little town carrying water for a farmer at eight dollars an hour, because this way he could get enough money every day for his bottles.

But this was not the end of his troubles and neither the end of mine. A year later work was getting hard to get for him; so he got into his head the best thing to do for him was to hurt me and my reputation. The insurance agent told me he will never deal with him again and many costumers told me they had to wait for him up to two years the get their roof repaired. Two years is a very long time; especially when the roof is leaking.

I guess he was watching me though, because in the middle of the afternoon he and his drinking partner came to get his tools. His friend's name was Frank and I could tell by their behaviours they came to cause me troubles at the same time and why else would he have left his equipment over there this long and until I get there.

The mayor himself was a man six foot four tall and the other one was at least two hundred and thirty pounds. Although the owner of the house I think had anticipated something like this to happen, because he stayed home all day even though he had a lot of other things to do. I could tell he was watching them as if they were mad dogs. They were all born in this area so they knew each other better than I did.

At the end of the day the owner paid me the twenty-two hundred dollars the insurance allowed for the work and I thanked him. He was satisfied, but he mentioned this was a lot of money for one day work even though it is hard work. He probably thought it would take me a few days by myself to complete the job. I took half of this money and I went to buy myself a compressor, a nailer and a couple of boxes of those nails that go with it. Then one more time I was in business and on my own. It is kind of shameful that a carpenter with years of experiences has a hard time to get thirty dollars an hour and a roofer with hardly any can get more than seventy.

This mayor told a few people I used him to build myself a clientele. It was certainly not me who did something to create the trouble between us. I worked my ass off for both of us for four months and this was to allow him to drink a little bit more.

The only thing I did is not letting him walk on my big toe, he was too heavy, besides, this is not a flaw for a businessman.

The insurance agent told this customer he will never give this drunk another contract even if he was the only one around to do it.

A short time later while this mayor was completely drunk and he fell in his stairs inside his house and split his head open, but he managed to get outside anyway and he walked to the corner of the street in front of his house. He apparently faint over there and someone called the police.

Someone else, an ex director of the school saw him too just before he fainted and he told the police there was nobody else around, but this drunk told the cops anyway that I beat him up with pieces of wood I got on the other side of the street and there were three other guys with me disguised as soldiers.

To this day I don't know anyone who would help me doing something like this and besides, I never counted on anyone else to defend myself except a lawyer maybe when it is absolutely necessary.

Luckily for me the cops didn't believe him.

On the other hand his drinking partner did believe him and he came after me one day when I was planting my potatoes in my garden. It was not really at my place, but on a piece of land I rented out just for this. He was as drunk as one could be without passing out; coming towards me swearing his head off. I didn't realize right away he was interested in me when I heard; 'Now I got you, you son of a bitch.'

I rather thought he was after his dog, but I changed my mind when he got closer to me.

He asked me what the hell I was doing on this land, this land wasn't mine and I had no business over there. I told him then I was busy and I had no time for this. Then he got closer to me saying he will kill me and bury me in my potatoes and at the same time he tried to hit me with a punch. I then moved on the side avoiding the hit and I gave him a good one, but I couldn't help noticing he had a real tough mouth. I told him then to go away and to leave me alone and I walked away trying to avoid a blood shed. But he came at me again and when he was close enough I turned around to face him and when he swung at me I swung too, but it was with the handle of my rake. I was aiming at his mouth, but I hit him on the forehead splitting it open for a couple of inches and this was enough for him to cool off a little bit.

Even though he was bleeding like a pig he was happy saying; 'Now I know you're the one who hurt my friend; now I know you did it. Now I found the guilty one'

He then went to his other drinking partner; the man I moved here from BC the previous year.

This man's wife called the police right away, but I too went home in the mean time to call the cops who came as soon as they could, because they were at my place pretty quick. The officer asked me many questions about the incident and he told me I could be charged for assault. He also said he wouldn't charge me because this man was very nasty with the ambulance people and also with them, the cops, this was easy enough to believe he could have been nasty with me as well. I told him all I did was defending myself.

This tough drunk spent two days at the hospital with a headache, this injury he really called for. The cop told me also to stay away from these two, because they were very dangerous, both of them.

I knew for hearing him myself the man I moved here from BC was, because he told me himself how he stabbed a little man in Ontario who was nagging him. He also told me how he got away with it with lies from him and his wife. He also told me how he and his brother-in-law were stealing semi-trailers in Ontario as well. He was a sort of an Al Capone Canadian.

He also told me the main reason to move away from BC was for him to avoid committing murder on another man name Dwaine who was also cruising his wife. I actually know this Dwaine who lives in Peachland BC. He showed me the sword he kept very sharp, which he was going to use to cut the head off this man. It was his wife who talked him into moving away from there before the worst happen. This man is the owner of the dog that gave me all of the troubles with my females, Angie's father.

I asked him why he had to stab a little man of one hundred and forty pounds; him who is as strong as Hercules and is built like a wrestler and weight at least two hundreds and eighty pounds. Of course he could not answer me on this one, but I think it was to cause permanent damage. He was a man who saw Hitler face to face during the war and was trading liquor for guns and bullets.

They moved away from here for a very similar reason; he was going to kill the man I hit in the forehead, his own drinking partner because him too was harassing his wife for sex. Both of them were called Frank and both of them died of a similar death, from a heart attack. One of them died here in the village in his house face down on the floor. I heard about the other one's death from one of his friends.

I personally think his wife is a tease, because she told me one day and this in front of her husband she has a tight vagina, which could very well be interesting to many men. One could just wonder why she would mention something like this anyway. She also let anyone who wants to hear it that her husband was impotent.

There was another character called Steve who also died from a heart attack most likely for having a fit over a dollar he lost at an auction.

I did a few little jobs for him and I had quite a time to get paid and I never got paid for the last one. That time he wanted me to come and install an antenna he bought from me, which I delivered to his place, but I didn't want to install, mainly because I was too busy. This was in the same period of time I was working on the church property and frankly; I had enough with my eight to ten hours a day on the roof in this hot temperature. But he really insisted and since he was an older man and I kind of felt sorry for him and one day I quit earlier and I went to the store to buy the material I needed to fix the antenna.

He was an ex school teacher. The material I bought amounted to five dollars. I went just after supper to install it. When I was done I told him he owes me eleven dollars. 'Ho no.' He said. 'I'll give you five dollars.'

I told him again he owes me eleven dollars and he handed me a five dollar bill. I simply told him to keep it and I just walked out on him.

He came to my place many other times begging me to do other little jobs for him, that I was the best one, that there was nothing I couldn't fix and so on, but for me there was no way I was going to be taken again by the same person twice. I forgave him, but I didn't want to have anything else to forgive him. I heard a story later on about him which made me laugh a little.

The Frank, the one I hit in the forehead worked for Steve on a farm for two full days when Steve offered the other guy to pay him with some chicken. Frank told Steve he wouldn't mind, that he liked this meat. So Steve went and got him a frozen chicken. Frank picked it up and a bit mocking he asked Steve if he didn't think this was too much. Steve then with all of the seriousness in the world said he would have cut it in a half, but the chicken was too hard.

Then this Frank, the one I sent to the hospital still had a grudge against me and he came to attack me another time one day when I was working in the village. So I had two choices ahead of me and this was to either send him again to the hospital or to call the police. So this man had to go to court and explain to a judge why he was harassing me. He received the order to stay away from me anywhere and at all times. He came after me two more times anyway.

The lady where I was working that day accused me of breaking her brand new window I installed in her house. The whole work was inspected by a government agent and everything had to be A one before they send the cheque over. She tried everything she could to make me pay for the repairs, but to no avail. It was her son, a farmer who didn't know how to use the handle who broke it. He just forgot to unlock it before and he just thought it was too tight. She died shortly after from a heart attack too.

My ex partner, Rod also died while he was drunk and he smashed his head on the sidewalk this time when he fell in a similar way he did it the previous year at his place. I worried a little at first, because the way they said it on the news, it sounded like he was murdered. I then thought, everyone will point the finger at me and I will be questioned by the police. He was in his late forties and apparently he was a psychopath.

There was another case a bit strange. A lawyer from a town of four thousands people situated at eighteen miles East of Goodadam called and asked me if I would go to Fenwood, a village the size of Goodadam. The new owner of this house received it in an inheritance and he was not interested in keeping it; so he wanted to know how much I would want to take it apart.

After looking at it I thought the house was just too nice to be demolished and I asked how much I would have to pay to get it. One thing I have to say here is the person who owned it before died in.

Even before I got an answer to it, the house was sold to someone else in the village of Fenwood. A mechanic called Normand bought it for one hundred dollars.

I made the mistake to mention it to one of my friend who was having coffee with Normand just about every day. I had no doubt when it comes to know where the information came from. In less than three months Normand died too from a heart attack. He was barely fifty. I could have sold this house anywhere between five and ten thousands dollars.

A few months earlier I met with Normand's cousin, who was called Charley also of Fenwood, because I needed him to cut a few big trees that fell on my dog's fence blown down by the strong wind. I knew he was a wood man and he had a good chainsaw.

I think he was forty-two. He plainly told me he wasn't interested in doing this. I know he could have done it in less than a half hour. He was also a man from whom I bought some firewood before.

Although, before I left him he asked me if I would help him getting a grant from the government to renovate his house. I plainly smiled and I left without saying another word. Two months later his friend who is also one of my customers founds him dead in his house, sat in his chair, holding a big bottle of liquor and choked with his vomit.

Another man in my village name Mike, a customer of mine was very mad at me because I didn't want to lie to the insurance agent concerning the damage done to his house. The valley was not done right and the rain pushed by the wind found its way to his kitchen ceiling causing quite a bit of damages. He died too a few months later from a heart attack. He seemed to be in a pretty good shape physically.

One of the only things I can say about all of these deaths is my enemies didn't have too much luck and this incites me to warn the others to be careful and to try not to hate me too much. It is as if God wants to show me I don't have to fear anything anymore from my enemies that He would take care of them Himself. In one way this is very reassuring.

CHAPTER 11

Although, there are good things too that happen in Saskatchewan and in Goodadam! Take for example about a month ago I had to go to the hospital to get an x ray and a blood test. Only fourteen minutes went by from the time I opened the door to enter and the time I opened the door to get out and this after I got what I needed. I could never get this kind of service in any other province in Canada.

The insurances for my antique light van only cost me ten dollars a month. I don't think any other province can beat this either.

I sold my property of five acres in British Colombia, a very rocky land for the amount of seventy-five thousands dollars. Here in Goodadam I bought four houses on four properties which amount to a little more than four acres four two thousands. Not only those are four pieces of land all together, but it is also the best top soil I ever saw. I just couldn't go wrong. In BC they wanted thousands of dollars just to separate my property in two pieces.

One summer in 2005 I planted potatoes just to see how they will grow. Let me tell you that I got thirty-five hundreds pounds of them out of a piece of land of forty feet by eighty.

I didn't stop there, because I bought another twenty-four other properties and among them are a restaurant, a two story community hall, a huge old garage, a couple of barns, another house a bit more decent to welcome my mom who visited me in 2005 and many pieces of land. I have to say here that my mom at eighty-four wanted to operate the restaurant. I have to say too that in 2003, when I moved here I still had a lot of ambition.

I even planed to create a sheltering center for homeless people that are not on drugs. I was telling myself; 'Why someone has to live in the street of big towns when here in Goodadam we can buy decent and liveable houses for five hundreds dollars or less. I actually bought three houses on nice pieces of land of one hundred and sixty feet wide by two hundred feet deep for one thousand. There were three hundred and thirty-three dollars each which is not even one month of welfare.

I wanted to create work for many people also. There is a school also which cost eight hundred thousands dollars to build and was for sale and was sold for four thousands dollars. This one would have made a wonderful home for elderly people by converting the classes into bachelors.

The mayor of the time, my ex partner was pretending to negotiate the purchase of it, apparently for a dollar and he would have sold it to me for ten thousands dollars. All this of course was going to be made in the name of the village. I surprised him one day pretending to discuss on the phone the sale with the person responsible for it, but there was nobody at the other end of the line. He was quite a bad actor. Of course this was before we split up.

I'm glad though the deal failed through in a way, because in reality I could not afford such a huge project even though it would have been one of the most interesting. It was just too big for me; I mean for my finances. Just to heat this building was an exorbitant amount of money. I would have needed a much more important cash flow to put such a wonderful project like this on its feet.

There was a huge income potential of thirty thousands dollars a month though; less the expenses naturally, which was nothing to spit on besides giving to many poor old people a standard of life a little more enjoyable. I was planning a trip out every week for everyone including the ones who just had a thin hundred dollar left from their pension cheque, which I meant to leave in their pocket and who could travel for shopping. Of course they would have to be able to do it physically too.

Although, the bus is about all I could afford, but the dream is still there and we never know; one day maybe it might come to reality.

The November 26th 2003 is an important date, because I think I invented an important program to help the itinerants, to pull these poor people out of the hell they are in and bring them to a little piece of paradise.

The Liberal government of British Columbia decided to cut off welfare from thousands of homeless and out of work people and in some of those cases people with no means at all to make a dollar. I personally think there is only one way to fight evil and this is with doing good to others.

Here is what I planned, what this program could do for them. Here in Saskatchewan, in many villages there are many houses that one can get for next to nothing. In fact, I will start by helping myself with this. I actually have an anecdote to tell you about this one.

An old guy I know fairly well, his name is Jeff and he bought some years ago a two story house on a pretty nice piece of land for the amount of five hundreds dollars, Yes, you read it right, $500.00. Ho, understand me now; it's not a castle, but nevertheless, it is a roof over his head.

One day in one of our conversations some time ago while we were talking about the authorities he said; 'These sons of a bitches; they doubled my taxes.'

So not showing too much emotion and very innocently I asked him how much he was paying now. He said very sadly; 'Thirty dollars a year!'

I felt a lot like bursting laughing, but I didn't.

"It's not the fact you have to pay thirty dollars a year that bothers you the most, but the fact they doubled your taxes, isn't it?" "Thirty dollars?" "This is not even ten cents a day and you're complaining."

He responded by saying they doubled his taxes and this was not right and not fair.

So I suggested to him he goes take a walk every day and pick up two pop cans and I know he likes to walk. This will be good for him anyway and also would take care of his taxes. If he pick up a beer can on top of it; this would take care of next year taxes. I told him if for some reasons he cannot walk anymore he just has to let me know that I will give him those couple of cans. I also know he likes to go to the dump and pick up a bunch of things that richer people don't mind throwing away.

One day he told me he sent $100,000.00 to his niece in Ukraine. I couldn't help telling him he was lying; that I didn't believe a single word of all this. The next day he was at my place with all the proofs to back him up. His niece received $96,000.00 and the cost of sending the money was $4000.00. I found out this year this was to buy her silence for what he did in the pass.

A few years later I was told by someone honest in the village that this old man was stealing boards from me, in my shop next to his place. I told myself I will not bother him or stir shit for a few pieces of boards. But they were not worthless boards, but three quarter inches full sheets of plywood which sell for around sixty dollars a piece in the store. When I confronted him about it he said he found them at the dump. I said 'Han, han, no one throws away sheets of plywood of this value and besides, I recognized the mark I made on it with my saw. You're lying and just know you cannot enter heaven with these stolen things.'

Now my plan is to run an ad in the papers sayings;

For you homeless!
Do you want a new life?
Do you want a roof over your head?
Do you want a job?
Are you ready to get training?
Are you ready to drop illegal substances?

Then I got a place for you.

First condition; wanted to get out of your troubles.

Second; want to work.

Third; want to at least try to be honest.

Fourth; want to be sober.

The next two are not mandatory.

Fifth; want to help others as well.

Sixth; want to be part of this program.

We need; construction workers; carpenters, plumbers, roofers, painters, drywallers, fence builders, tapers, sheet metal installers, electricians!

Also in restoration; dishes cleaners, waiters, waitresses, cooks!

Gardens; gardeners, farmer's help for fruits and vegetables and harvesting!

Maintenance mechanics, wreckers, car scrapping!

Sales persons, males, females!

Helpers for aged people!

Dogs trainers, groomers!

Office workers; book keepers, Internet specialists, WebPages masters and programmers!

We have a lot of fun activities and sports.

Fishing and ice fishing, small and big games hunting, curling, ball, dog's sleigh riding and racing, horses riding, horse shoes games, bingo, dancing, skating, hockey, ball and many others.

I am afraid though it is getting too late for me to put this project together; at least for what I can do myself.

It is good to work and it is good to have fun too in a healthy way anyway. But yet, we never know.

As far as I am concerned; all I can say is after having so many hits and low blows it comes to a point where it is hard to get back on your feet, but for as long as I will be able to get up either physically or financially I will give everything I got.

Although, wanted to do and being able to do are two different things even if it was said; 'When there is a will, there is a way.'

All I can say about all of this is I do what I can and not always what I want, but yet, may the will of God be done. God allowed me to do a lot for people; especially to open their eyes spiritually instead of helping people materially.

I know Jesus did the same thing and with all the power he had; he never helped people getting out of poverty and neither helped them to get richer in any way at least according to the scripture.

I really appreciated the six months my mom spent here with me in 2005. You should have seen her catching her first pickerel of twenty-two inches long, sat with me in the fishing boat in a beautiful sunny day.

The fish wasn't biting much and she started getting impatient and she was doing crazy moves with her line when I started to tell her to calm down; she was going to scare the fish away and at the same time her fish bit on her bait. I have to say this might just have been a trick I didn't know yet. She was eighty-four then and again last Sunday while I was talking to her she mentioned the next time we'll go fishing together again. She is now eighty-nine years old.

One of the things she didn't like at all in the West is the wood ticks. She asked me to make a garden for her, but she never put her foot in it after she heard of those little creatures.

She was not too crazy either about the gossipers of the village and she put an end to it fairly quick, at least in our house.

Then things started to deteriorate for me in the falls of 2008; when my doctor told me I was hit by a very common problem on ageing people. Oh yes, I was told I had a bad case of arthritis which forbid me not only to walk more than five hundred feet but to work also.

For one and a half year I had a very hard time taking care of my dogs even though they have never at anytime missed anything; except walking as they used to maybe. There were some days where I had to try twice to do the one hour chore.

Since I always been a self-employed there was no compensation at all for me, no UI or anything else. I always thought I could help myself at any time and in every situation!

The situation was not rose at all. I sure have a lot of things to sell, but as you probably know; when we have to sell something, people see you coming and you don't even get half of its value.

I also had to return my almost new minivan to the dealer, because the monthly payments were just too high for a non working man.

All this though didn't affect me too much; probably because I already knew what it was like to be poor and this for most of my life. I experienced the highs and lows.

I still have a roof over my head and I think this is the most important.

My dogs were never short of food or water as always, it's rather my power bill that suffered a little. Ho sure, I had to borrow money from friends a couple of times, but they knew they weren't going to lose anything with me and besides, I owned a lot of things they are interested in.

I was due to get my old age pension in April 2009, but a little detail, something happened in 1959 came back to haunt me. I have to say I forgot about it completely, but this caused me quite a bit of a problem.

When I got on the work force at fifteen and a half years old I had to lie about my age to get a job and a sin number. I told the responsible person I was born in 1943 instead of 1944 and I forgot about it afterwards. I was certainly not thinking about my old age pension back then.

When I asked for my pension in 2008 I was told there was no problem, but when it was time to pay me there was one. Three months after I was due to get something I was told then my sin number didn't match with my birth date. I argued with them saying I was born in 1944 and this is what it's written on my driver's licence. Of course for them I was only an impostor!

They then asked me to supply them with my birth certificate and I asked them where I could get it. They gave me a phone number in Regina where I could get a form and this without asking me where I was born. There I was told I have to make a demand by writing and they sent me the famous form like two months later. So I filled up this form and I returned it along with the fifty dollars they have demanded. Three months later I received a letter telling me I have to make the demand in the province where I was born. The least I can say is, it makes you feel like swearing.

A few months later again I received my birth certificate from Quebec, but then it was written all over it, get the hold of this; 'Nil.' It is written at least thirty times. So I sent a copy of it to the government office as I was asked to do, but guess what. They too could not understand why it was written nil all over it and they asked me to come and meet them in person with my original birth certificate. They finally found out from Quebec this was just normal and it was a process to fight frauds.

I had to go through almost all the same experiences to finally receive the old age supplement. Life is not always easy, that's for sure.

In the month of April 2009 I had a visitor coming from Saskatoon; a BAAC officer came to inspect my twenty-three dogs. The report was absolutely clear and simple. 'Everything is normal with plenty of dogfood, plenty of water, shelter better than usual, because the dogs have a real house like humans, a large fenced run for them to run and play, barking two on five, which is normal and all of them seem to be healthy.'

In the evening of the same day there was a meeting in the town village office with two special guests, but I wasn't one of them even though I was the main attraction and I was not interested and neither impressed. The authorities of the village got through their heads I must get rid of some dogs.

The mayor argued his wife who used to walk by my place was afraid to do it now because she's scared of the dogs. I thought poor idiot, if you cannot walk with her you just had to ask me and I would walk her around. On the other hand; if she is paranoid; it is not very interesting. I have enough dogs to control.

I don't really know if the two cops were invited in to inform us or to intimidate. The mayor as if he didn't know what else to say kept asking me why I didn't learn from my experiences in British Columbia. It was very clear to me the pressure came from the BC BAAC, as if they were thinking they didn't cause me enough problems.

Harassment continues. If the pressure came from the BC BAAC, the complaint came from the authorities of the village and from someone else I discovered afterwards.

Although I had with me the fresh report of the morning from the BAAC officer and this was all to my honour and to my advantage. One of the two police officers read it and told the others they had nothing against me to nail me with and I realized this was the reason they were there for. But then again the mayor was still bringing back what happened to me in BC about my dogs. I finally told him that dogs in heat were not as easy to control as teenagers. His son just got a young girl pregnant for the second time; which makes his mom cry every day.

I told them anyway that I contacted a few dog's rescue institutions trying to find homes for a dozen of my dogs. They gave me thirty day to get rid of them. One of the cops said it was fine to get rid of the dogs, but we have to know what will happen to them. It's nice to see I'm not the only one who cares about the dogs. I asked them if it was illegal to keep twenty dogs and I was told it wasn't. So I told them to stop their threats in this case. The village has no by-law about it and it bothers them a lot and apparently it is expensive to create one.

When I contacted the dog's rescue, Pawsitiveness Match in Calgary on the seventeen of March 2010, I asked for help to find homes for a dozen of my dogs telling them I didn't want to be judged that I just wanted to save the lives of a dozen of my dogs. I talked to a very nice lady by the name of Jennifer who made many efforts to find people, other rescue nearer to me here in Saskatchewan. She too tried to find people who would try to find home for my dogs and also help me with the dogfood.

It was from the National Newscast on TV I heard one evening the name of Pawsitive Match who was bringing dogs from Mexico. I told myself then if they could bring dogs from this far they might be able to take some of mine over here in the same country and dogs much closer. It was there and then I moved on the project of asking for help.

I was asked right away for pictures of my dogs I succeeded to send with the help of a friend, because I didn't have a camera anymore. They wanted to know the age of my dogs, their health condition, their sex, etc. After she heard about my problems the nice lady told me they will do everything in their power to help me with the dogfood and the adoption.

So I asked when the dogfood should arrive, because I couldn't pay for both, all the food I needed and the power bill the same month. I was already threatening to be cut from my electricity. I trusted the help would come and I went to pay the power bill and for this reason I bought quite a bit less dogfood.

So just like by a mere chance a few days later, on April 13 2010, I had the visit of a BAAC officer from Saskatoon again. I guessed he tried to catch me with no dogfood at all. I let him conduct his investigation till the end when he mentioned a female dog of mine which just showed up with a breast cancer. From then on I knew who did make a call to the BAAC beside the village. A woman from Regina by the name of Stacy had offered me to pay for a vet visit to my place. This vet just confirmed what I already knew, but the BAAC officer could only find this out from the dog's rescue lady.

Despite of my demand not to be judged and despite risking the lives of my dogs and without seeing the condition of my animals this woman made a complaint to the BAAC. Some people have strange ways to help others in need. The BAAC officer had already told me that if he takes my dogs they most likely going to die.

I asked for help on March the seventeen 2010, but I got another visit from the same officer on the 23rd of June of the same year. Again the report was clear, everything was normal concerning all of my dogs without exception.

Although, it was very clear to me too they tried everything they could to trap me. For sure twenty three beautiful dogs in good health would pay more than a dozen; especially when someone can get them for free.

All of this happened after eighty-five Emails in a bit better than four months and I kept a copy of everyone of them just in case they want to seize my computer one day. A hell of a good thing the whole situation was in a hurry!

The day after his visit the BAAC officer called me to say that if I didn't get rid of all my dogs but five within six days he will seize them all without any exception. I asked him again if it was illegal to keep twenty dogs and he told me it wasn't. I asked him why then he was threatening me like this. He told me then he received the order from his boss to seize all my dogs within six days if I didn't reduce the number of them down to five. I told him I want to keep ten. I can't understand how come I didn't throw a fit at him, because I was just boiling inside.

I called the provincial and the federal deputies telling them I had in my hands reports from the BAAC officer and everything was fine with my dogs, with food and water, with shelters and everything else and there was no law to forbid me to keep them all, but they wanted to seize them anyways.

They understood there was something very strange in all of this, but they could not do anything about it. I also call my lawyer, but when she heard what it was all about, the BAAC, she told me she couldn't take the case any farther. She knew there was basically no chance to win against such a big machine even if we didn't do anything wrong.

I also went to see the police at their station with the two reports in my favour to be told they had no jurisdiction over the BAAC. They can steal, they can kill and the police can't do anything about it. One officer told me to contact the person who wanted to steal from me, the head of the BAAC in Saskatoon.

My very last option was to call the thief who wanted to harm me, to take my animals away and to kill them or to get someone else to sell them even if this was illegal. Do you still wonder why I can't wait to get to the future world?

On the sixth of July they all came together at my place to give me shit because of my two last puppies, one from Fannie and the other one from my Princess, the one I had to put down because of her cancer. They were mad at me because I found them a home before the rescue people did.

Robin, one of the rescue people from Moosejaw was totally furious and I think it was because she had already sold these puppies before having them. The BAAC officer told me that finding home for the dogs was costing a lot of money and the puppies would have help her getting some of the money back. She complained about the expenses, but she drove one hundred and fifty miles one way just to come to give me shit about the two puppies I didn't want to rid of in the first place.

I had by the time acquired enough experiences to know how they were operating and to see them coming. They all went around all my buildings trying to get these two puppies back in the hope to put their hands on them. I told them they were sold to a man who went to Calgary when they asked. I told them also it was up to me when it comes to which dog would leave my property. These two puppies were my last hope to have the chance to continue this breed of mine, my mutesheps.

The previous year I called one of this rescue outfits in Regina and I was told they wanted one hundred and eighty dollars per dog to rescue them. I told them then that if I had this kind of money I could simply feed them.

One of them, Lori who lives in Melville came on the sixth of July had already offered me to come and walk my dogs to give them some exercise. I told her then I thought of sharing the ownership of the male pup with her to get him to get use of strangers and get exercise at the same time. She told me then she would have loved this. But now I know I can't trust any of them for any reason.

Another woman who was with them told me I have very nice dogs. I said yes and they all are healthy.

I had the chance to have a bit of conversation with them anyway and the BAAC officer mentioned another breeder a little south west of Regina he was trying to trap, but until now he had no luck with him.

I told him I did everything in my power to find homes for my dogs and I had many Emails he could read to prove it. Guess what he said then. His own words; 'I know, I read them all.'

Obvious conclusions, the BAAC seize (steal) animals that belongs to people like me, breeders and they go as far as to spread shit on the ground and inside animal's pens to get the population on their side.

They always come with cameras to get pictures and videos to show the public what is not always the reality. Then they pass the animals to dog rescue institutions, which already have a network around the country and even as far as Mexico. What ever they cannot sell they put them down and this not always in a human way like they did it in Tofino and this is also witnessed by their own employees. All of this financed by people of the population with a golden heart and who don't hesitate to give for what they think is to save lives of these poor animals. In fact and this in many cases what these people do is double paying these monsters to do the exact opposite of protecting the animals.

My only mistake or crime was to have wonderful dogs that were in demand. You can see them on my Website and see and judge for yourself if any of my dogs were malnourished.

Now, I won't let anyone anymore tell me that what they do is in the best interest of the animals. I will continue until my death if I have to, to ask for either a public inquiry or a private investigation until the governments of this country establish an agency to overlook what the BAAC is doing all over this country to our animals. This is what is called protection against cruelty made to the animals and to human beings.

At least forty of my wonderful dogs were put down by the BC BAAC of Tofino, which means all the dogs they couldn't sell, but my dogs could very well continue to live even if this would have meant to leave them alone at my place. They were costing me money, but they were alive, happy and well treated.

It is time now to switch to something else and is there a need to say this was very painful to me? It took me over seven years to almost get over it, which is not completely done to this day.

Then last year the young man whom they say is blond, son of the actual mayor came to my place to give me a fifty dollar deposit on the 1986 Camero I still keep behind my house. I told myself; finally, it is about time he made up his mind after seven years of turning around the bush.

He told me he will bring the rest, the two hundred dollars in a couple of days. A week later he was at my place again with a cheque of two hundred dollars he said his uncle from Regina wrote to him. Of course I wasn't born the day before and I told him I couldn't take the cheque and the bank wouldn't cash a cheque from a third party either. He tried to explain to me how good it was, that it was a good cheque and all this and I had nothing to fear about it.

Then I told him if the cheque was good as he was saying he shouldn't have any problem going to the bank, cash it and bring me the money. One month later his mother stopped at my place asking me if I have seen her cat and giving me the description and all this. I told her I haven't seen it and I told her to tell her son to come and discuss with me about the car. She told me then her son had no money. I told her to tell him anyway. She then said it again that her son had no money.

One month later this young blond man came to see me. He had his girlfriend with him, the mother of his children. He asked me for the fifty dollar deposit back that he gave me earlier. I told him business doesn't work this way. He then got out of his truck, walked to the back of it and grabbed a baseball bat and brandishing it in front of my face, he ordered me to dig into my packets and give him the money.

His girlfriend pleaded with him to give up this idea, but he didn't want to hear anything. Lucky for me there was someone else over there, a middle age man who was shopping for a bumper for his 1968 Chevelle and he told the young lad to think this over only to be told to shut up or else I'll get the same thing I will. He just told me he will knock my head off.

I felt the pressure building up when I started thinking of what I will have to do to neutralize this man. I knew very well of what I was capable of, but we never know what the consequences could be. I knew I could break his back and make him invalid for the rest of his life if I had to do it to defend myself, but I decided to let the justice take care of him instead.

I also know it's never easy for a poor man to defend himself in court against a man who has millionaires for parents. I knew too, because I lived through it many years ago that a lawyer who is not paid too much can be bought and reduced to silence.

This young man finally calmed down and when doing so he said it would be better for me to never make him mad again. At that moment I was dreaming of one thing only and this was to be able to get on a boxing ring with him. He gave me a huge desire to break his face or at least give him a lesson he obviously never got at home.

During his rage of affection towards me this young man mentioned that no one wanted me here in this village and I should return to France where I came from.

I'm sure he's not the first youngster who doesn't know his geography, because truly, Quebec is far from the old country. I didn't know how this situation would turn out, but it seems to me there was a little bit of politics in this statement on top of racism.

When he and his girlfriend were gone the other man and I discussed our option about telling the police concerning the situation. This man told me he had to go to town anyway to get money from the bank to buy the bumper he was interested in. He then left me at the police station and he went to the bank.

After I filled up my report the police officer told me it would have been a lot simpler just to give this guy the money. To him too I had to explain businesses don't work this way. I asked him if he knew that by law the head person of authority has to run his business to the best of his knowledge to make his enterprise succeed. A business is not necessarily a charity organization and even if it was it shouldn't be to support jerks.

So the other man too came to fill up a report about the incident, which kind of forced the cop to do something about it against his will.

The cop told me then this young man was arrested and released many times already before, but see, he is the son of a rich mayor who is friend with many cops; so the situation was not too easy. So because of it this young man got away with a lot of mischief. The cop told me though that if the young man doesn't sign a restricting order which forbids him to come near me, he will spend the night in jail and so on until he does. At least this was a little something.

A week later there was a big celebration in the village of Goodadam. It was its hundredth anniversary. Since many people in this village gave me some reasons to protest; being dirtier than dogs can be, I was not going to miss such an opportunity.

So I prepared for the occasion what I could dare call a manifestation. For sure it was not all for one, but rather all against one, all against me. I have to say here that I went on strike for three days once back in 1975 on a more than three thousands men project in James Bay, north Quebec and I won my point.

Here is what I prepared and exposed all day long during this parade. I was lucky in a way, if I can say to own twenty-eight properties; so I didn't have to trespass anywhere to set my work of arts. Here it is.

Goodadam, Good place to live, Good administration.

I was told seven years ago I would have no problem with my animals over here in Goodadam, but of course this was from the previous administration.

Raymore, a little town situated at about one hundred miles West of Goodadam was hit by a tornado lately, but it was in the news the help came from all over for the victims of the disaster. Congratulation to the good souls!

Here in Goodadam as you will be able to notice the one hundred miles an hour wind blew down my shop and destroyed it all the same day, but I received no help of any kind nor any offer of help and neither a word of compassion from anybody. I got to say though, because it's the truth that I received a letter from the village office ordering me to clean up. Good place to live, a place to fine the joy of life.

Now this administration is talking about an animal by-law and a building by-law and what else now, I wonder???? I'm a dog breeder and a general contractor.

The administration did everything in its power to get the BAAC to come and get all the dogs they can out of me. My dogs have never hurt anyone, not here or anywhere else.

They raised my taxes over night from $1300.00 to $3300.00 a year, this they were very good for.

I think they want to run this little village of less than sixty people like the town of Toronto; maybe it's time to have a protestation like they have in Toronto. I won't break any window though; I'm not this kind of guy.

I was told last week to get my shit out of here and go back to France where I was told I came from; that nobody wants me here in Goodadam.

I'm sorry for you, but it will take a bit more than your threats and your intimidation to get me out of here.

Now I'm sure most people will understand I don't really feel like celebrating with all the rest of you and don't feel sorry for me, I don't. I suggest you rather feel sorry for the poor judgement of this administration.

John Prince, Goodadam Saskatchewan.

Of course this was the talk of the day and this all day long and this made many people mad also, but it takes what it takes; even if it only helps slowing down their attack against me.

This young man only received a little sentence. He was put on probation for six months and during this time since he has to pass in front of my house to make it to his parents' place, only he does it at eighty miles an hour on a gravel street. I had to call the cops again to calm him down.

He has committed five criminal actions in about five minutes when he attacked me and he got away with it with hardly a slap on the hand and this is pushing it. This was an assault with a weapon on a person, he made death threats on a person with a weapon, he made death threats to another person with the same weapon, he also made an attempt to steal from me with a weapon and he also made racist comments by telling me to go back to France. I just wonder what I would get if I try to do the same thing. Ten years maybe! There are some cops who have killed people a lot less threatening for their own defence here in Canada.

When I think I was taken all the way to court for a perch my old friend left by mistake in my pail of fish, there are certainly reasons for questioning.

The justice system is not really for the honest people of this world. I didn't really want this guy to go to jail, but it seems to me that at least an order to go take a temper management could have been fair. I can easily say I succeeded to control my dogs better than his parents did with this young man and I didn't complain to the BAAC; even though he is much more vicious and dangerous than any of my dogs.

I have a young puppy of four months old in my house and he is not allow in my kitchen and the only thing which stops him from coming in is a two foot high piece of plywood he can easily climb, but he wont do it and the only thing that stops him is obedience. This is true even if I'm gone up to six hours at the time and my cat is challenging him all the time.

Before ending this chapter and crossing over to the other world I would like to introduce a few testimonies from people who saw from their own eyes the assassination of my dogs by the Tofino BAAC in BC. I collected these testimonies from the animaladvocates. com Website. Since they collected information on my Website I thought I have the same right.

CHAPTER 12

The following pages are testimonies from people who witnessed the BAAC behaviour and this is public property.

"It was with shock and horror that I received the news regarding the deaths of 10 "Elkford" dogs at the Tofino shelter on Friday, January 31, 2003. These animals were allegedly euthanized in order to "protect" the public. Yet volunteers and ex-staff who had worked extensively with the dogs claimed that they were not a danger, and were progressing favourably with a walking program and socialization. Further, I quote an excerpt from a Victoria Times Colonist article (Thursday, January 30, 2003): "Animal trainer Don Sullivanos believes abused dogs can quickly recover from their emotional scars, provided their new owners firmly discipline their animals... Sullivanos has been successful with his tough-love approach...." ("Dogs, poultry saved from living in filth").

I strongly believe that the BAAC has made a serious judgment error, and ten beautiful dogs have recently paid the price. Therefore, I call upon the BC BAAC to completely oversee the operations of its individual shelters, and to enforce the existing no-kill policy. According to volunteers, most of these animals would have been adoptable within a reasonable period of time, and some could even have been adopted out immediately. Already exhibiting sociable behaviour, they would have continued to improve--particularly when removed from unnatural confinement. Therefore, there was no excuse for this mass killing.

Yours truly,"

TOP STORY

SEIZE AND KILL! or RESCUE AND SAVE?

TWO CASES: A COMPARISON AND OUTCOME

CASE ONE: TOPAN CREEK DOGS: RESCUED AND SAVED BY CRESTONIAL PAWS SOCIETY

CASE TWO: ELKFORD DOGS: SEIZED AND KILLED BY THE TOFINO BAAC

Fifty some odd northern mixed-breed dogs tied to trees, neglected and dissocialized for years. One group in Topan Creek BC, one in Elkford BC.

Two remarkably similar situations, handled by two remarkably different organizations with radically different strategies and outcomes. Scientists themselves couldn't have created two better control groups.

DATES OF REMOVAL OF DOGS

Topan Creek: Between July 2, 2002 and July 28, 2002. Dogs were rescued and removed as foster space became available by a small rescue organization, Crestonial PAWS.

Elkford: July 3, 2002. Seized by the Tofino BAAC.

LENGTH OF TIME THE BAAC KNEW OF THE DOGS

Topan Creek: a minimum of three years.

Elkford: Ten years that the BAAC admits to; John Prince had been breeding dogs in Elkford for 12 years, according to media reports. (This is completely false for I never knew where Elkford was before 1995 and I knew nobody in there either. John Prince) (Prince had been on the AAS web page for over a year before the Tofino BAAC acted: Animal Advocates Society of BC | Puppymill Investigations)

NUMBER OF DOGS RESCUED OR IMPOUNDED

Topan Creek: 56

Elkford: 46 (47 adult dogs were seized: one was returned to Prince: a number of (sellable) pups were also seized)

NUMBER OF DOGS EUTHANIZED

Topan Creek: 2

Elkford: 34 (to date to the best of our knowledge: BAAC figures are confusing)

BREED OF DOGS

Both cases mainly husky type crosses.

FINANCIAL RESOURCES AVAILABLE

Topan Creek: little to none, from day to day

Elkford: BC BAAC: $20 million a year

LIVING CONDITIONS IN WHICH DOGS WERE KEPT

Topan Creek: Some of the dogs were chained to trees, others were chained to objects, out in the open, without adequate food and water, with numerous diseases and untreated wounds. Some of these dogs were suffering under the PCA Act definition of "critical distress" which permits immediate seizure.

Elkford: Dogs were not tied directly to trees, but rather tied by chains to 10 metre nylon ropes strung between trees, allowing them some degree of unfettered movement. The dogs had wooden doghouses and some buildings, as shown in the pictures on Prince's website hubcap.bc.ca/dog_breeding.html. None of the dogs were suffering "critical distress" and may not have been suffering even "simple distress".

PHYSICAL CONDITION OF DOGS WHEN REMOVED

Topan Creek: Eleven of the Topan Creek dogs had wounds on their bodies, from lick granulomas to severe open and abscessed bite wounds. Many wounds were infested with maggots. One dog had a chain embedded into the skin of his neck. One dog was malformed, suffering from an exposed penis shaft and deformed testicles, resulting in numerous urinary tract fissures and lesions as well as a severe and chronic bladder infection. One dog's leg wound was so severe and longstanding that infection had spread to the bone. Many dogs had scars. One dog was covered in an oily substance, which Mr. Meyers claimed was motor oil. All dogs appeared to have tick wounds on their ears and necks. All dogs had hair missing from around their necks from chains rubbing the skin. (Photos and report of Topan Creek dogs' injuries given to the BAAC: animaladvocates.com/ TopanCreekDogs.htm)

Elkford: According to BAAC spokesperson Loren Chortok the dogs were seized due to "suffering from neglect and illness without necessary food, water, and housing". BAAC staff had reported to the media that "some of the dogs looked thin and malnourished". The dogs were treated for Giardia, a common and easily-treated intestinal protozoa. None of the dogs look unhealthy, no diseases, infections or injuries were ever described by the BAAC. (pictures of Elkford dogs can be seen at Prince's web site hubcap.bc.ca/dog_breeding. html **and at** animaladvocates.com/Elkford-photos.htm

PSYCHOLOGICAL CONDITION OF DOGS WHEN REMOVED

Topan Creek: The dog "Raven" with the wound that was exposed to the bone was completely unapproachable for treatment due to extreme pain and fear. (animaladvocates.com/TopanCreekDogs.htm) According to Crestonial PAWS' report, "all the dogs displayed varying degrees of fear aggression or terror." Again, according to Crestonial PAWS' report, "During the month that it took to remove all dogs from Meyer's property intensive psychological rehabilitation was begun. Every day until we were able to bring the last dog down, we spent time with each dog as we fed and watered it, talking, petting, treating wounds, and some grooming, to help them overcome their terrors and learn to trust."

Elkford: At the time of their seizure Tofino BAAC investigator Tom Kuish was quoted as saying "They've had no socialization with people. It will take them time to adjust." After four months of living in cells at the Tofino BAAC, spokesperson Lorie Chortok says of the Elkford dogs: "Because some have been tethered, they're terrified of doorways and floors. All they know is the confined environment of the tether. We can't just send these animals to a family. It could lead to aggressive behaviour. If some of the dogs show signs of severe psychological problems, the BAAC will euthanize them as a last resort." But numerous volunteers were allowed to walk the dogs in public and reported that the dogs were friendly and well-socialized. (See volunteers statements: animaladvocates.com/Elkford-volunteers/htm

VETERINARIAN ATTENTION

Topan Creek: All dogs' conditions received immediate medical attention. All wounds were treated, all were treated for parasites, all dogs were spayed and neutered and vaccinated. **Elkford:** The dogs were treated for Giardia, a common intestinal parasite. All were reportedly dewormed and vaccinated. None were spayed or neutered, some became impregnated and had litters of puppies while at the Tofino BAAC. Some of the mother dogs were euthanized also.

METHODS OF EUTHANASIA

Topan Creek: Humane and painless intravenous injection administered by a vet.

Elkford: BAAC has not said, but it appears that at least some of the dogs were euthanized using cardiac puncture administered by BAAC staff. Cardiac puncture in the heart if not missed. If the heart is missed, it can result in the Euthanyl flooding the abdominal cavity or lungs and slow, agonizing death. Independent veterinary opinion is that this method is sometimes used on dogs if the administrators are not trained or proficient in finding veins for intravenous injection. The BC VMA does not approve it as a method of euthanasia for dogs. BAAC admits that shelter staff euthanized the dogs, not a veterinarian.

FATE OF DOGS DECIDED BY

Topan Creek: Crestonial PAWS Society and numerous individual rescuers, foster homes, and small, independent organizations, all of them with much personal experience with dogs, especially dogs in need of socialization.

Elkford: The BC BAAC: From the Tofino BAAC Manager to the Regional Manager to the BC BAAC Head Office to the BC BAAC Board of Directors. Head Office would decide the ultimate disposition of the Elkford dogs, including sending the BC BAAC' s "assessment" team to assess the dogs and to pronounce them aggressive and not rehabilitatable. The assessment team members may have more university degrees than personal knowledge of dog behaviour. Hired "experts" in every field are frequently used to justify decisions or actions and to deflect questions of actions that are otherwise questionable. "Experts" were used by the BAAC to justify the killing of thirty-four dogs that many volunteers and one staff member say were gentle and friendly. That the dogs were not aggressive is confirmed by the fact that the Tofino BAAC allowed volunteers free and unsupervised access to the dogs for up to six months. The BAAC kept the Elkford dogs in sterile cells, with little human interaction and unneutered, all factors which are commonly understood, even by those without degrees, to contribute to high stress levels and then the BC BAAC experts said they were unrehabilitable and would have to be euthanized.

REHABILITATION OF DOGS

Topan Creek: All dogs placed in foster homes - All dogs received individual human care, socializing and attention while in foster care. None had litters. All dogs were sterilized immediately. No puppies were conceived under Crestonial PAWS custody. None were subjected to psychological drug therapy or to "expert" assessments.

Elkford: Dogs were housed in chain link runs at Tofino BAAC for as long as seven months. Prolonged confinement by caging adds to des-socialization and stress in dogs. Dogs were interacted with and walked by volunteers during shelter hours (11 am - 4pm). The remaining nineteen hours a day were spent without outside stimuli. No dogs were spayed or neutered during their rehabilitation period at the Tofino BAAC. Spaying and neutering helps to reduce stress levels in dogs by reducing hormone levels. Staff and volunteers witnessed multiple fights between unaltered males over females in heat, as well as copulation between unaltered males and females in heat who were housed together.

(I, John Prince have never allowed such an orgy at my place in Elkford nor anywhere else.)

Some staff claimed to have witnessed the conception of, and to have helped deliver as many as three litters of pups. Interior Regional Manager Robert Busch admits that at least one litter of pups was conceived within, and sold by, the Tofino BAAC. The dogs were also subjected to drug therapy. According to media reports, they were given Clomicalm (chlomipramine hydrochloride) an anti-anxiety drug that is contraindicated in dogs with a propensity to bite, including those who are fear-biters, as the drug decreases inhibition, thus increasing the likelihood of the dog biting*. The BAAC claims these dogs were aggressive and fearful. If this is true, why did the BAAC give them a drug that could make them worse? The Elkford dogs were confined in cages in a stressful BAAC environment for seven months. The BAAC claimed they were under intensive rehabilitation, and were being "assessed". Intensive rehabilitation cannot happen when an animal lives at an BAAC facility. Intensive rehabilitation can only happen when an animal is placed in a home environment, with as little stress and demand on it as possible. BAAC facilities are stressful for animals.

(I, John Prince would add to this statement that it is scary for humans too)

The new BAAC "assessment tool" should not be used to fail dogs that the BAAC has not permitted a chance to be socialized. To "assess" an animal's temperament in a high stress shelter situation is unfair. Being confined in an enclosed space with a stranger and being poked at with a plastic hand is terrifying. The BAAC's new "assessment tool" is not designed to reveal a dog's true temperament, as true temperaments don't show themselves under times of extreme stress. Assessment tests are not designed to help animals pass; they are designed to expose the failures. So far, 34 Elkford "failures" have been killed by the BAAC. Hence, the new "assessment tool" may be just the BAAC's latest excuse for killing. The question begs to be asked: If the Elkford dogs were so aggressive that the BAAC had to kill them, why were volunteers allowed to handle them and walk them in public places? (See letters from volunteers: TOFINO BAAC VOLUNTEERS SPEAK FOR THE ELKFORD DOGS)

DISPOSITION OF THE DOGS

Topan Creek: All but two of the fifty-six Topan Creek dogs were rehabilitated and rehomed. Two dogs, Raven and Sumac, were euthanized for humane reasons. Raven suffered from a large wound that penetrated to the bone, was in obvious pain, and was completely unapproachable for treatment. Sumac suffered a severe physical deformity of his genital organs that was painful and unalterable.

Elkford: Thirty-four dogs killed by BAAC (to date March 30/03). This number does not include pups that died while in the custody of the BAAC (eaten or shaken by adult dogs, low birth-weight, other causes). Of the original 47 adults seized, one was returned to Prince. Of the 46 adult dogs impounded at the Tofino BAAC 34 have been killed and 7 remain and so 5 may be in foster homes or have been sold. The BAAC's figures have been confusing because it sometimes includes puppies, both those seized from Prince and those conceived and born while in the custody of the Tofino BAAC, but as anyone can sell puppies and needn't kill them, puppies are not germane to this issue and to include them in statistics is misleading.

CHARGES

Topan Creek: Any BAAC investigation was so botched that charges were never laid. BAAC Local Agent Marg Truscott said to PAWS president when being urged to seize the dogs, "Well, what can we do? We can't just shoot 'em all", and "You can't fault a fellow for having a dream"! (The dream Truscott referred to was Meyers' plan to use the dogs in a dog-sledding business.) "Distress" under the PCA Act is a summary offence and prosecutions for summary offences must be initiated within six months. The BC BAAC Board of Directors discussed the Topan Creek case at its board meeting of November 23rd, four months after the last dog was removed from Meyers by Crestonial PAWS and with still 2 months in which to send a report to Crown. No legal action has been taken. The BAAC permitted the press and TV to give it credit for the rescue of the Topan Creek dogs. This taking of credit very possibly resulted in the loss of thousands of dollars in donations for Crestonial PAWS and the gain of those thousands of dollars in donations for the BAAC.

(I, John Prince wrote it before that the BAAC has a good business, good in the sense of making money, not good for people and even less for animals.)

Crestonial PAWS begged the BAAC to act and when it didn't, PAWS was forced to act itself and to assume responsibility for all expenses. The agency that did nothing got the credit and the money; the agency that did everything got the dogs and the bills. (AAS sent $500 to Crestonial PAWS.) Meyers will not be prosecuted. Is this because to put this case before the media and public again would reveal that the BAAC neglected these dogs, some of them in critical distress for years, and then took credit for their rescue?

Elkford: Charges were laid against John Prince. Quotes from various news sources: John Prince: (July 2, 2002) "I'm stuck with too many adults. I hate to put them down. I offered the BAAC 20 months ago to take 12-20 dogs. They said they weren't adoptable." Cindycal Soules, BC BAAC: (July 9, 2002) reported as saying that there are no plans at this time to put down any of the animals. October 9, 2002: BAAC gains possession of dogs, demands Prince pay $12,000 if he wants them back. (BAAC is willing to return dogs to Prince after getting untold thousands in donations from publicity and if it gets a further $12,000 from the man it has accused of neglecting the dogs.)

(I, John Prince have to bring a little adjustment here; it was not twelve thousands I was asked to pay, but $110,000.00.)

Prince is quoted: "I can't afford it. To get them back I'd have to do like the BAAC does - cry to the public to get some funds." Nov. 1, 2002, Prince pleaded not guilty to three criminal charges laid against him by BAAC. His trial is scheduled for Sept. 16 and 17, 2003.

Fifty-six Topan Creek dogs had the great fortune to be ignored by the BAAC. Forty-six Elkford dogs had the misfortune to be seized by the Tofino BAAC.

Topan Creek rescued dogs in the Crestonial Parade, May 17/03

Here are a few testimonies from people who have seen, heard and experimented some behaviours of the people of the Tofino BAAC in British-Colombia.

By: Connie Mahoney
Date: 2/6/2003, 8:34 am
In Response To: Tofino BAAC kills 10 more "Elkford Dogs" (AAS)

Subject: Elkford dogs

"I am writing to you because of the latest mass killings of the "Elkford dogs" at the Tofino BAAC.

Under the care of the BAAC, dogs became pregnant, at least twenty eight were killed, they were caged with others who were incompatible causing fights and they were dealt with negative reinforcement. Some were hidden away from the public and barely socialized. When the caring public inquired about them the staff was very secretive and would not give out any information.

When dedicated and concerned staff or volunteers questioned the treatment of the dogs and the decisions that were made they were liable to be fired or banned from the shelter. I know this for a fact. I am a past director of the Tofino BAAC and the chair of Citizens For Circuses Without Animals which lobbied for a successful ban on wild and exotic animals in circuses in Tofino. I complained about the dirty, wet and cold conditions of the dog kennels and a serious safety concern (a live electrical wire sitting in a puddle of water) and for my concern the manager Robin Rogers banned me from the shelter and revoked my volunteer "privileges". A very special caring employee was fired two days after her own dog had died on the operating table just before Christmas of 2000. The manager fired her because she cared for the animals and would question decisions that were not made in the best interest of the animals. These are not unique situations. Also, others have been fired recently who cared about the animals. This week two dedicated volunteers were banned from the shelter. The Tofino BAAC has the reputation of being very unfriendly for both animals and people. When asked about the Elkford dogs; staff were very secretive and wouldn't answer any questions about the dogs. Volunteers always have the threat of being banned or sued. The manager threatened to sue me when I complained.

Last spring the BC BAAC announced a moratorium on euthanasia except for health and temperament reasons, and decisions had to be made by a vet. I guess that didn't include the Tofino BAAC. The latest batch of twenty eight Elkford dogs were killed here. Was a qualified Vet consulted about these important decisions and actually responsible for doing the procedures, or was it just staff? I also walked some of those dogs and I cannot accept their excuse that all of them were aggressive and not adoptable. I don't believe the BAAC did all they said they were going to do to help the dogs socialize and get used to their new world. I am not aware of any qualified dog trainers working regularly with them.

You have to wonder what is going on when ALL the other animal groups are criticizing the BAAC. These are caring, dedicated, and responsible people in these organizations who all have at least two things in common. They all love and want to help animals and they are all critical of how the BAAC operates and they want things to change for the better for the animals in our communities. Connie Mahoney Tofino BC."

By: Mandy Rawson
Date: 2/5/2003, 2:06 pm
In Response To: Tofino BAAC kills 10 more "Elkford Dogs" (AAS)

"The so called rescue of the Elkford dogs seems to me to be ill conceived from the very beginning. All the animal groups in the Okanogan area have heard complaints for years about the conditions these dogs were living in. Animal rescuers have even gone as far as taking Elkford puppies and breeding females because the BAAC could not or would not act. For the shelter staff to move in and confiscate over fifty dogs on one day was an overwhelming task.

Where were the logistics about where and how these animals were to be placed? What would become of the countless other dogs being surrendered to an already full shelter? I have been told that some dogs were sent to the Penticton shelter, which was already overcrowded. What was their fate? I suspect that the dramatic, media saturated rescue was no more than an attempt to garner waning public support and fill shelter bank accounts.

Then, to take these so called unsocialized dogs from their lives on ropes tied to trees and place them together with other unsocialized, unfixed dogs in metal cages with concrete floors, is, in my opinion, simply exchanging one hell for another. It is impossible to accurately assess the temperament of animals in such a stressful environment. Dog walkers report that the animals were friendly towards people and other animals. The walkers were also given permission to walk the Elkford dogs in areas which were highly public.

The most unconscionable act in this whole debacle is the BAAC allowing these dogs to breed and produce litters while they were in the shelter. The BC BAAC states on its website that "pet overpopulation is still a serious problem in British Columbia". Why on earth would they add to this serious problem by allowing dogs with "questionable" temperaments to breed indiscriminately? Could it be because puppies are cute and easier to sell than large, unfixed, unsocialized adult dogs? How much does the shelter get for each puppy sold? Enough to cover the euthanasia costs of the adult dogs anyway. With the BC BAAC stating so emphatically that it has "proactive spaying and neutering programs" there is no excuse, in my opinion, for these puppies to have been born in the first place.

This latest incident has galvanized animal lovers throughout the Okanogan to speak out against the Tofino shelter. For me, it is the final straw in a long list of unforgivable incidents. In memory of all the euthanized Elkford dogs, I urge animal lovers to support the small animal groups who really do help the animals. Mandy Rawsonl."

(I, John Prince, I say that if these people from animals groups didn't put as much pressure on the BAAC to take my dogs away, most of my dogs would have had a chance to live their whole life. If they had really come to my place in Elkford, they would have seen that I had many dogs alright, but they would have seen also that they were all in good health and well treated and that they had a nice place to live. If they wanted to help my dogs this much, why they didn't do it while it was still time to do it and when I begged people disparately for help against the Tofino BAAC, because I wanted to protect my dogs against these killers?)

The Culling of the Elkford Dogs: Here are the numbers again.

Posted By: Joann Bessler
Date: Thursday, 6 February 2003, at 8:37 a.m.
In Response To: Tofino BAAC kills 10 more "Elkford Dogs" *(AAS)*

"22 Elkford dogs were killed in November 2002. We have BAAC press releases, reports in the media, and information from an ex-employee listing each dog by name and its kill date.

On 3 July 2002 the BAAC seized 53 dogs from John Prince, 47 adults and 6 pups.

On 4 November 18 adults were killed.
On 7 November 1 adult was returned to Prince.
On 8 November 4 adults were killed.
On 31 January 2003 10 adults were killed.

Of the original 47 adult dogs seized by the BAAC, 32 have been killed so far and one was returned, leaving only 14 of the original adult dogs alive.

Joann"

"On Tofino radio news tonight it was announced that 18 of the 53 husky crosses seized from John Prince's property in Elkford 4 months ago were euthanized today. Inability to guarantee that the dogs were not capable of

224

aggressive behaviour was cited as the reason. I heard 3 separate newscasts regarding this matter today, and at no point was the BAAC ever named. They were simply identified as "officials." I reserve father comment on this matter until I learn more details, but suffice it to say that I am suspicious of the BAAC's history of using the media: when they're actually enforcing the PCA act they have no qualms about glorifying themselves through the media, but when they execute innocent dogs, because it is part of the job they have chosen as pound keepers and/or open surrender facility rather than a closed, no kill, real shelter, they magically become simply nameless "officials". Is the BAAC hoping no one will notice that its New Direction looks very much like its old direction to me.

Rest in peace, you 18 poor innocent souls, who were ever given a real chance."

TOFINO BAAC VOLUNTEERS SPEAK FOR THE ELKFORD DOGS.

Email to Kim Munro, BC BAAC

March 11/03.

Dear Mrs. Munro:

"I am Hellena Pol, a retired high school teacher, living in Tofino for more than 20 years. For the past 6 years, I have been a member of the Okanogan Humane Society, a non-profit charity that assists low-income families with the cost of spaying/neutering their pets. I foster around 25 animals year around and find them homes once they are fixed and vaccinated. In the past 5 years, I have placed over 600 animals for the OHS.

I have also been a volunteer and a supporting member of the BAAC for 7 years. I have observed and worked closely with 4 professional dog trainers in Tofino, trying to learn as much as possible about "man's best friend." I have walked, fostered and arranged adoptions for both the OHS and the BAAC -- about 1,400 dogs altogether.

Many people, including myself, were very enthusiastic when the BAAC rescued 53 dogs from Elkford last summer. The problem there had been recognized for many years. In November, about half of the dogs were put down -- something which nobody questioned at the time: we assumed it was absolutely necessary.

(I, John Prince say that you guys assumed also that my dogs were in distress, which was not the case at all.)

I learned from the management that the dogs had been through heavy drug therapy and that 2 teams of experts had assessed them. Apparently, they strongly disagreed with each other. The dog walking started in the middle of December, so few of us got involved. The dogs were surprisingly friendly, considering they had no human contact for 16 hours a day when the shelter is closed, were not neutered, and lived in confined areas with up to 3 males together. All that, plus the fact that dogs are not solitary animals, increases the stress level substantially.

During the weeks of walking along Mission Creek Greenway, we met many folks with their dogs, often off leash. Not once did we experience any problem with aggressiveness or growling. Many passers-by complimented the dogs on their good behaviour and asked why they were not available for adoption. We spent a lot of time writing detailed reports about each dog and its reaction to everything. Sadly, that proved to be a total waste of time. It's absolutely amazing that the same BAAC that repeatedly worried about the safety of the public allowed us to walk the dogs in a public park on daily basis. Neither did anybody worry about the children in Kae's Youth group (staff member) who brought the children several times to the back area of the shelter to play with the pups and some adult dogs.

In the middle of January, I learned from the management that the fate of the dogs would be decided at BC BAAC that week. I was extremely pleased to be invited to a meeting with BAAC management and District Manager Bob Busch. At the meeting, I was told there was no need for panic and the next day *Capital News* said, in part, "This week, animal groups were in frenzy after a RUMOR [my emphasis] circulated that the dogs would be destroyed. The rumour was false..." Well, 2 weeks later the rumour became sad reality.

Why did Bob Busch and the management deceive the public and me? When I asked this question at the AGM of BAAC on February 24th, Bob Busch said they simply meant the dogs would not be killed that week. What a joke! What a silly excuse! When asked why none of the "experts" suggested immediate spay/

neuter in November, Bob Busch came with another amazing answer: "There were 92 of them, too many!" Well, the arithmetic doesn't add up, considering that, by Christmas, 24 adults were dead and the shelter had about 25 other puppies and dogs in the kennels -- that simply means that there must have been at least 40 Elkford pups in the shelter! Yet, when asked how many pups were actually born as a result of breeding in the shelter, Bob said one litter! Really?? We know there must have been 2 - 3 litters.

When asked why BAAC couldn't share the experience and use the help of other groups of dedicated volunteers like the one in Crestonial which had successfully handled a similar disaster with the same breed of dogs in the same period of time at Topan Creek, the answer was, "Those were quite different dogs, bred for dog sled teams... no comparison with the Elkford dogs." What a misrepresentation! We saw the colour pictures of terribly injured, neglected dogs covered with urine and feces and read the detailed e-mails about their dreadful condition. Of the 56 Topan Creek dogs, 54 were fixed and found homes.

Okanogan Collie Rescue, a local animal welfare group, deals with horribly abused and neglected dogs every week -- 28 just in the month of January. Some of the dogs have been kept in wooden boxes, never seeing the light of day. At OCR, with no shelter and no government support, the dogs are all spayed/neutered, fostered and ultimately find new homes, thanks to tireless dedicated volunteers.

In the last 4 years, ONE very ill dog was put down; more than 80 were placed last year!

The madness in the press following the killing of 10 Elkford dogs at the end of January is hard to describe. The local paper, *Capital News,* printed only pro-BAAC articles. All volunteers were totally discredited and labelled intolerant, self-righteous activists, radicals, freaks, bullies -- even terrorists! The public was made to believe that these lunatics were threatening and harassing the BAAC staff on a daily basis! I have not seen such vicious attacks, false accusations and pitiful tactics since I left a Communist country 30 years ago. There was even a picture of a terribly scarred human face (one of the worst bites of the decade in town). The picture had nothing whatever to do with the Elkford case, yet it was placed directly in the article about "aggressive" Elkford dogs! What hysteria and how utterly unprofessional of the press! How did the picture get there? Only Dog Control officers had those slides.

Do you know, Kim that many women belonging to local animal charities and rescue groups have been cooperating with the BAAC for years; do you know that many of us contribute hundreds of dollars to help fix and place dozens of animals and pay the vet bills, constantly digging into our savings. All my nice clothes, jewellery and even antiques are gone for a good cause. Do you know where many of our animals, mostly abused and neglected ones came from? Yes, an BAAC shelter where they were considered unadoptable. Would you like to meet some of them?

Do you know, for example, that the Okanogan Humane Society is a small group of volunteers, mostly middle-aged and senior women, who, with their very limited funds, have been assisting low-income families with spay/neuter for the last 7 years? We started 4 years before the Regional District awarded the local BAAC $25,000 annually to do the same thing. We get $2,500, yet we have managed to fix 3,500 animals so far.

Why is the BAAC such an untouchable empire when everybody, including senators, ministers and priests make mistakes? Why is every person who dares to have a different opinion labelled an enemy? Why are compassionate employees fired and volunteers asked to leave? I have kept quiet for more than 6 years. Now it is time to speak up. Would you like to know why Robin Rogers (the manager) asked me to leave 6 years ago? I guess I was stupid to give up my whole summer. I worked at the shelter 6-8 hours a day, 7 days a week cleaning up the cat cages. I also ran 4-5 miles a day with 8-10 dogs each day. Almarie Bowers (an incredible volunteer and dog expert) and I worked closely with professional dog trainer Hugh Devlin. According to staff, the three of us were completing more than 80% of all the shelter's successful dog adoptions. We were so happy; we thought we were really making a difference. Wrong! It apparently wasn't appreciated by the Board of Directors and some of the staff. The atmosphere in the shelter was always depressing. We have never felt welcome. There was no greeting, no smile. Well, we were there for the animals.

My mother and I adopted out 2 badly abused dogs (one of them was returned to the shelter 3 times and 1 needed eye surgery) and 3 cats. I paid full fee for all of them in spite of the fact that they were considered unadoptable. Poor Sasha, the cat was half dead, had hardly any fur left and was due to be euthanized. I still had to pay the full $70.00 for her. I could see that I became a person looked at with suspicion and fear: What does she want, why is she here every day? I assured everybody I had a very good teacher's salary but it didn't help. I brought my husband to a meeting with Robin Rogers who basically kicked me out of the shelter. This was later confirmed by a letter from the Board. We read such stupid accusations as: "leaving the shelter through the wrong door,... disrupting work of staff." I would bring dozens of small cardboard boxes, carved holes in them, and put them inside the cages for kittens (sometimes 3-5 in one cage) begging desperately to get out of there. I knew it would reduce their stress in the misery of such a small confinement, but the staff was throwing them out and complained about it. Well, guess what? A year ago, I was shown exactly the same boxes -- now called domes -- that were "developed" by some expert at BC BAAC and I read how proud of them they were in the newsletter. Elizabeth Turnell (assistant manager) just looked at me and laughed her head off when I pointed this out to her. She remembered. I was also told that I worked too fast and that was causing the staff stress. Poor souls!

My husband dragged me out of there saying: "You don't need this BS. Forget the shelter and have some fun." But I could not stay away from the animals. I became a member of TRACS and soon after OHS. I started fostering, trapping ferals, and adoptions. Four years ago I became a Board member of OHS and started cooperating with all other animal charities as well as the BAAC. Looking after animals takes all my free time; I have not had a day off for 4 years.

A few summers ago, there was a big fire in town. The folks from Magic Estates were not allowed to go home for 2 days and were asked to report to the Fire Hall. Guess who was standing there for hours, offering help to people and their pets? Everybody thought we were from BAAC. We had pretty crowded homes and gardens for a few days. When, a few weeks later, that fierce forest fire reached Salmon Arm, would you like to know who drove there in the middle of the night, through police road blocks and offered help to the BAAC? My girlfriend and I were scared and inhaled lots of smoke. We felt sick for quite a few days afterwards. But, we saved 25 cats and later placed all but one of them here in town -- with the permission of the BAAC in Salmon Arm, of course.

Then when we returned to Tofino, we were surprised to receive harassing phone calls from the local BAAC. They demanded we surrender the cats to them. Yet we knew they had not even been in touch with the Salmon Arm BAAC to offer help. Besides, Tofino BAAC had no room for the additional 25 cats as they were full to the rooftop.

I invited the staff to visit the cats any time. I had no cages. They lived in luxury. When the phone calls continued, I got angry. I phoned the manager of Field

Operations, Carl Ottosen, and then everything stopped. The public has never heard of this because our main concern has always been to help animals and had not learned to exploit the news media for publicity. On February 2, 2003, as I was leaving the shelter completely exhausted and still completely shattered by the latest killing of dogs, I said quietly to a staff member that I have known for 7 years now, "How do you guys sleep at night? I don't." The following morning the manager Robin Rogers called me and announced that I wasn't allowed in the shelter anymore. We have known each other for 7 years and attended many meetings together. I have sponsored some of the dogs in the shelter, and helped to place couple of old dogs. Why couldn't he approach me personally and discuss such a silly little comment like an adult? Why did he have to blow it out of proportion by going to the press?

A friend of mine, like me, was upset by the killing of the dogs. We had both known them so well. Neither of us could sleep or eat properly for weeks. My friend offered to foster and possibly adopt one of the remaining 11 dogs she had become quite attached to. The answer from Robin Rogers was, "No."

When I questioned him about it a few days ago, stressing how experienced and caring this couple was and how much time they could spend with the dog, he repeated, "Not even a remote chance! Never!" So, the dogs were punished and one of the best potential homes was refused because of personal pride, power seeking and a difference of opinion. Foolishly, I thought it was the animals who were the most important, and that finding

233

suitable homes was a priority. Sadly, the BAAC also lost 2 of their long time friends and supporters.

I am so incredibly discouraged with everything, but I don't give up easily. I am determined to conquer the obstacles and improve each situation. I believe the BC BAAC was trying, about 2 years ago, to do the same thing when it hired an independent group to travel to several BC cities to hold public hearings (I was present in Tofino) on the future direction of the BAAC.

After reading recently in the local paper the manager's statement that the future of 5 of the 11 remaining Elkford dogs was uncertain, I alerted 2 directors of the local animal charities and a professional dog trainer. Also, I told Manager Robin Rogers that the dog trainer was willing to start working with those dogs immediately, and her expenses would be paid by the 2 charities. He said the money was no problem and after about a week we were invited to the shelter. I put a lot of effort into assuring the dog trainer that her help would be appreciated and that the dogs would, of course, benefit from her expertise. The dog trainer was certified in Vancouver and runs very successful classes and gives lessons in town. Well, it turned out to be another shocking and embarrassing situation..Rogers didn't even greet the dog trainer. Instead, he directed both of us straight away to the young staff that looks after the dogs, saying, "Always check with them. Don't give them a rough time. Don't talk to anybody about this. Just take the dogs to the creek or wherever." We went to check a couple of the dogs in the kennels, when Rogers came back, saying that some of the staff were uncomfortable with our presence. I said, "We are here to work with the dogs, not to bother staff". Still, I was most willing to talk to the staff in the office. I started talking to them in a friendly way. The office manager (Jan) didn't look at me and indicated strongly that she was not willing to talk. After a few minutes of some confusion; we were asked to leave. "After all," said the manager, "We have to keep the staff happy. You will have to go." I wanted to say very loudly, "So who IS the manager here, you or her?" but the dog trainer was already out of the door, completely shocked and bewildered. Before she left she just managed to ask, "How about the damn dogs? Does anybody care about them?"

Another disaster -- The office manager has never worked with the dogs and, as she has admitted to me several times, does not know them at all. So again the poor dogs were punished and deprived of important social skills, human contact and compassion. It seems like a bad dream that comes much too often. The dog trainer, who has never said anything about the killings or commented on any decision of the shelter is so upset she does not want to talk to anybody or have her name released.

The next morning this same office manager referred a very upset lady who needed at least $800 for her cat's surgery to me. I asked Jan as well as the other staff not to give my phone number to people who need money for vet bills–I live on a pension and our small charity does not have even 10% of the money available to BAAC! Yet, it keeps happening! I have and always will refer the clients looking for a certain type of dog or cat to BAAC;

animals need to find homes regardless what shelter or group they are coming from; it would sure be nice if the staff could have a bit more consideration.

I would like to ask you to remedy this situation immediately. The trainer deserves a written apology. The behaviour of the office manager was rude and totally unacceptable. By now, I have just about had enough too. I would like to ask you to send me a reply to this e-mail address within 4 days, please. After that I will approach anybody from the media who will be willing to listen, as well as Animal Advocates. I hope that will not be necessary.

Yours very truly,
Hellena Pol"
(Hellena has not received a reply)
By:AAS <office@animaladvocates.ocm>

Date: 2/3/2003, 10:38 pm
In Response To: Tofino BAAC kills 10 more "Elkford Dogs" (AAS)

"As for the dogs getting pregnant there, there is no rumour, I saw them get impregnated and I helped deliver the litters, Jenny is still alive and well. Half of her litter didn't make it she killed them. She ate one of the puppies and shook two others to death, leaving 4 puppies I believe. Blondie I think may have been killed but I am not positive and she got pregnant at the shelter by a dog named Morley. So here is the right total:

November 4th = 18 dogs killed.

November 8th = 4 dogs killed.

January 30th = 10 dogs killed.

Total = 32 dead dogs.

These dogs got pregnant while at the Tofino BAAC:

17. Becky: killed November 4th, 2002- had a litter - got pregnant at the BAAC.
19. Lena: killed November 4th, 2002- had a litter - got pregnant at the BAAC.
32. Blondie: not sure - had a litter - got pregnant at the BAAC.
33. Jenny: Alive - had a litter got - pregnant at the BAAC.

1. Mickey: killed November 4th, 2002.
2. Growly: killed November 4th, 2002.
3. Matthew: killed November 8th, 2002.
4. Mona: killed November 4th, 2002.
5. Ben: killed November 4th, 2002.
6. Fudge: killed November 4th, 2002.
7. George: killed November 8th, 2002.
8. Benson: killed November 8th, 2002.
9. Nova: killed November 4th, 2002.
10. Stu: killed November 4th, 2002.
11. Austin: killed November 4th, 2002.
12. Bowser: killed November 4th, 2002.
13. Kaluha: killed November 4th, 2002.
14. Tundra: killed November 4th, 2002.
15. Trixie: killed November 4th, 2002.
16. Stella: killed November 4th, 2002.

17. Becky: killed November 4th, 2002- had a litter - got pregnant at the shelter.
18. Blake: killed November 4th, 2002.
19. Lena: killed November 4th, 2002- had a litter - got pregnant at the shelter.
20. Niko: killed November 4th, 2002.
21. Melinda: killed November 4th, 2002.
22. Chewy (the dog I begged to adopt): killed January 30th, 2003.
23. Bobby: killed January 30th, 2003.
24. Bronson: killed January 30th, 2003.
25. Bosco: adopted - Lucky boy got to escape the BAAC
26. Zack: alive.
27. Carter: killed January 30th, 2003.
28. Felix: killed January 30th, 2003.
29. Morley: killed January 30th, 2003.
30. Josie: Alive.
31. Lucy: killed January 30th, 2003.
32. Blondie: not sure - had a litter - got pregnant at the shelter.
33. Jenny: Alive - had a litter got - pregnant at the shelter.
34. Kola: not sure.
35. Gollum: not sure.
36. King: alive.
37. Ziggy: alive.
38. Jerome: alive.
39. Morris: killed January 30th, 2003.
40. Clyde: alive.
41. Shirley: killed January 30th, 2003.

42. Laverne: alive.

43. Flower: alive.

44. Taffy: killed January 30th, 2003 - had a litter - pregnant when seized.

45. Mouse: alive.

46. Joe: alive.

47. Grandpa: went home to Jacques - lucky boy got to escape the BAAC. Kat Riley"

AAS: puppies impregnated and born at the BAAC were sold.

Re: 53 Elkford Dogs seized by the Tofino BAAC July 2002.

"I used to be an officer at the Tofino BAAC but lost my job due I believe to the fact that my morals didn't allow me to watch those innocent dogs die.

The Tofino BAAC killed 21 of those dogs (November 2002) without trying to properly rehabilitate them or anything...leaving 22 more for 3 more months in the kennels, one of which, 'Chewy', I love immensely.

After the termination of my job I was granted a measly few minutes twice a week to visit Chewy and my visitation was taken away from me on Monday.

I have since received an email from the BAAC Regional Manager (Bob Busch) stating that Chewy, the dog I want to adopt so badly, will be put to death along with most of the remaining 22 dogs.

These dogs were rescued from a puppy mill to spend 7 months in a cage awaiting their euthanization. Chewy is said to be aggressive, but I am telling you that is not true. They simply do not want to admit I was right about the wrongful euthanizations they did and to do so they terminated my employment and now are going to euthanize Chewy. He deserves a second chance...he deserves to live, and I want him here with me and my family, I am pretty sure it is too late and that they killed him this morning (January 31/03)

Kat Riley"

"My name is Helen Schiele. I live in Tofino and have been a volunteer dog-walker for the Tofino BAAC since January 2002. On July 3rd, the volunteer dog walking program was put on hold and the next day we learned the reason: About 50 dogs were removed by the Tofino BAAC from an alleged puppy mill in Elkford on July 4th.

The case against John Prince, owner of the Elkford dogs was settled some time in October. Shortly after, when the dogs became BAAC property, 28 were euthanized because they were deemed unsuitable for adoption or foster homes.

In December, one of the dogs, "Grandpa" was returned to the owner, as part of the settlement.

On January 31, another ten dogs were euthanized, among them two black and silver young dogs that I had taken for an hour's walk just two days earlier.

Although I had taken a few other Elkford dogs for walks with my husband earlier in January, these two, Felix and Morley were far more socialized (not pulling) and a pleasure to walk. A man walking a Golden Retriever was so attracted to them he insisted his dog should meet our two, even when we told him they belonged to the BAAC. He just said "my dog is friendly". So they sniffed, happily.

When on Jan.31st I drove to the shelter in the afternoon to walk what I expected to be Felix and Morley, I learned they had been put down just that morning. Around 4:30 in the afternoon, as I was taking a second Elkford dog for a walk, I passed a man who was emptying a large freezer just inside the garage. I realized then that the green bags contained the bodies of the 10 helpless Elkford dogs.

Later I learned that the dogs had been euthanized not by a vet, but by a senior member of the shelter staff with the assistance of a junior. It may be coincidence, but three of the dogs that I had walked before the Jan.31 euthanasia session, appeared a great deal more stressed than they had been before Jan.31st.

Yesterday, one of the dogs refused to enter the garage where the freezer is located. Not wishing to add to his distress I took him back to the kennel by another entry. He was ok with that. Also yesterday, I met a young girl (perhaps still a teenager) while walking "Joe". As she was walking "Josie" also a Elkford dog, so we began walking together. She told me how devastated she was to learn that the dog she had been socializing, "Shirley", had been among the ten to die. She said Shirley was extremely timid with other people, but the minute she came to see Shirley, Shirley would run up greet her. The girl had even brought her mother to see Shirley because she hoped to foster her.

This morning I asked my husband to walk dogs with me because I wanted him to see a small Elkford female called "Mouse". She is very nervous, and extremely thin, but I believed if I could foster her it might be a step toward adoption. I know the shelter still deems the remaining 11 dogs unadoptable, so I did not want to use the word "adopt".

When I asked to foster Mouse, I was directed to speak with the assistant manager, Elizabeth Turnell. She said I could not foster Mouse because they had to do some "reassessments" and the dogs needed to "settle down". Then she added they were supposed to be spayed later in the week. They might consider letting Mouse be fostered on Friday. I then said I would have Mouse spayed myself. No, they would do the spaying themselves. I said I had considerable experience with dogs.

Then the assistant manager said I could not foster because I had two cats. She said their rules did not allow foster dogs to go to a family with other pets. No matter what I said, the answer was no. Try on Friday, she said.

As I understand she had personally killed the 10 dogs on Jan.31, I feared that Friday might be the end for the remaining 11. So when the manager walked by me I asked him if I could foster Mouse. He replied with the same excuses, dogs need to be assessed. At that point, I'm afraid I lost my temper very badly. I told him the BAAC had been assessing the dogs since July 4th. How much longer did they need? I said something like "you killed 28 then 10.... you seem determined to kill the remaining 11. He then said I could not foster. The dog would not be given to me. I said you won't see another penny from me... The only thing I regret saying was "If the dogs are so vicious, why are volunteers permitted to walk them along the Mission Greenway?" I fear my outburst may jeopardize a very excellent dog-walking program.

Although I have not been officially barred from the shelter, I will not go back because I am so disgusted that an BAAC could behave worse than the puppy mill operator. When the dogs were removed in July the owner said that the BAAC would just kill them all. Sadly, he was right and people who already hesitate calling the BAAC about animal abuse may well remember the owner's words and do nothing.

What worries me as well in the feeling that the ten who were euthanized on Jan.31 were the more socialized and beautiful. When they come to do in the remaining 11, it may be that much easier to say "See, after all our efforts, they are still unsocialized". I hope I am wrong.

Helen Schiele Tofino."

Here some of John Prince's commentaries!:

The authorities of the Tofino BAAC have proven a few things to the whole population.

That they are crueller than I ever was!

That they are no better than me to train dogs!

That they don't love animals!

That they like money more than I do!

That they are unfair with volunteers and the employees, especially the ones who have compassion!

That they lied to judges to get warrants against me!

That they forged false proofs!

That they are corrupted to the bone!

That if they have Mouse, a very thin dog within their walls, means she was malnourished, something they couldn't find at my place. And more. Besides, how many of my dogs were sold or killed by the Tofino BAAC before these dogs have actually become their properties knowing that puppies sell better when they're young?

John Prince

----- Original Message -----

From: Robin Schiele
To: Capital News
Cc: ross freake
Sent: Monday, February 03, 2003 9:06 PM
Subject: Tofino BAAC

Letter to the Editor

"I can't believe that the Tofino BAAC of all groups has forgotten its own principles. Does the group not remember what the P stands for in its name? Instead of "preventing" cruelty, it perpetrates it. Its treatment of the Elkford dogs over the past few months has been nothing short of scandalous. Of the 50-odd dogs (the number used by the media seems to vary with each story) 38 (not 28 as reported on Feb. 2) have so far been euthanized. Two of those dogs my wife and a friend took for a walk only the day before they met their death. Indeed, we discussed whether we should adopt them. An BAAC official in Vancouver claims the animals were "vicious." Does that mean the Tofino officials willingly and knowingly allowed unsuspecting volunteers like her to take these vicious dogs for a social walk? If they were so vicious, how come they met another dog on the walk, sniffing each other nose to nose and wagging their tails quite happily? Sad to say; the slaughter was done; as I understand it at the hands of a senior BAAC employee, not a vet as one would expect. Some of the dogs remaining at the Casorso Road site are now terrified

245

of the green bags which were used as body bags and the freezer where the corpses were kept at what has become a slaughterhouse for those poor animals.

Robin Schiele,"

MEDIA RELEASE:
BAAC ACTIONS QUESTIONED, WHILE CITIZENS MOURN KILLING OF ELKFORD DOGS

Candlelight Vigil
When: Friday, February 7, 2003, 7 p.m.
Where: Highway 97 (Harvey Ave.) in front of Petcetera

"In response to the recent Elkford dog tragedy, the following organizations would like to express our profound grief and dismay regarding the actions of the Tofino BAAC; whereby ten rescued dogs met the same fate as eighteen others killed at the same shelter in 2002. For the following reasons; we feel that the BAAC, a society that claims to "speak for those who cannot speak for themselves," has betrayed not only the animal victims entrusted into their care, but public donors and supporters who have expected a higher level of insight, compassion and patience in the handling of these very unfortunate, neglected dogs:

1) Numerous dog-walking volunteers, as well as two ex-employees (all of whom had extensively handled the Elkford dogs), have repeatedly expressed the opinion that these animals were

"not vicious", but simply in need of more handling, training, and patience, and that they should not have been kept in shelter confinement for such an extended period of time.

2) Several individuals who had successfully handled the dogs and were witness to improved behaviour had expressed the wish to adopt some of the animals, yet their repeated requests were turned down by shelter management.

3) The Tofino shelter relied heavily upon the advice of two non-local "experts" in dog behaviour, whose opinions allegedly influenced the recent decision to terminate the lives of the ten dogs. Yet other animal trainers have reported an excellent success rate with severely neglected dogs; in fact, a local dog trainer who had contact with the Elkford dogs last year, described them as being "not at all vicious" and was optimistic that they could be rehabilitated.

4) The BC BAAC announced a moratorium on euthanasia last year and, to our knowledge, this has not been lifted. Why was a group of neglected, basically timid dogs considered exempt from this protective ruling?

5) Two compassionate employees who had worked closely with the Elkford dogs state that they were fired from the Tofino shelter. Young, inexperienced staff were hired on as replacements. Was this a decision based on logic, and in the best interests of animals needing expert care and training?

6) Quoting Lorie Chortok, General Manager of Community Relations, BC BAAC: "It is indeed local shelter staff who carry out assessments on animals coming into the shelter and who determine the type of remedial care that the animals need..." However, numerous witnesses have stated that Tofino shelter management had, when questioned specifically about the fate of the Elkford dogs, referred to this as a "head office" responsibility. Where is the truth in all of this?

7) Several local animal charities offered financial assistance to the Tofino BAAC (for spaying and neutering the Elkford dogs). This offer was rejected. The Tofino branch was made fully aware of community interest and support with regard to these dogs, yet the BAAC's silence and non-acceptance of this help was astounding. On January 17th, 2003, the Capital News reported that "...animal groups were in a frenzy after a rumour circulated that the dogs would be destroyed on Thursday. The rumour was false...." ("Plight of apprehended dogs questioned"). Just over two weeks later, a mass killing quietly took place on Casorso Road. Many citizens were stunned by the news, and are now demanding answers.

With heavy hearts, we will publicly mourn our killed canine friends this Friday. Our thoughts and prayers will also be with the remaining animals in the Tofino shelter."

What is following is not part of this report.

I, John Prince was there that night and I thought and I still do that most people who were there that night should keep their prayers for the employees of the BAAC; including the manager, Robin Rogers and the assistant manager, Elizabeth Turnell and all the people responsible for the death of my dogs. They went as far as lying twice to a judge to get warrants against me. Pray for them; they will need your prayers to get God's forgiveness if this is possible for all the crimes they have committed and for them to receive the pardon from the Creator of these animals; these creatures totally innocent and without any viciousness. That these dogs feared their executioners and they could distrust the ones who took them away from their master they all loved I understand, because I believe them to be smart enough to figure out who is good for them and who is not. My dogs knew from the moment they left my yard they were in danger to die and I did too.

If there is one thing I can add to these testimonies over this whole situation is; it made a lot of people talked about it and it confirmed one other thing and this is my dogs were murdered, executed like criminals in some States, them that didn't do a single thing wrong to anyone and neither did I.

This confirms too that basically all the charity groups and pet shops who put so much pressure on the BAAC to act against me contributed to the sad destiny of my dogs and their death. I repeat that Robin Rogers and all the others from the BAAC didn't have anything to nail me with in more than ten years and believe it; they were at my place more often than they were invited in. My dogs are way too intelligent not to know who could be good or bad to them. The BAAC killed so many of them that one has to wonder if they don't make dogfood with them like it was done in Ontario a few years back.

The last time I talked with Robin Rogers I told him he won an inning, but the whole game was not over yet. This book I'm finishing now will make him known across the world; him and his accomplices and all the atrocities they have committed. May God come to their rescue better than they came to the rescue of my dogs! Maybe they will have a better luck than my dogs had.

But all of this did one thing in particular and this is to prepare me for the kingdom of heaven; where I will be a lot better than I ever was in this world full of plots and traps from enemies that I see fall one after another. I have here a few good things for them and everybody else to read. One is in Isaiah 66, 3; 'He who sacrifices a lamb is like the one who breaks a dog's neck.' The Christians dare say that God did this, see John 3, 16. It is written this is an abomination. The other one is in Ecclesiastes 9, 4; 'Surely a live dog is better than a dead lion.'

There have been many years since I could see Sheba again; this was the day I could give her this book you're reading now. If I would have gone to BC before I could pay the fine I got because of these crooks and got caught; they would have put me in jail until it was paid off.

It is time now to introduce you to one more of my dreams, my vision of the kingdom of heaven; where I will live happy forever after with people I love and none of them who doesn't like me.

CHAPTER 13

THE TEN VIRGINS AND THE KINGDOM OF HEAVEN

Here is the first little town of the kingdom of heaven without any kind of problem. It is without problem simply because the devil, Satan and his angels, all of his demons like the ones who led the people of the Tofino BAAC to act and do all they have done simply don't have a place among the good people anymore. They have been chained for a thousand years and people who have followed Jesus can now live in peace. There is no more money, which means the big banks with huge profits are out, because they have been eliminated too. There is no injustice neither; so no more courthouse, no judge, no lawyer, no cop, no prison and nothing with regards of the injustice system.

We don't hear about war anymore either, which means all the soldiers of all armies had to find themselves another job. Of course I'm talking about those who loved the Lord here.

It is the same thing for the hospitals, because there is no sickness, no more disease, no more pain of any kind; for God took them all away from his people. All the fruit trees are our medicine cabinet and the word of God takes care of everything. One grape takes care of a headache, one orange takes care of heartburn and if a woman eats a tomato the day before her delivery; she will feel no pain at all when the time comes for the baby to join us. This is how all the pain is treated.

All of the transactions are made through fair and impartial exchanges. I'm myself a carpenter and I built a house for the baker and all the bread and the pastries will be supplied to me and my posterity endlessly.

I also built a barn for M. Grognon, the farmer who will supply me with all the vegetables my family will ever need. It is also with vegetables the same farmer obtained all the construction's material he needed from the lumberjack who also has a sawmill. He's got five employees who are please to work for the material who will in turn trade it for anything they need.

It is just a little town of three hundred people and we all are very happy. The wives are faithful to their husbands and vice versa. The children are obedient to their parents and the parents do have time for their children who grow up loved and in full bloom and with a lot of happiness.

None of us have to worry about tomorrow; none have any problem for trading, because there is always someone who can use our talent and our participation what ever it is.

There are fifteen farmers and all of them produce about twenty times of all the food we need. All of the surplus is use to trade from other communities similar to ours; for all of the other things we need and those we're not producing.

There are also five factories in our little town. In one of them we make shoes and footwear of all kind and sizes for everyone. Another one makes all the clothing the body needs and all the linen needed for the house.

There are no more cars; for they were the main killing tools of the beast, the system. This is one of the reasons why we didn't see any war in North America in the last sixty years, because the diseases like cancer, AIDS, cigarettes, drugs, etc. were killing enough people so the beast could control the population of the world down while at the same time it was saving his weaponry for the big one. The second commandment from God was to fill up the earth, but the devil knew that when the earth would be full it would be the end of him.

He is wicked maybe, but not crazy. He is actually very crafty. See 2 Corinthians 12, 16; 'Myself; nevertheless, crafty fellow that I am, I took you in by deceit.'

The ox and the horse are happy for having been returned to work for the Creator and his people and they sure can do a terrific job.

There is another factory where we produce our nails, wires, utensils and tools of all kind and just about all of what concern the hardware.

Our only government is the will of God and his word is respected by everyone. No one has more right than the others and each and everyone appreciate it. We all are brothers and sisters, princes and princesses, because our Father is the greatest King. The justice reigns and so is the word of God and everybody is happy about it.

In the forth factory we make windows and glasses for the needs of everyone. Everyone needs them and everyone contributes to the well-being of the glass maker.

In the fifth and last one, but not the least we make the floor covering of all kind. Everything we have in surplus in our little town is use to import what ever we don't make and we can use.

There is nobody who is poor. We all have wealth in our soul and in our hearts and the body lack nothing at all.

There are also many great artists. One of them makes pottery vases and dishes. Another one can paint whatever we want in it and most everyone chooses to have their house painted inside their dishes, which is very convenient after the parties to know who it belongs to. This artist is often hired to decorate the houses also.

We also have four distributors who carry just about anything imaginable of the things we have and the things we can export, which means when we need something or else when we have something to trade we take it to one of the distributors, usually the one who is most likely to get what we need. Everyone of them keeps a long list of the things that are available from our town and from elsewhere.

Every day is a feast and it is very rare we have to wait any link of time for anything. We can borrow anything from the others and unlike we had in the world; everyone knows and remembers where the borrowed article belongs to.

The clothes lines are back, no one is ashamed of them and the man who used to be the machine repair man is our Jack of all trades, but rather than to be bored to death as he was, now he's the busiest and the most considerate of all. He is busy because he's the one who helps everyone else in town. His name is Jack, the Jack of all trades. No one is happier than he is for the simple reason he makes everyone happy. No one can keep him very long though, because there's always someone else who needs and is waiting for him.

He came and spent one day with me once to help me put the rafters up on a house. When it was time to pay him back, he categorically refused to take anything saying that what he learned from me during the day was worth more than anything I could give him. So we went for lemonade together and I grabbed my guitar to sing Praises to My Lord. He then took my banjo to accompany and in less than a mark of the day half of the town was around us with all kind of instruments. You should have heard this chorus of all these people who love the Almighty singing with us praises to my Lord. I rarely heard something as touching as this in my entire life. I'm sure also the Almighty loved it and this is one of the reasons why our little community receives so many blessings.

Praises to My Lord

I want to sing praises to my lord with the angels, with the angels of heaven.

And I want to be happy up there with the angels and Adam, Eve and Abel.

I want to sing praises to my Lord with the angels, with the angels of heaven.

And I want to be happy up there with the angels and with all of his children.

1-6

Listening to Jesus, to Jesus and Moses, this is how I have known the Father as my own.

And because they told me, this is why I can see.

Yes now I can see through and I believe the truth.

2

I'll be able to meet the great Job and Jacob.

Shake hands with Abraham, I am one of his fans.

I don't need Cadillac to meet with Isaac.

I'll sing with the angels, Daniel and Ezekiel.

3

I will seal with Noah and walk with Jeremiah.

I'll fish with Hosea also with Isaiah.

I will build some mentions with David and Samson.

Be with the apostles and Jesus' disciples.

4

My heart is with Joseph who in prison was kept.

Was like me a dreamer didn't want to be sinner.

So my God was with him, kept him away from sin.

I'll meet him when ever there at the Lord supper.

5

Now's the great gathering, will you be there to sing,

With all of us one day in the heavens to pray?

The Lord is powerful; He's with whom is faithful.

He will not let you down; come join us in the round.

6

Listening to Jesus, to Jesus and Moses, this is how I
have known the Father as my own.
And because they told me, this is why I can see.
Yes now I can see through and I believe the truth.

I want to sing praises to my lord with the angels, with
the angels of heaven.
And I want to be happy up there with the angels and
Adam, Eve and Abel.
I want to sing praises to my Lord with the angels, with
the angels of heaven.
And I want to be happy up there with the angels and
with all of his children.

We have absolutely nothing to envy from anyone
and neither from any other part of the universe. The bad
souls have a lot to envy from us though. This must be
hell for them.
We all have what we need. My family and I miss
nothing at all. We actually have more to give away than
we need for ourselves.
The other day a family of six members arrived to
our town and they had nothing but what they had on
themselves. In less than ten days they too had a house
with a garden, a horse and a buggy and a job for the
man. And what a job he's got for he is a messenger, a
kind of pony express. He goes from town to town, from
province to province, from country to country, reporting
all the good news; all the novelties and innovations there
are. If there is something we are looking for no matter

where it is; we find out where it is, how to get it and what we have to give to get it. There are thousands of those guys who do this job in the kingdom which is one of the most interesting.

I left with my dear wife one day for another province and while I was building a little shed for my friend John; Madeleina, his charming wife, such an artist made a very pretty dress for my Sheba; who never ceased to be the very prettiest Princess of all time.

The dress and the hat to match it just suit her to perfection. Believe me; it was worth the trip. We used this opportunity to bring to each of our children a piece of her confection too.

I owe them some labour and John told me he'll need a little barn in a few years from now. He didn't seem to worry when I told him I'll come back when he's ready. We brought back also a bunch of little gadgets we didn't have at home. On our arrival at home they had a feast for us which lasted fifteen days.

All the way through our trip it was a renewal of our honeymoon. Everywhere we went and stopped everyone was hospitable. The only thing which made us a bit sorry was the fact our children were left behind.

All the way through our journey everyone wanted to keep us longer than we could really stay. We simply promised to do the trip again with our kids next time. We also have invited everyone of them to visit us at their convenience.

The exchanges of ideas are always welcome by everyone and this is how I learn to form a chain work, which is the most efficient at the time of harvesting. For example when it's time to pick up potatoes, sixty or more people get together to pick, clean and store them. The whole population benefits it. Those potatoes are of a much better quality now without the chemicals they used towards the end and the chain creates such an unequal brotherhood.

This way the farmers don't have to work twenty hours a day like they had to and many of them lost their properties toward the end of their lives, because they were tired and buried in debts.

This way when the harvesting is over the farmers can pay everyone back either with vegetables or with some labour. The lumberjacks appreciate particularly their help, because they are strong and knowledgeable. Each and everyone once their job is over turn toward someone else to help and none of us is left alone. Our life insurance is the honesty and the fairness of all the others. There are no keys and no locks and it is not necessary either. Each and everyone can sleep well without sleeping pills for there is nothing to fear from anybody. The stress, depression and everything that was hard on our nerves are now non-existent.

Denise, the florist and her husband Albert were missing things one day; so they decided to give a party to let the others know about their needs. Albert doesn't really have a trade anymore, because he was one of the rare honest cops appointed to banks before and now he helps Denise with her flowers production. Denise has never changed; she always helps others to succeed and to be happy. This has simply continued for her and if she is short right now this is the reason. She has always been humble and generous.

Joe Labrecque who is a linen maker was one of the attendants at her party. He ordered sixty bouquets of flowers to give away to all the people in the community who has supported him in exchange for all what her family will need in the next two years. Two farmers gave her two big loads of top soil already fertilized to grow her flowers. Another one gave her the manure she'll need for the rest of the year. This was to thank her and Albert for their help at the harvesting.

The owner of an orchard traded her all the fruits she needs for her and her family for six bouquets of flowers.

One of the distributors asked her to change all the floral arrangements in his building against all what her and her family need. Finally she was just overwhelmed by this reception and started crying of joy. Albert went to hug her for support.

All a person has to do when is in need is to let the others know and in no time at all the whole community contributes to his well-being. Most of the time the neighbour sees the need of his neighbour before it becomes urgent.

All of the children can see their dreams and desires come through. In the winter we make a mountain of snow to make a huge slide out of it. This is the farmers' job and what a job they do. They used to go South in the hot sunny states, but now they have discovered the pleasure to please the children, which brings them a lot more joy than feeding the beast by spending their money on luxurious beaches. It seems that even horses have a smile on their faces and have a lot of fun doing this. It has been a very long time since I have seen something as funny as this. I've seen a black horse once tried the slide before anyone else down the white mountain. No one could miss it. The horse started to dance at the bottom of the hill happy to make this many people laugh this much and then they laugh even more. If it wasn't for the owner the horse would have started all over again.

The hoisting is slow but secure and without any efforts for it is operated by the horses with the help of a cable and a pulley. We also have the sleigh rides either pulled by horses or by dogs.

Also a major part of a farm is use to make a wonderful ice rink and even there many people brought their help to this; so no one has to exhaust himself on the job and everyone can enjoy it.

I personally prefer snaring wild rabbits, which kind of keeps a certain control on their population and allows me to feed my dogs.

I make slippers, mittens, Jackets, hats, floor mats and sleeping bags with their fur, which is the most thermos of all fur. With their meat and the beef meat I make all the food all of my dogs need. Those dogs are my main way of transport; they just love doing it, they are happy, they are loved and they love me back. They are fast and very faithful. They're not the man best friend anymore though, but certainly good second best. Well, God is our best friend then your wife is; our family and everybody else and then your dogs followed by horses. Let me tell you; it is good to have no more enemies around.

You should see these dogs when I take out the harnesses. They can hardly control their excitement. On a trip I always have fourteen of them; seven who pull and seven who play and rest waiting for their turn. Before the working seven get too tired I replace them by the other seven who were just anxious to take their turn.

One day on one of my trip a big black bear wanted to give me a bad time and all of my dogs got at him; a bit like the wolves would have done. After an hour or so the bear was totally exhausted and kind of wanted to sleep. My dogs did the whole job without hurting the animal and without getting hurt also. I'm sure this bear will remember this experience for a long time to come and maybe forever.

I was extremely proud of my team of mutesheps which come originally from a pure big male malamute and a pure German shepherd female champion for listening and beauty. Bad people from the last world tried very hard though to eliminate this wonderful breed of dogs by killing some and neutering others.

Then I rang the bell for lunch as a mark of appreciation. They understood very quickly that I was happy with them. If this had been necessary; I had my bow and arrows also. My friend, my dogs are the very best alarm system there is. They detect the enemy thousands of feet away and sense the danger ahead of time. They are fast and their needs are very minimal.

One day on another one of our trips we were completely out of food. I then sent my dogs to get us something, whatever they could find. They brought us back a very pretty big deer, which allowed us to survive and continued on our journey. We got home with all kind of goodies and we were appreciated from all of the others.

It is a wonderful life with no pressure what so ever. The stress is now something unheard of. The weekends, the ends of months, the ends of years are not more important than the rest. Our only government is the justice that comes from God. We love Him with all of our heart and we sure have good reasons to do so.

Each year we celebrate the feast of the town and everyone of us without exception from the youngest to the oldest participate. The youngest do it often while crying, but there are always some babysitters willing to take care and calm him down. They love babies and dream of the day that in turn they will have some. They even prefer doing this rather than dancing which they like to do too. The oldest participate with yawning, but they do their share too.

All of the music instruments are heard that day and each and every musicians have a chance to execute her or himself either he is the least or the most talented. They do it to the joy of everyone too. I make my contribution with the fiddle, Jack on the banjo, Sheba at the mandolin, Denise on the piano and at least half a dozen of guitarists. We played them a few quadrilles. It is still a dance the most love and appreciate. Then I play them a beautiful old time waltz, one I wished I could dance too. After a little while we leave our places to other musicians and we go dancing.

JAMES PRINCE

The feast continued to the early hours of the morning for those who were the most energetic. The oldest went to bed earlier and so did the kids who fell asleep despite their desire to stay up. The very last hour we spent it singing praises to our Lord; Who sure gave us a little paradise on earth. It is with a lot of cheerfulness that we finally went to bed.

Of course the ones who went to bed early were the most rested and they were the ones who prepared the meals the next day. We all enjoy a delicious diner, an unequal feast, one that is absolutely unforgettable.

We have three feasts like this one in a year. This one I just described, one at Easter and one more for Thanks Giving. The one at Easter to recognize it is God who allows the earth to renew life; the growing of our food for everyone year after year. The one at Thanks Giving because we have the proof before our own eyes that God has done it again. The one I just described, because we live in a place absolutely magnificent surrounded by wonderful friends.

We also have other reunions not as important every week. We have others a little more important each month, but the ones of the year are simply unique and everyone participate in it one way or the other.

Each year there is something a little different than the previous years. There are a few new musicians, a few new songs and a few new hymns. The participation is totally exceptional. I am always impressed by the youngest with an inventive mind like the little Nathia, who did a tap dance of sixty different steps on a silk handkerchief without moving it even a centimetre. She learned it from her cousin Leo who did just as many steps with a glass of water on top of his head without loosing a single drop. It's something else to see. It takes an extraordinary concentration and requires an enormous number of hours in practice.

Now what to say about the tale teller? What a talent! And the one who sing songs which require the participation of all, like questions and answers. All of this is a lot of fun that doesn't cost much.

The party is not yet over that many of us already think of what we'll do next time. I already think of practising a few different tunes on the fiddle without neglecting the ones I played in case someone asks them again. I almost always have a few new songs and a few new hymns to sing to the Lord like this one called:

You Told Me Lord

You told me oh my Lord; You brought to us the sword.
The kingdom of heaven belongs to your children.
You made beautiful things, for You I'll be pleading.
I found You amazing and for You I will sing.

You are the Father of the heavens and the earth.
You know all the secrets of the earth and the sea.
Some want to take over what you created first.
Only You knows how to control the universe.

Only You knows to change our hearth and our thoughts.
What can I do for You? For You I love so much.
From your word came my faith, now I do know my fate.

For You I want to sing, the Master of all things.

You are the Father of the heavens and the earth.
You know all the secrets of the earth and the sea.
Some want to take over what you created first.
Only You knows how to control the universe.

You showed me oh my Lord that life is not a game.
Many mock you my Lord, everywhere is the shame.
Everything goes down hill, enough to make me ill.
Sing is my destiny for the eternity.

You are the Father of the heavens and the earth.
You know all the secrets of the earth and the sea.
Some want to take over what you created first.
Only You knows how to control the universe.
Only You knows how to control the universe.

Do I have to mention that everyone without exception; from the youngest to the oldest who knows the words participates in the singing one way or the other? Some do it while grumbling, others while humming or mumbling, but they do bring their contribution and I know for sure that God the Father hears everyone of us no matter how it is done or who we are.

Here it is not as much the quality of the voice that is appreciated, but the quality of the song and mainly the sincerity of the words. The sincere words that come from the heart and have a gracious signification are appreciated by God and by everyone. Everyone of us can be heard one way or the other either with a poem, a song, a hymn, a story or even a single fact that happened during the day. It could also be telling the way a trip went like the adventure with my dogs against the bear and the way they brought me a deer to feed us during our last trip.

The travellers always have nice tales to tell too that are very interesting. Very often they are gone for a year, but when they're back they have to spend at least six months with their families before going out again. Many of them take their family along, which is a bit more cumbersome, but a lot less boring. It is nice to hear there are thousands of nice places along the road, but none of them is as wonderful as ours. I just know from the bottom of my heart that here we are very blessed. I appreciate it; I'm thankful for it and I love it.

We also have a few little lakes which give us a lot of fish, mainly because the fish too quit eating each other. There is so much of it that we have to export some of it to allow the rest to have enough space. We feed the fish with corns since we know about it. In the pass; when we were still getting thunder storms, the pouring rain would take down to the lake a lot of worms, but this is not the case anymore. Since the day of the big change we only have light showers when we need them.

We still get the overturning of the waters though, which allows the feeding of the bigger fish in the winter. During the summer days the water is cooler in the bottom, which the big fish appreciate a lot, but when comes the colder days just the opposite happens. The water then becomes colder on top and many little minnows cannot survive the change, which feeds the remaining fish all winter long.

We're still feeding corns to the fish in the winter; even though it is in a lot less quantity just to make sure it doesn't get back to the old habit.

Just like I used to do; once or twice a month I organize a huge supper for the whole community. Either some great pickerel or perch serve with slices of potatoes fried just right. Next time it will be some greenbass. There are others who do basically the same thing with turkey or chicken or yet a good beef stew, but never with pork, because as always this is unclean to the children of God. See Leviticus 11, 7.

No matter what is served; it is a real feast each time. There are no more poor people among us; so no need to make an eternal collect, because everyone of us has something to satisfy his appetite.

At the end of the previous world the corruption was so great; such that a very small amount, a very small percentage of the money collected by charities actually got to the needy. Not only the needy received very little, but most of the time it took from twelve to thirty months to get to them.

Many of them died before the dollar which could have saved their life actually got to them. They just threw their bodies in a community mass burial without even a box or a single bed sheet to cover them. In fact, I would take more care to bury a dog that died of old age than they did to bury human beings with their bulldozers.

Just about all sports became some products of the organized crime. It all came to me with an idea a bit crazy when I mentioned to Angie, my little miracle female dog some names of people and organizations including governments that my suspicions increased substantially. When I mentioned the Liberal party of Canada I had a heck of a time to get her to quiet down. It was a bit less when I mentioned the liberal government of Quebec. But watch, when I mentioned the Block Quebecois, I had to muzzle her and this wasn't enough; I had to lock her up for the night, because I went as far as mentioning the separatists.

She just couldn't get over it. She was just howling terribly when I mentioned to her the most corrupted.

This reminded me Jesus when he wept over Jerusalem. It was the same thing when I mentioned the mayors of towns and villages. Even in my small village of Goodadam, the mayor had a tendency towards the criminals. One day I asked him how much he would take me to push some snow in front of my house; just enough to put my car in the yard. This was less than a ten minutes job. He was already out in his backhoe. He told me it would be $70.00. I couldn't help asking him if he got hit on the head. He told me then it was twenty dollars for the snow and $50.00 I got from his son. I couldn't help telling him his son is a criminal and thanks to his dad he will most likely end his days in jail despite of all his money. Ironically enough; the son tried to get this money with a baseball bat and his father tried to get it with a backhoe.

But the very worst were no doubt the construction dealers and the organized sports.

Angie was lying down very peacefully each time I mentioned Sheba, which is a special and great comfort to me. She became though quite irrational when we were driving close to the police stations. This says it all. I was convinced for a long time by then we would never get a better world until God separate the good from the bad.

Many have told me too that I have a way to piss off people, but I always responded be saying they miss a word. When they asked me which word was that; I told them I have a way to piss off <u>bad</u> people.

No matter what I was talking about with Angie; either it was about boxing or hockey, football, soccer, tennis or any other organized sport; it was according to Angie corrupted to the bone.

I had already quite a few doubts before all this came to light. Too many time I heard sport commentators say things like; 'What a setting of a play!' Yet something like; 'It couldn't have been better if the act was written before the game.' Again I heard; 'He played his role to the perfection.' I also noticed a scene in a hockey game where our friend kovacalev was totally alone with the opposite goaltender while all of his teammates were stocked in his zone. The pass of the act was late to come, but it did and our friend went to score as the whole setup; the whole scene was planned. It was obvious to me that both teams knew the act ahead of time.

These things were known for a long time in the wrestling world, but not as much in the other sports. Of course when a person is paid millions of dollars to play we can understand that a certain percentage of this money is used to buy their silence and just like movies actors, they are well paid to act and being professionals they can act without showing too much it is an act.

For example; I am a carpenter and I would have no problem at all acting one, because this is what I've done most of my life. I could also act as a fiddler, a guitar player, a banjo player, a mandolin player and a keyboard player, but I could never play games with the population like they did.

When spectators pay hundreds of dollars to watch a game, which is already tricked ahead of time by a producer who has determined the winner according to the bets that were made before the game! When the spectators pay something like $20.00 for a small paper glass of beer; you can call this heavy corruption.

Yet, I don't feel sorry for those who have been caught in these scams, because it's their own fault if they chose athletes, the singers, the artists, the politicians and thousands of saints for idols instead of turning to God. Then they deserve their poor destiny.

No one can say it is because God didn't warn them about it, because the Bible was the book the most sold in the world. Everyone had the choice between the truth and the lie, between the true prophet and the false prophet, between right and wrong, between God and the devil, between Jesus' teaching and Paul's teaching. God has actually left everyone without exception free to choose. This means that each and everyone can either congratulate himself or blame himself for his choice.

I personally have chosen God and I'm glad God chose me. He is my Father and I am his son. I love Him with all my heart and soul and he loves me more yet.

When it comes to my lawyer, Bill Clarke, I really think he did everything he could to help and to defend me. Just like me and my dogs; he was facing a huge monster to battle, a monster who is a terrible killer. When I say in my song they are more vicious than my dogs; I have the proof when I talk about my Princess that gave life to Chewy and she also gave her life to save him, but they, (BAAC cowardly killed him, a beautiful dog that didn't even have a single vicious bone in him. All I wanted for my dogs and this above anything is for them to find a good home where they would be loved and taken care of. If Kat Riley would have come to my place to adopt Chewy I would have been glad to give him to her.

If I was one of those who fill the pockets of the veterinarians, of the lawyers and of the politicians and all of these suckers; I would probably have had a little more support from the public in general, but my soul was not and is not for sale.

Even the man from Westside who made the three harnesses for my dogs chose to keep his mouth shut under the pretension he had to make his way to politic. I think he missed the boat; he missed his chance to make himself known as an honest man, because he knew very well the condition of my dogs and how well they were treated at my place. He used to be a dog man too.

The Carmi millionaire, the one who came to my place the day of the disaster; him who was a witness that there was nothing true at all in the accusations against me by the BAAC could also come to my defence and tell the authorities about it, but he chose to keep his mouth shut also. He's the one who bought my property for $75,000.00 while I was asking $160,000.00. During all the negotiations he kept saying he was not interested in anything but the land. When I suggested to identify everything I was taking he repeated that he was not interested in any of it. I thought he was my friend, but I found out his friend is money. There were some cars I wanted to keep and other things, but once the property was transferred to his name it was a total different story. Let me tell you that with friends like him nobody needs any enemies. Luckily for me it was written I was to keep my house that I was planning to take apart and to move away. He didn't mind this one mainly because he always thought I could never do it and this is what he told one of my friends that he thought was his friend too.

He had quite a fit when he found out I sold some parts of it to a man in Elkford. They were insulated panels that this man needed to put under his concrete floor. This man invited me for breakfast one morning in a restaurant and it was there and then he told me the property he was really interested in was mine. He also told me he was ready to pay up to $150,000.00 for it. I told him I would have finished the house for this amount, labour wise. He also told me he went to see the Carmi millionaire and my employee in Taylor trying to get my phone number, which both of them refused to give him. Even the realtor refused to give me my phone number. I think she too was controlled by this millionaire, who always pretends he is good to his neighbours. Good my eye!

Nonetheless, as you could read for yourselves; I was the victim of hundreds of attacks from all sides and from many different people and I didn't mention them all. I was attacked by some people like some Moslems do; who really think they're doing good and go as far as killing their neighbours in the name of their god, but the devil who is using them knows exactly what he's doing.

I'm finishing this book and the corrections on April 22, 2011, just in time for Easter, the celebration of the resurrection of our master Jesus-Christ, the son of God.

The millions of Christians in the world did and still do make a huge feast to celebrate Easter, the resurrection of Jesus and Christmas, the supposedly date of his birth; cooking ham, pork, and eat pork bacon just about every day; the exact meat God doesn't want his children to ever touch it in any way, shape or form; so even less put it in your belly. Do they know that without the nitrate they use in it the bacon would be grey and ham would be green? See Isaiah 65, 4, Isaiah 66, 17 and Leviticus 11, 6-8. 'The rabbit also, for though it chews cud, it does not divide the hoof, it is unclean to you, and the pig, for though it divides the hoof, thus making a split hoof, it does not chew cud, it is unclean to you. You shall not eat of their flesh nor touch their carcasses; they are unclean to you.'

From James Prince, an author who believes that John Prince was maliciously attacked by many people, many demons, but the attack by the Tofino BAAC is to me beyond understanding. I could see tonight on TV, on a show called (enquete, inquiry) about the cruelty to the animals by The Berger Blanc in Montreal, the horrible way John's dogs were put down by an official of the BAAC of Tofino. This was an awful spectacle to the common human being, but to realize this is the way your own loved animals suffered before they actually died justify John's request to get an inquiry into what was done to his dogs.

Finally the dog that came between John and Sheba and had his mouth broken by John in his dream at the beginning of this book is no doubt the Tofino BAAC of BC. Canada, who forced him to move away from Sheba, his love one.

John is like me a Jesus' disciple and happy to be one and I hope my stories will help you understand how the devil works; enough to be aware of evil and trust in God and his disciples. I also hope these stories will help you understand what is happening in your life. I wish everyone good luck and may my God, the God of Israel bless you!

James Prince on behalf of John Prince